FORCE 10 FROM NAVARONE

ALASTAIR MACLEAN, the son of a Scots Minister, was brought up in the Scottish Highlands. In 1941 at the age of eighteen, he joined the Royal Navy; two and a half years spent aboard a cruiser was later to give him the background for *HMS Ulysses*, his first novel, the outstanding documentary novel on the war at sea. He is now the author of twenty-one best-selling novels, of which *Sea Witch* is the most recent; sixteen of them have now sold more than a million copies throughout the world.

Many of his novels have also been filmed – *The Guns of Navarone* and *Where Eagles Dare* are among the most famous – and there are plans to film many more books including *The Golden Gate*.

ALISTAIR MACLEAN

Force 10 from Navarone

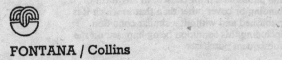

FONTANA / Collins

First published in 1968 by William Collins Sons & Co Ltd
First issued in Fontana Books 1970
Nineteenth Impression October 1978

© 1968 Cymbeline Productions Ltd.

Printed in Canada

To Lewis and Caroline

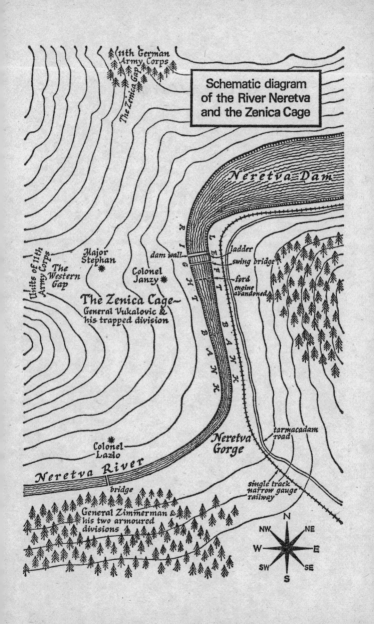

Schematic diagram of the River Neretva and the Zenica Cage

11th German Army Corps

The Zenica Gap

Neretva Dam

Units of 11th Army Corps

Major Stephan

The Western Gap

Colonel Janzy

The Zenica Cage—
General Vukalovic &
his trapped division

dam wall

R I G H T   B A N K

L E F T   B A N K

ladder

swing bridge

ford

engine abandoned

Colonel Lazlo

Neretva Gorge

Neretva River

bridge

tarmacadam road

single track narrow gauge railway

General Zimmerman &
his two armoured divisions

N
NW   NE
W   E
SW   SE
S

I

PRELUDE: THURSDAY 0000-0600

Commander Vincent Ryan, RN, Captain (Destroyers) and commanding officer of His Majesty's latest S-class destroyer *Sirdar*, leaned his elbows comfortably on the coaming of his bridge, brought up his night-glasses and gazed out thoughtfully over the calm and silvered waters of the moonlit Aegean.

He looked first of all due north, straight out over the huge and smoothly sculpted and whitely phosphorescent bow-wave thrown up by the knife-edged forefoot of his racing destroyer: four miles away, no more, framed in its backdrop of indigo sky and diamantine stars, lay the brooding mass of a darkly cliff-girt island: the island of Kheros, for months the remote and beleaguered outpost of two thousand British troops who had expected to die that night, and who would now not die.

Ryan swung his glasses through 180° and nodded approvingly. This was what he liked to see. The four destroyers to the south were in such perfect line astern that the hull of the leading vessel, a gleaming bone in its teeth, completely obscured the hulls of the three ships behind. Ryan turned his binoculars to the east.

It was odd, he thought inconsequentially, how unimpressive, even how disappointing, the aftermath of either natural or man-made disaster could be. Were it not for that dull red glow and wisping smoke that emanated from the upper part of the cliff and lent the scene a vaguely Dantean aura of primeval menace and foreboding, the precipitous far wall of the harbour looked as it might have done in the times of Homer. That great ledge of rock that looked from that distance so smooth and regular and somehow inevitable

7

could have been carved out by the wind and weather of a
hundred million years: it could equally well have been cut
away fifty centuries ago by the masons of Ancient Greece
seeking marble for the building of their Ionian temples: what
was almost inconceivable, what almost passed rational
comprehension, was the fact that ten minutes ago that
ledge had not been there at all, that there had been in its
place tens of thousands of tons of rock, the most impregnable
German fortress in the Aegean and, above all, the two great
guns of Navarone, now all buried for ever three hundred
feet under the sea. With a slow shake of his head
Commander Ryan lowered his binoculars and turned to look
at the men responsible for achieving more in five minutes than
nature could have done in five million years.

Captain Mallory and Corporal Miller. That was all he
knew of them, that and the fact that they had been sent on
this mission by an old friend of his, a naval captain by the
name of Jensen who, he had learnt only twenty-four hours
previously—and that to his total astonishment—was the
Head of Allied Intelligence in the Mediterranean. But that
was all he knew of them and maybe he didn't even know
that. Maybe their names weren't Mallory and Miller. Maybe
they weren't even a captain and a corporal. They didn't look
like any captain or corporal he'd ever seen. Come to
that, they didn't look like any soldiers he'd ever seen. Clad
in salt-water- and blood-stained German uniforms, filthy,
unshaven, quiet and watchful and remote, they belonged to
no category of men he'd ever encountered: all he could
be certain of as he gazed at the blurred and blood-shot
sunken eyes, the gaunt and trenched and stubbled-grey
faces of two men no longer young, was that he had never
before seen human beings so far gone in total exhaustion.

'Well, that seems to be about it,' Ryan said. 'The troops
on Kheros waiting to be taken off, our flotilla going north
to take them off and the guns of Navarone no longer in
any position to do anything about our flotilla. Satisfied,
Captain Mallory?'

'That was the object of the exercise,' Mallory agreed.

Ryan lifted his glasses again. This time, almost at the

range of night vision, he focused on a rubber dinghy closing in on the rocky shore-line to the west of Navarone harbour. The two figures seated in the dinghy were just discernible, no more. Ryan lowered his glasses and said thoughtfully:

'Your big friend—and the lady with him—doesn't believe in hanging about. You didn't—ah—introduce me to them, Captain Mallory.'

'I didn't get the chance to. Maria and Andrea. Andrea's a colonel in the Greek army: 19th Motorized Division.'

'Andrea *was* a colonel in the Greek army,' Miller said. 'I think he's just retired.'

'I rather think he has. They were in a hurry, Commander, because they're both patriotic Greeks, they're both islanders and there is much for both to do in Navarone. Besides, I understand they have some urgent and very personal matters to attend to.'

'I see.' Ryan didn't press the matter, instead he looked out again over the smoking remains of the shattered fortress. 'Well, that seems to be that. Finished for the evening, gentlemen?'

Mallory smiled faintly. 'I think so.'

'Then I would suggest some sleep.'

'What a wonderful word that is.' Miller pushed himself wearily off the side of the bridge and stood there swaying as he drew an exhausted forearm over blood-shot, aching eyes. 'Wake me up in Alexandria.'

'Alexandria?' Ryan looked at him in amusement. 'We won't be there for thirty hours yet.'

'That's what I meant,' Miller said.

Miller didn't get his thirty hours. He had, in fact, been asleep for just over thirty minutes when he was wakened by the slow realization that something was hurting his eyes: after he had moaned and feebly protested for some time he managed to get one eye open and saw that that something was a bright overhead light let into the deck-head of the cabin that had been provided for Mallory and himself. Miller propped himself up on a groggy elbow, managed to get his second eye into commission and looked without enthusiasm at the other two occupants of the cabin: Mallory was seated by a table, apparently transcribing some kind of message, while Commander Ryan stood in the open doorway.

'This is outrageous,' Miller said bitterly. 'I haven't closed an eye all night.'

'You've been asleep for thirty-five minutes,' Ryan said. 'Sorry. But Cairo said this message for Captain Mallory was of the greatest urgency.'

'It is, is it?' Miller said suspiciously. He brightened. 'It's probably about promotions and medals and leave and so forth.' He looked hopefully at Mallory who had just straightened after decoding the message. 'Is it?'

'Well, no. It starts off promisingly enough, mind you, warmest congratulations and what-have-you, but after that the tone of the message deteriorates a bit.'

Mallory re-read the message: SIGNAL RECEIVED WARMEST CONGRATULATIONS MAGNIFICENT ACHIEVEMENT. YOU BLOODY FOOLS WHY YOU LET ANDREA GET AWAY? ESSENTIAL CONTACT HIM IMMEDIATELY. WILL EVACUATE BEFORE DAWN UNDER DIVERSIONARY AIR ATTACK AIR STRIP ONE MILE SOUTH-EAST MANDRAKOS. SEND CE VIA SIRDAR. URGENT 3 REPEAT URGENT 3. BEST LUCK. JENSEN.

Miller took the message from Mallory's outstretched hand, moved the paper to and fro until he had brought his bleary eyes into focus, read the message in horrified silence, handed it back to Mallory and stretched out his full length on his bunk. He said, 'Oh, my God!' and relapsed into what appeared to be a state of shock.

'That about sums it up,' Mallory agreed. He shook his head wearily and turned to Ryan. 'I'm sorry, sir, but we must trouble you for three things. A rubber dinghy, a portable radio transmitter and an immediate return to Navarone. Please arrange to have the radio lined up on a pre-set frequency to be constantly monitored by your WT room. When you receive a CE signal, transmit it to Cairo.'

'CE?' Ryan asked.

'Uh-huh. Just that.'

'And that's all?'

'We could do with a bottle of brandy,' Miller said. 'Something—anything—to see us through the rigours of the long night that lies ahead.'

Ryan lifted an eyebrow. 'A bottle of five-star, no doubt, Corporal?'

'Would you,' Miller asked morosely, 'give a bottle of three-star to a man going to his death?'

As it happened, Miller's gloomy expectations of an early demise turned out to be baseless—for that night, at least. Even the expected fearful rigours of the long night ahead proved to be no more than minor physical inconveniences.

By the time the *Sirdar* had brought them back to Navarone and as close in to the rocky shores as was prudent, the sky had become darkly overcast, rain was falling and a swell was beginning to blow up from the south-west so that it was little wonder to either Mallory or Miller that by the time they had paddled their dinghy within striking distance of the shore, they were in a very damp and miserable condition indeed: and it was even less wonder that by the time they had reached the boulder-strewn beach itself, they were soaked to the skin, for a breaking wave flung their dinghy against a sloping shelf of rock, overturning their rubber craft and precipitating them both into the sea. But this was of little enough account in itself: their Schmeisser machine-pistols, their radio, their torches were securely wrapped in waterproof bags and all of those were safely salvaged. All in all, Mallory reflected, an almost perfect three-point landing compared to the last time they had come to Navarone by boat, when their Greek caique, caught in the teeth of a giant storm, had been battered to pieces against the jaggedly vertical—and supposedly unclimbable—South Cliff of Navarone.

Slipping, stumbling and with suitably sulphuric comments, they made their way over the wet shingle and massively rounded boulders until their way was barred by a steeply-angled slope that soared up into the near-darkness above.

Mallory unwrapped a pencil torch and began to quarter the face of the slope with its narrow, concentrated beam. Miller touched him on the arm.

'Taking a bit of a chance, aren't we? With that thing, I mean?'

'No chance,' Mallory said. 'There won't be a soldier left on guard on the coasts tonight. They'll all be fighting the fires in the town. Besides, who is left for them to guard against? We are the birds and the birds, duty done, have flown. Only a madman would come back to the island again.'

'I know what we are,' Miller said with feeling. 'You don't have to tell me.'

Mallory smiled to himself in the darkness and continued his search. Within a minute he had located what he had been hoping to find—an angled gully in the slope. He and Miller scrambled up the shale- and rock-strewn bed of the gully as fast as the treacherous footing and their encumbrances would permit: within fifteen minutes they had reached the plateau above and paused to take their breath. Miller reached inside the depths of his tunic, a discreet movement that was at once followed by a discreet gurgling.

'What are you doing?' Mallory enquired.

'I thought I heard my teeth chattering. What's all this "urgent 3 repeat urgent 3" business in the message, then?'

'I've never seen it before. But I know what it means. Some people, somewhere, are about to die.'

'I'll tell you two for a start. And what if Andrea won't come? He's not a member of our armed forces. He doesn't have to come. *And* he said he was getting married right away.'

Mallory said with certainty: 'He'll come.'

'What makes you so sure?'

'Because Andrea is the one completely responsible man I've ever met. He has two great responsibilities—one to others, one to himself. That's why he came back to Navarone—because he knew the people needed him. And that's why he'll leave Navarone when he sees this "urgent 3" signal, because he'll know that someone, in some other place, needs him even more.'

Miller retrieved the brandy bottle from Mallory and thrust it securely inside his tunic again. 'Well, I can tell you this. The future Mrs Andrea Stavros isn't going to be very happy about it.'

'Neither is Andrea Stavros and I'm not looking forward to telling him,' Mallory said candidly. He peered at his luminous watch and swung to his feet. 'Mandrakos in half an hour.'

In precisely thirty minutes, their Schmeissers removed from their waterproof bags and now shoulder-slung at hip level, Mallory and Miller moved swiftly but very quietly from shadow to shadow through the plantations of carob trees on the outskirts of the village of Mandrakos. Suddenly, from directly ahead, they heard the unmistakable clink of glasses and bottlenecks.

For the two men a potentially dangerous situation such as this was so routine as not even to warrant a glance at each other. They dropped silently to their hands and knees and crawled forward, Miller sniffing the air appreciatively as they advanced: the Greek resinous spirit *ouzo* has an extraordinary ability to permeate the atmosphere for a considerable distance around it. Mallory and Miller reached the edge of a clump of bushes, sank prone and looked ahead.

From their richly-befrogged waistcoats, cummerbunds and fancy headgear, the two characters propped against the bole of a plane tree in the clearing ahead were obviously men of the island: from the rifles across their knees, their role appeared to be that of guards of some kind: from the almost vertical angle at which they had to tip the *ouzo* bottle to get at what little was left of its contents, it was equally apparent that they weren't taking their duties too seriously, nor had been for some considerable time past.

Mallory and Miller withdrew somewhat less stealthily than they had advanced, rose and glanced at each other. Suitable comment seemed lacking. Mallory shrugged and moved on, circling around to his right. Twice more, as they moved swiftly into the centre of Mandrakos, flitting from the shadow of carob grove to carob grove, from the shadow of plane tree to plane tree, from the shadow of house to house, they came upon but easily avoided other ostensible sentries, all busy interpreting their duties in a very liberal fashion. Miller pulled Mallory into a doorway.

'Our friends back there,' he said, 'What were they celebrating?'

'Wouldn't you? Celebrate, I mean. Navarone is useless to the Germans now. A week. from now and they'll all be gone.'

'All right. So why are they keeping a watch?' Miller nodded to a small, whitewashed Greek Orthodox church standing in the centre of the village square. From inside came a far from subdued murmur of voices. Also from inside came a great deal of light escaping through very imperfectly blacked-out windows. 'Could it be anything to do with that?'

Mallory said: 'Well, there's one sure way to find out.'

They moved quietly on, taking advantage of all available cover and shadow until they came to a still deeper shadow caused by two flying buttresses supporting the wall of the ancient church. Between the buttresses was one of the few more successfully blacked-out windows with only a tiny chink of light showing along the bottom edge. Both men stooped and peered through the narrow aperture.

The church appeared even more ancient inside than on the outside. The high unpainted wooden benches, adze-cut oak from centuries long gone, had been blackened and smoothed by untold generations of church-goers, the wood itself cracked and splintered by the ravages of time: the whitewashed walls looked as if they required buttresses within as well as without, crumbling to an extinction that could not now be long delayed: the roof appeared to be in imminent danger of falling in at any moment.

The now even louder hum of sound came from islanders of almost every age and sex, many in ceremonial dress, who occupied nearly every available seat in the church: the light came from literally hundreds of guttering candles, many of them ancient and twisted and ornamented and evidently called out for this special occasion, that lined the walls, the central aisle and the altar: by the altar itself, a priest, a bearded patriarch in Greek Orthodox robes, waited impassively.

Mallory and Miller looked interrogatively at each other and were on the point of standing upright when a very deep and very quiet voice spoke behind them.

'Hands behind the necks,' it said pleasantly. 'And straighten very slowly. I have a Schmeisser machine-pistol in my hands.'

Slowly and carefully, just as the voice asked, Mallory and Miller did as they were told.

'Turn round. Carefully, now.'

So they turned round, carefully. Miller looked at the massive dark figure who indeed had, as he'd claimed, a machine-pistol in his hands, and said irritably: 'Do you mind? Point that damned thing somewhere else.'

The dark figure gave a startled exclamation, lowered the gun to his side and bent forward, the dark, craggy, lined face expressing no more than a passing flicker of surprise. Andrea Stavros didn't go in very much for registering unnecessary emotional displays and the recovery of his habitual composure was instantaneous.

'The German uniforms,' he explained apologetically. 'They had me fooled.'

'You could have fooled me, too,' Miller said. He looked incredulously at Andrea's clothes, at the unbelievably baggy black trousers, the black jackboots, the intricately ornamented black waistcoat and violently purple cummerbund, shuddered and closed his eyes in pain. 'Been visiting the Mandrakos pawn-shop?'

'The ceremonial dress of my ancestors,' Andrea said mildly. 'You two fall overboard?'

'Not intentionally,' Mallory said. 'We came back to see you.'

'You could have chosen a more convenient time.' He hesitated, glanced at a small lighted building across the street and took their arms. 'We can talk in here.'

He ushered them in and closed the door behind him. The room was obviously, from its benches and Spartan furnishings, some sort of communal meeting-place, a village hall:

illumination came from three rather smoky oil-lamps, the
light from which was most hospitably reflected by the scores
of bottles of spirit and wine and beer and glasses that
took up almost every available inch of two long trestle
tables. The haphazardly unaesthetic layout of the refresh-
ments bespoke a very impromptu and hastily improvised
preparation for a celebration: the serried rows of bottles
heralded the intention of compensating for lack of quality
by an excess of quantity.

Andrea crossed to the nearest table, picked up three glasses
and a bottle of *ouzo*, and began to pour drinks. Miller fished
out his brandy and offered it, but Andrea was too preoc-
cupied to notice. He handed them the *ouzo* glasses.

'Health.' Andrea drained his glass and went on thoughtfully: 'You did not return without a good reason, my
Keith.'

Silently, Mallory removed the Cairo radio message from its
waterproof oilskin wallet and handed it to Andrea, who
took it half-unwillingly, then read it, scowling blackly.

He said: 'Urgent 3 means what I think it means?'

Again Mallory remained silent, merely nodding as he
watched Andrea unwinkingly.

'This is most inconvenient for me.' The scowl deepened.
'*Most* inconvenient. There are many things for me to do in
Navarone. The people will miss me.'

'It's also inconvenient for me,' Miller said. 'There are many
things *I* could profitably be doing in the West End of
London. They miss me, too. Ask any barmaid. But that's
hardly the point.'

Andrea regarded him for an impassive moment, then
looked at Mallory. '*You* are saying nothing.'

'I've nothing to say.'

The scowl slowly left Andrea's face, though the brooding
frown remained. He hesitated, then reached again for the
bottle of *ouzo*. Miller shuddered delicately.

'Please.' He indicated the bottle of brandy.

Andrea smiled, briefly and for the first time, poured some
of Miller's five-star into their glasses, re-read the message and

handed it back to Mallory. 'I must think it over. I have some business to attend to first.'

Mallory looked at him thoughtfully. 'Business?'

'I have to attend a wedding.'

'A wedding?' Miller said politely.

'Must you two repeat everything I say? A wedding.'

'But who do *you* know?' Miller asked. 'And at this hour of night.'

'For some people in Navarone,' Andrea said drily, 'the night is the only safe time.' He turned abruptly, walked away, opened the door and hesitated.

Mallory said curiously: 'Who's getting married?'

Andrea made no reply. Instead he walked back to the nearest table, poured and drained a half-tumbler of the brandy, ran a hand through his thick dark hair, straightened his cummerbund, squared his shoulders and walked purposefully towards the door. Mallory and Miller stared after him, then at the door that closed behind him: then they stared at each other.

Some fifteen minutes later they were still staring at each other, this time with expressions which alternated between the merely bemused and slightly stunned.

They were seated in the back seat of the Greek Orthodox church—the only part of any pew in the entire church not now occupied by islanders. From where they sat, the altar was at least sixty feet away but as they were both tall men and sitting by the central aisle, they had a pretty fair view of what was going on up there.

There was, to be accurate, nothing going on up there any more. The ceremony was over. Gravely, the Orthodox priest bestowed his blessing and Andrea and Maria, the girl who had shown them the way into the fortress of Navarone, turned with the slow dignity becoming the occasion, and walked down the aisle. Andrea bent over, tenderness and solicitousness both in expression and manner, and whispered something in her ear, but his words, it would have seemed, bore little relation to the way in which they were expressed for half-way down the aisle a furious altercation broke out between them. Between, perhaps, is not the right word: it was less an altercation than a very one-sided monologue. Maria, her face flushed and dark eyes flashing, gesticulating and clearly mad through, was addressing Andrea in far from low tones of not even barely-controlled fury: Andrea, for his part, was deprecatory, placatory, trying to hush her up with about the same amount of success as Canute had in holding back the tide, and looking apprehensively around. The reaction of the seated guests varied from disbelief through open-mouthed astonishment and bafflement to downright horror: clearly all regarded the spectacle as a highly unusual aftermath to a wedding ceremony.

As the couple approached the end of the aisle opposite the pew where Mallory and Miller were seated, the argument, if such it could be called, raged more furiously than ever. As they passed by the end pew, Andrea, hand over his mouth, leaned over towards Mallory.

'This,' he said, *sotto voce*, 'is our first married quarrel.'

He was given time to say no more. An imperative hand seized his arm and almost literally dragged him through the church doorway. Even after they had disappeared from sight, Maria's voice, loud and clear, could still be heard by everyone within the church. Miller turned from surveying the empty doorway and looked thoughtfully at Mallory.

'Very high-spirited girl, that. I wish I understood Greek. What was she saying there?'

Mallory kept his face carefully expressionless. 'What about my honeymoon?'

'Ah!' Miller's face was equally dead-pan. 'Don't you think we'd better follow them?'

'Why?'

'Andrea can take care of most people.' It was the usual masterly Miller understatement. 'But he's stepped out of his class this time.'

Mallory smiled, rose and went to the door, followed by Miller, who was in turn followed by an eager press of guests understandably anxious to see the second act of this unscheduled entertainment: but the village square was empty of life.

Mallory did not hesitate. With the instinct born from the experience of long association with Andrea, he headed across the square to the communal hall where Andrea had made the earlier of his two dramatic statements. His instincts hadn't betrayed him. Andrea, with a large glass of brandy in his hand and moodily fingering a spreading patch of red on his cheek, looked up as Mallory and Miller entered.

He said moodily: 'She's gone home to her mother.'

Miller glanced at his watch. 'One minute and twenty-five seconds,' he said admiringly. 'A world record.'

Andrea glowered at him and Mallory moved in hastily.

'You're coming, then.'

'Of course I'm coming,' Andrea said irritably. He surveyed without enthusiasm the guests now swarming into the hall and brushing unceremoniously by as they headed, like the camel for the oasis, towards the bottle-laden tables. 'Somebody's got to look after you two.'

Mallory looked at his watch. 'Three and a half hours yet before that plane is due. We're dead on our feet, Andrea. Where can we sleep—a safe place to sleep. Your perimeter guards are drunk.'

'They've been that way ever since the fortress blew up,' Andrea said. 'Come, I'll show you.'

Miller looked around the islanders, who, amid a loud babel of cheerful voices, were already quite exceptionally busy with bottles and glasses. 'How about your guests?'

'How about them, then?' Andrea surveyed his compatriots morosely. 'Just look at that lot. Ever known a wedding reception yet where anybody paid any attention to the bride and groom? Come.'

They made their way southwards through the outskirts of Mandrakos to the open countryside beyond. Twice they were challenged by guards, twice a scowl and growl from Andrea sent them back hurriedly to their *ouzo* bottles. It was still raining heavily, but Mallory's and Miller's clothes were already so saturated that a little more rain could hardly make any appreciable difference to the way they felt, while Andrea, if anything, seemed even more oblivious of it. Andrea had the air of a man who had other things on his mind.

After fifteen minutes' walk, Andrea stopped before the swing doors of a small, dilapidated and obviously deserted roadside barn.

'There's hay inside,' he said. 'We'll be safe here.'

Mallory said: 'Fine. A radio message to the *Sirdar* to send her CE message to Cairo and—'

'CE?' Andrea asked. 'What's that?'

'To let Cairo know we've contacted you and are ready for pick-up . . . And after that, three lovely long hours' sleep.'

Andrea nodded. 'Three hours it is.'

'Three *long* hours,' Mallory said meditatively.

A smile slowly broke on Andrea's craggy face as he clapped Mallory on the shoulder.

'In three long hours,' he said, 'a man like myself can accomplish a great deal.'

He turned and hurried off through the rain-filled night. Mallory and Miller looked after him with expressionless faces, looked at each other, still with the same expressionless faces, then pushed open the swing doors of the barn.

The Mandrakos airfield would not have received a licence from any Civil Air Board anywhere in the world. It was just over half a mile long, with hills rising steeply at both ends of the alleged runway, not more than forty yards wide and liberally besprinkled with a variety of bumps and potholes virtually guaranteed to wreck any undercarriage in the aviation business. But the RAF had used it before so it was not impossible that they might be able to use it at least once again.

To the south, the airstrip was lined with groves of carob trees. Under the pitiful shelter afforded by one of those, Mallory, Miller and Andrea sat waiting. At least Mallory and Miller did, hunched, miserable and shivering violently in their still sodden clothes. Andrea, however, was stretched out luxuriously with his hands behind his head, oblivious of the heavy drips of rain that fell on his upturned face. There was about him an air of satisfaction, of complacency almost, as he gazed at the first greyish tinges appearing in the sky to the east over the black-walled massif of the Turkish coast.

Andrea said: 'They're coming now.'

Mallory and Miller listened for a few moments, then they too heard it—the distant, muted roar of heavy aircraft approaching. All three rose and moved out to the perimeter of the airstrip. Within a minute, descending rapidly after their climb over the mountains to the south and at a height of less than a thousand feet, a squadron of eighteen Wellingtons, as much heard as seen in the light of early dawn, passed directly over the airstrip, heading for the town of Navarone. Two minutes later, the three watchers both heard the detonations and saw the brilliant orange mushrooming of light as the Wellingtons unloaded their bombs over the shattered fortress to the north. Sporadic lines of upward-flying tracers, obviously exclusively small-arm, attested to the ineffectuality, the weakness of the ground defences. When the fortress had blown up, so had all the anti-aircraft batteries in the town. The attack was short and sharp: less than two minutes after the bombardment had started it ceased as abruptly as it had begun and then there was only the fading dying sound of de-synchronized engines as the Wellingtons pulled away, first to the north and then the west, across the still-dark waters of the Aegean.

For perhaps a minute the three watchers stood silent on the perimeter of the Mandrakos airstrip, then Miller said wonderingly: 'What makes us so important?'

'I don't know,' Mallory said. 'But I don't think you're going to enjoy finding out.'

'And that won't be long now.' Andrea turned round and looked towards the mountains to the south. 'Hear it?'

Neither of the others heard it, but they did not doubt that, in fact, there was something to hear. Andrea's hearing was on a par with his phenomenal eyesight. Then, suddenly, they could hear it, too. A solitary bomber—also a Wellington—came sinking in from the south, circled the perimeter area once as Mallory blinked his torch upwards in rapidly successive flashes, lined up its approach, landed heavily at the far end of the airstrip and came taxiing towards them, bumping heavily across the atrocious surface of the airfield. It halted less than a hundred yards from where they stood: then a light started winking from the flight-deck.

Andrea said: 'Now, don't forget. I've promised to be back in a week.'

'Never make promises,' Miller said severely. 'What if we aren't back in a week? What if they're sending us to the Pacific?'

'Then when we get back I'll send you in first to explain.'

Miller shook his head. 'I don't really think I'd like that.'

'We'll talk about your cowardice later on,' Mallory said. 'Come on. Hurry up.'

The three men broke into a run towards the waiting Wellington.

The Wellington was half an hour on the way to its destination, wherever its destination was, and Andrea and Miller, coffee-mugs in hand, were trying, unsuccessfully, to attain a degree of comfort on the lumpy palliasses on the fuselage floor when Mallory returned from the flight-deck. Miller looked up at him in weary resignation, his expression characterized by an entire lack of enthusiasm and the spirit of adventure.

'Well, what did you find out?' His tone of voice made it abundantly clear that what he had expected Mallory to find out was nothing short of the very worst. 'Where to, now? Rhodes? Beirut? The flesh-pots of Cairo?'

'Termoli, the man says.'

'Termoli, is it? Place I've always wanted to see.' Miller paused. 'Where the hell's Termoli?'

'Italy, so I believe. Somewhere on the south Adriatic coast.'

'Oh, no!' Miller turned on his side and pulled a blanket over his head. 'I *hate* spaghetti.'

II

THURSDAY 1400-2330

The landing on Termoli airfield, on the Adriatic coast of Southern Italy, was every bit as bumpy as the harrowing take-off from the Mandrakos airstrip had been. The Termoli fighter air-base was officially and optimistically listed as newly-constructed but in point of fact was no more than half-finished and felt that way for every yard of the excruciating touch-down and the jack-rabbit run-up to the prefabricated control-tower at the eastern end of the field. When Mallory and Andrea swung down to terra firma, neither of them looked particularly happy: Miller, who came a very shaky last, and who was widely known to have an almost pathological loathing and detestation of all conceivable forms of transport, looked very ill indeed.

Miller was given time neither to seek nor receive commiseration. A camouflaged British 5th Army jeep pulled up alongside the plane, and the sergeant at the wheel, having briefly established their identity, waved them inside in silence, a silence which he stonily maintained on their drive through the shambles of the war-torn streets of Termoli. Mallory was unperturbed by the apparent unfriendliness. The driver was obviously under the strictest instructions not to talk to them, a situation which Mallory had encountered all too often in the past. There were not, Mallory reflected, very many groups of untouchables, but his, he knew, was one of them: no one, with two or three rare exceptions, was ever permitted to talk to them. The process, Mallory knew, was perfectly understandable and justifiable, but it was an attitude that did tend to become increasingly wearing with the passing of the years. It tended to make for a certain lack of contact with one's fellow-men.

After twenty minutes, the jeep stopped below the broad-flagged steps of a house on the outskirts of the town. The jeep driver gestured briefly to an armed sentry on the top of the steps who responded with a similarly perfunctory greeting. Mallory took this as a sign that they had arrived at their destination and, not wishing to violate the young sergeant's vow of silence, got out without being told. The others followed and the jeep at once drove off.

The house—it looked more like a modest palace—was a rather splendid example of late Renaissance architecture, all colonnades and columns and everything in veined marble, but Mallory was more interested in what was inside the house than what it was made of on the outside. At the head of the steps their path was barred by the young corporal sentry armed with a Lee-Enfield .303. He looked like a refugee from high school.

'Names, please.'

'Captain Mallory.'

'Identity papers? Pay-books?'

'Oh, my God,' Miller moaned. 'And me feeling so sick, too.'

'We have none,' Mallory said gently. 'Take us inside, please.'

'My instructions are—'

'I know, I know,' Andrea said soothingly. He leaned across, effortlessly removed the rifle from the corporal's desperate grasp, ejected and pocketed the magazine and returned the rifle. 'Please, now.'

Red-faced and furious, the youngster hesitated briefly, looked at the three men more carefully, turned, opened the door behind him and gestured for the three to follow him.

Before them stretched a long, marble-flagged corridor, tall leaded windows on one side, heavy oil paintings and the occasional set of double-leather doors on the other. Half-way down the passage Andrea tapped the corporal on the shoulder and handed the magazine back without a word. The corporal took it, smiling uncertainly, and inserted it into his rifle without a word. Another twenty paces and he stopped before the last pair of leather doors, knocked, heard a muffled acknowledgment and pushed open one of the doors, standing aside to let the three men pass him. Then he moved out again, closing the door behind him.

It was obviously the main drawing-room of the house—or palace—furnished in an almost medieval opulence, all dark oak, heavily brocaded silk curtains, leather upholstery, leather-bound books, what were undoubtedly a set of Old Masters on the walls and a flowing sea of dull bronze carpeting from wall to wall. Taken all in all, even a member of the old-pre-war Italian nobility wouldn't have turned up his nose at it.

The room was pleasantly redolent with the smell of burning pine, the source of which wasn't difficult to locate: one could have roasted a very large ox indeed in the vast and crackling fireplace at the far end of the room. Close by this fireplace stood three young men who bore no resemblance whatsoever to the rather ineffectual youngster who had so recently tried to prevent their entry. They were, to begin with, a good few years older, though still young men. They were heavily-built, broad-shouldered characters and had about them a look of tough and hard-bitten competence. They were dressed in the uniform of that élite of combat troops, the Marine Commandos, and they looked perfectly at home in those uniforms.

But what caught and held the unwavering attention of Mallory and his two companions was neither the rather splendidly effete decadence of the room and its furnishings nor the wholly unexpected presence of the three commandos: it was the fourth figure in the room, a tall, heavily built and commanding figure who leaned negligently against a table in the centre of the room. The deeply-trenched face, the authoritative expression, the splendid grey beard and the piercing blue eyes made him a prototype for the classic British naval captain, which, as the immaculate white uniform he wore indicated, was precisely what he was. With a collective sinking of their hearts, Mallory, Andrea and Miller gazed again, and with a marked lack of enthusiasm, upon the splendidly piratical figure of Captain Jensen, RN, Chief of Allied Intelligence, Mediterranean, and the man who had so recently sent them on their suicidal mission to the island of Navarone. All three looked at one another and shook their heads in slow despair.

Captain Jensen straightened, smiled his magnificent sabre-toothed tiger's smile and strode forward to greet them, his hand outstretched.

'Mallory! Andrea! Miller!' There was a dramatic five-second pause between the words. 'I don't know what to say! I just don't know what to say! A magnificent job, a magnificent—' He broke off and regarded them thoughtfully. 'You—um—don't seem all that surprised to see me, Captain Mallory?'

'I'm not. With respect, sir, whenever and wherever there's dirty work afoot, one looks to find—'

'Yes, yes, yes. Quite, quite. And how are you all?'

'Tired,' Miller said firmly. 'Terribly tired. We need a rest. At least, I do.'

Jensen said earnestly: 'And that's exactly what you're going to have, my boy. A rest. A long one. A *very* long one.'

'A *very* long one?' Miller looked at him in frank incredulity.

'You have my word.' Jensen stroked his beard in momentary diffidence. 'Just as soon, that is, as you get back from Yugoslavia.'

'Yugoslavia!' Miller stared at him.

'Tonight.'

'Tonight!'

'By parachute.'

'By *parachute*!'

Jensen said with forbearance: 'I am aware, Corporal Miller, that you have had a classical education and are, moreover, just returned from the Isles of Greece. But we'll do without the Ancient Greek Chorus bit, if you don't mind.'

Miller looked moodily at Andrea. 'Bang goes your honeymoon.'

'What was that?' Jensen asked sharply.

'Just a private joke, sir.'

Mallory said in mild protest: 'You're forgetting, sir, that none of us has ever made a parachute jump.'

'I'm forgetting nothing. There's a first time for everything. What do you gentlemen know about the war in Yugoslavia?'

'What war?' Andrea said warily.

'Precisely.' There was satisfaction in Jensen's voice.

'I heard about it,' Miller volunteered. 'There's a bunch of what-do-you-call-'em—Partisans, isn't it—offering some kind of underground resistance to the German occupation troops.'

'It is probably as well for you,' Jensen said heavily, 'that the Partisans cannot hear you. They're not underground, they're very much over ground and at the latest count there were 350,000 of them tying down twenty-eight German and Bulgarian divisions in Yugoslavia.' He paused briefly. 'More, in fact, than the combined Allied armies are tying down here in Italy.'

'Somebody should have told me,' Miller complained. He brightened. 'If there's 350,000 of them around, what would they want us for?'

Jensen said acidly: 'You must learn to curb your enthusiasm, Corporal. The fighting part of it you may leave to the Partisans—and they're fighting the cruellest, hardest, most brutal war in Europe today. A ruthless, vicious war with no quarter and no surrender on either side. Arms, munitions, food, clothes—the Partisans are desperately short of all of those. But they have those twenty-eight divisions pinned down.'

'I don't want any part of that,' Miller muttered.

Mallory said hastily: 'What do you want us to do, sir?'

'This.' Jensen removed his glacial stare from Miller. 'Nobody appreciates it yet, but the Yugoslavs are our most important Allies in Southern Europe. Their war is our war. And they're fighting a war they can never hope to win. Unless—'

Mallory nodded. 'The tools to finish the job.'

'Hardly original, but true. The tools to finish the job. We are the *only* people who are at present supplying them with rifles, machine-guns, ammunition, clothing and medical

supplies. And those are not getting through.' He broke
off, picking up a cane, walked almost angrily across the
room to a large wall-map hanging between a couple of
Old Masters and rapped the tip of the bamboo against
it. 'Bosnia-Herzegovina, gentlemen. West-Central Yugoslavia.
We've sent in four British Military Missions in the
past two months to liaise with the Yugoslavs—the Partisan
Yugoslavs. The leaders of all four missions have disappeared without trace. Ninety per cent of our recent airlift
supplies have fallen into German hands. They have broken
all our radio codes and have established a network of
agents in Southern Italy here with whom they are apparently
able to communicate as and when they wish. Perplexing
questions, gentlemen. Vital questions. I want the answers.
Force 10 will get me the answers.'

'Force 10?' Mallory said politely.

'The code name for your operation.'

'Why that particular name?' Andrea asked.

'Why not? Ever heard of *any* code name that had *any*
bearing on the operation on hand? It's the whole essence
of it, man.'

'It wouldn't, of course,' Mallory said woodenly, 'have
anything to do with a frontal attack on something, a
storming of some vital place.' He observed Jensen's total lack
of reaction and went on in the same tone: 'On the Beaufort
Scale, Force 10 means a storm.'

'A storm!' It is very difficult to combine an exclamation
and a moan of anguish in the same word, but Miller managed
it without any difficulty. 'Oh my God, and all I want is
a flat calm, and that for the rest of my life.'

'There are limits to my patience, Corporal Miller,' Jensen
said. 'I may—I say *may*—have to change my mind about a
recommendation I made on your behalf this morning.'

'On my behalf?' Miller said guardedly.

'For the Distinguished Conduct Medal.'

'*That* should look nice on the lid of my coffin,' Miller
muttered.

'What was that?'

'Corporal Miller was just expressing his appreciation.'

Mallory moved closer to the wall-map and studied it briefly. 'Bosnia-Herzegovina—well, it's a fair-sized area, sir.'

'Agreed. But we can pin-point the spot—the approximate location of the disappearances—to within twenty miles.'

Mallory turned from the map and said slowly: 'There's been a lot of homework on this one. That raid this morning on Navarone. The Wellington standing by to take us here. All preparations—I infer this from what you've said—laid on for tonight. Not to mention—'

'We've been working on this for almost two months. You three were supposed to have come here some days ago. But —ah—well, you know.'

'We know.' The threatened withholding of his DCM had left Miller unmoved. 'Something else came up. Look, sir, why us? We're saboteurs, explosive experts, combat troops—this is a job for undercover espionage agents who speak Serbo-Croat or whatever.'

'You must allow me to be the best judge of that.' Jensen gave them another flash of his sabre-toothed smile. 'Besides, you're lucky.'

'Luck deserts tired men,' Andrea said. 'And we are very tired.'

'Tired or not, I can't find another team in Southern Europe to match you for resource, experience and skill.' Jensen smiled again. 'And luck. I have to be ruthless, Andrea. I don't like it, but I have to. But I take the point about your exhaustion. That's why I have decided to send a back-up team with you.'

Mallory looked at the three young soldiers standing by the hearth, then back to Jensen, who nodded.

'They're young, fresh and just raring to go. Marine Commandos, the most highly trained combat troops we have today. Remarkable variety of skills, I assure you. Take Reynolds, here.' Jensen nodded to a very tall, dark sergeant in his late twenties, a man with a deeply-tanned aquiline face. 'He can do anything from underwater demolition to flying a plane. And he will be flying a plane tonight. And, as you can see, he'll come in handy for carrying any heavy cases you have.'

Mallory said mildly: 'I've always found that Andrea makes a pretty fair porter, sir.'

Jensen turned to Reynolds. 'They have their doubts. Show them you can be of some use.'

Reynolds hesitated, then stooped, picked up a heavy brass poker and proceeded to bend it between his hands. Obviously, it wasn't an easy poker to bend. His face turned red, the veins stood out on his forehead and the tendons in his neck, his arms quivered with the strain, but slowly, inexorably, the poker was bent into a figure 'U'. Smiling almost apologetically, Reynolds handed the poker over to Andrea. Andrea took it reluctantly. He hunched his shoulders, his knuckles gleamed white but the poker remained in its 'U' shape. Andrea looked up at Reynolds, his expression thoughtful, then quietly laid the poker down.

'See what I mean?' Jensen said. 'Tired. Or Sergeant Groves here. Hot-foot from London, via the Middle East. Ex-air navigator, with all the latest in sabotage, explosives and electrics. For booby-traps, time-bombs and concealed microphones, a human mine-detector. And Sergeant Saunders here —a top-flight radio-operator.'

Miller said morosely to Mallory: 'You're a toothless old lion and you're over the hill.'

'Don't talk rubbish, Corporal!' Jensen's voice was sharp. 'Six is the ideal number. You'll be duplicated in every department, and those men are *good*. They'll be invaluable. If it's any salve to your pride, they weren't originally picked to go with you: they were picked as a reserve team in case you —um—well—'

'I see.' The lack of conviction in Miller's voice was total. 'All clear, then?'

'Not quite,' Mallory said. 'Who's in charge?'

Jensen said in genuine surprise: 'You are, of course.'

'So.' Mallory spoke quietly and pleasantly. 'I understand the training emphasis today—especially in the Marine Commandos—is on initiative, self-reliance, independence in thought and action. Fine—if they happen to be caught out on their own.' He smiled, almost deprecatingly. 'Otherwise

I shall expect imm⌐   ⌐nquestioning and total compliance
with orders. M⌐⌐   ⌐ant and total.'

'And if not? Reynolds asked.

'A superfluous question, Sergeant. You know the wartime
penalty for disobeying an officer in the field.'

'Does that apply to your friends, too?'

'No.'

Reynolds turned to Jensen. 'I don't think I like that, sir.'

Mallory sank wearily into a chair, lit a cigarette, nodded
at Reynolds and said, 'Replace him.'

'What!' Jensen was incredulous.

'Replace him, I said. We haven't even left and already he's
questioning my judgment. What's it going to be like in
action? He's dangerous. I'd rather carry a ticking time-bomb
with me.'

'Now, look here, Mallory—'

'Replace him or replace me.'

'And me,' Andrea said quietly.

'And me,' Miller added.

There was a brief and far from companionable silence in
the room, then Reynolds aproached Mallory's chair.

'Sir.'

Mallory looked at him without encouragement.

'I'm sorry,' Reynolds went on. 'I stepped out of line. I
will never make the same mistake twice. I *want* to go on
this trip, sir.'

Mallory glanced at Andrea and Miller. Miller's face registered only his shock at Reynolds's incredibly foolhardy enthusiasm for action. Andrea, impassive as ever, nodded
almost imperceptibly. Mallory smiled and said: 'As Captain
Jensen said, I'm sure you'll be a great asset.'

'Well, that's it, then.' Jensen affected not to notice the
almost palpable relaxation of tension in the room. 'Sleep's
the thing now. But first I'd like a few minutes—report on
Navarone, you know.' He looked at the three sergeants.
'Confidential, I'm afraid.'

'Yes, sir,' Reynolds said. 'Shall we go down to the field,
check flight plans, weather, parachutes and supplies?'

Jensen nodded. As the three sergeants closed the double

doors behind them, Jensen crossed to a side door, opened it and said: 'Come in, General.'

The man who entered was very tall, very gaunt. He was probably about thirty-five, but looked a great deal older. The care, the exhaustion, the endless privations inseparable from too many years' ceaseless struggle for survival had heavily silvered the once-black hair and deeply etched into the swarthy, sunburnt face the lines of physical and mental suffering. The eyes were dark and glowing and intense, the hypnotic eyes of a man inspired by a fanatical dedication to some as yet unrealized ideal. He was dressed in a British Army officer's uniform, bereft of insignia and badges.

Jensen said: 'Gentlemen, General Vukalovic. The general is second-in-command of the Partisan forces in Bosnia-Herzegovina. The RAF flew him out yesterday. He is here as a Partisan doctor seeking medical supplies. His true identity is known only to us. General, those are your men.'

Vukalovic looked them over severally and steadily, his face expressionless. He said: 'Those are tired men, Captain Jensen. So much depends . . . too tired to do what has to be done.'

'He's right, you know,' Miller said earnestly.

'There's maybe a little mileage left in them yet,' Jensen said mildly. 'It's a long haul from Navarone. Now then—'

'Navarone?' Vukalovic interrupted. 'These—these are the men—'

'An unlikely-looking lot, I agree.'

'Perhaps I was wrong about them.'

'No, you weren't, General,' Miller said. 'We're exhausted. We're completely—'

'Do you mind?' Jensen said acidly. 'Captain Mallory, with two exceptions the General will be the only person in Bosnia who knows who you are and what you are doing. Whether the General reveals the identity of the others is entirely up to him. General Vukalovic will be accompanying you to Yugoslavia, but not in the same plane.'

'Why not?' Mallory asked.

'Because his plane will be returning. Yours won't.'

'Ah!' Mallory said. There was a brief silence while he,

Andrea and Miller absorbed the significance behind Jensen's words. Abstractedly, Andrea threw some more wood on the sinking fire and looked around for a poker: but the only poker was the one that Reynolds had already bent into a 'U'-shape. Andrea picked it up. Absent-mindedly, effortlessly, Andrea straightened it out, poked the fire into a blaze and laid the poker down, a performance Vukalovic watched with a very thoughtful expression on his face.

Jensen went on: 'Your plane, Captain Mallory, will not be returning because your plane is expendable in the interests of authenticity.'

'Us, too?' Miller asked.

'You won't be able to accomplish very much, Corporal Miller, without actually putting your feet on the ground. Where you're going, no plane can possibly land: so you jump—and the plane crashes.'

'That sounds very authentic,' Miller muttered.

Jensen ignored him. 'The realities of total war are harsh beyond belief. Which is why I sent those three youngsters on their way—I don't want to dampen their enthusiasm.'

'Mine's water-logged,' Miller said dolefully.

'Oh, do be quiet. Now, it would be fine if, by way of a bonus, you could discover why eighty per cent of our airdrops fall into German hands, fine if you could locate and rescue our captured mission leaders. But not important. Those supplies, those agents are militarily expendable. What are not expendable are the seven thousand men under the command of General Vukalovic here, seven thousand men trapped in an area called the Zenica Cage, seven thousand starving men with almost no ammunition left, seven thousand men with no future.'

'We can help them?' Andrea asked heavily. 'Six men?'

Jensen said candidly: 'I don't know.'

'But you have a plan?'

'Not yet. Not as such. The glimmerings of an idea. No more.' Jensen rubbed his forehead wearily. 'I myself arrived from Alexandria only six hours ago.' He hesitated, then shrugged. 'By tonight, who knows? A few hours' sleep this afternoon might transform us all. But, first, the report on

Navarone. It would be pointless for you three other gentlemen to wait—there are sleeping-quarters down the hall. I
daresay Captain Mallory can tell me all I want to know.'

Mallory waited till the door closed behind Andrea, Miller
and Vukalovic and said: 'Where shall I begin my report,
sir?'

'What report?'

'Navarone, of course.'

'The hell with Navarone. That's over and done with.' He
picked up his cane, crossed to the wall, pulled down two
more maps. 'Now, then.'

'You—you *have* a plan,' Mallory said carefully.

'Of course I have a plan,' Jensen said coldly. He rapped
the map in front of him. 'Ten miles north of here. The
Gustav Line. Right across Italy along the line of the Sangro
and Liri rivers. Here the Germans have the most impregnable defensive positions in the history of modern warfare.
Monte Cassino here—our finest Allied divisions have broken
on it, some for ever. And here—the Anzio beach-head. Fifty
thousand Americans fighting for their lives. For five solid
months now we've been battering our heads against the
Gustav Line and the Anzio perimeter. Our losses in men
and machines—incalculable. Our gains—not one solitary
inch.'

Mallory said diffidently: 'You mentioned something about
Yugoslavia, sir.'

'I'm coming to that,' Jensen said with restraint. 'Now, our
only hope of breaching the Gustav Line is by weakening the
German defensive forces and the only way we can do *that*
is by persuading them to withdraw some of their front-line
divisions. So we practise the Allenby technique.'

'I see.'

'You don't see at all. General Allenby, Palestine, 1918. He
had an east-west line from the Jordan to the Mediterranean.
He planned to attack from the west—so he convinced the
Turks the attack was coming from the east. He did this
by building up in the east a huge city of army tents occupied
by only a few hundred men who came out and dashed
around like beavers whenever enemy planes came over on

reconnaissance. He did this by letting the same planes see large army truck convoys pouring to the east all day long —what the Turks didn't know was that the same convoys poured back to the west all night long. He even had fifteen thousand canvas dummies of horses built. Well, we're doing the same.'

'Fifteen thousand canvas horses?'

'Very, very amusing.' Jensen rapped the map again. 'Every airfield between here and Bari is jammed with dummy bombers and gliders. Outside Foggia is the biggest military encampment in Italy—occupied by two hundred men. The harbours of Bari and Taranto are crowded with assault landing-craft, the whole lot made of plywood. All day long columns of trucks and tanks converge on the Adriatic coast. If you, Mallory, were in the German High Command, what would you make of this?'

'I'd suspect an airborne and sea invasion of Yugoslavia. But I wouldn't be sure.'

'The German reaction exactly,' Jensen said with some satisfaction. 'They're badly worried, worried to the extent that they have already transferred two divisions from Italy to Yugoslavia to meet the threat.'

'But they're not certain?'

'Not quite. But almost.' Jensen cleared his throat. 'You see, our four captured mission leaders were all carrying unmistakable evidence pointing to an invasion of Central Yugoslavia in early May.'

'They carried evidence—' Mallory broke off, looked at Jensen for a long and speculative moment, then went on quietly: 'And how *did* the Germans manage to capture them all?'

'We told them they were coming.'

'You did what!'

'Volunteers all, volunteers all,' Jensen said quickly. There were, apparently, some of the harsher realities of total war that even he didn't care to dwell on too long. 'And it will be your job, my boy, to turn near-conviction into absolute certainty.' Seemingly oblivious of the fact that Mallory was regarding him with a marked lack of enthusiasm, he wheeled round dramatically and stabbed his cane at a large-scale map of Central Yugoslavia.

'The valley of the Neretva,' Jensen said. 'The vital sector of the main north-south route through Yugoslavia. Whoever controls this valley controls Yugoslavia—and no one knows this better than the Germans. If the blow falls, they know it must fall here. They are fully aware that an invasion of Yugoslavia is on the cards, they are terrified of a link-up between the Allies and the Russians advancing from the east and they *know* that any such link-up must be along this valley. They already have two armoured divisions along the Neretva, two divisions that, in the event of invasion, could be wiped out in a night. From the north—here—they are trying to force their way south to the Neretva with a whole army corps—but the only way is through the Zenica Cage here. And Vukalovic and his seven thousand men block the way.'

'Vukalovic knows about this?' Mallory asked. 'About what you really have in mind, I mean?'

'Yes. And the Partisan command. They know the risks, the odds against them. They accept them.'

'Photographs?' Mallory asked.

'Here.' Jensen pulled some photographs from a desk drawer, selected one and smoothed it out on the table. 'This is the Zenica Cage. Well-named: a perfect cage, a perfect trap. To the north and west, impassable mountains. To the east, the Neretva dam and the Neretva gorge. To the south, the Neretva river. To the north of the cage here, at the Zenica gap, the German 11th Army Corps is trying to break through. To the west here—they call it the West Gap— more units of the 11th trying to do the same. And to the south here, over the river and hidden in the trees, two armoured divisions under a General Zimmermann.'

'And this?' Mallory pointed to a thin black line spanning the river just north of the two armoured divisions.

'That,' Jensen said thoughtfully, 'is the bridge at Neretva.'

Close-up, the bridge at Neretva looked vastly more impressive than it had done in the large-scale photograph: it was a massively cantilevered structure in solid steel, with a black asphalt roadway laid on top. Below the bridge rushed the swiftly-flowing Neretva, greenish-white in colour and swollen with melting snow. To the south there was a narrow strip of green meadowland bordering the river and, to the south of this again, a dark and towering pine forest began. In the safe concealment of the forest's gloomy depths, General Zimmermann's two armoured divisions crouched waiting.

Parked close to the edge of the wood was the divisional command radio truck, a bulky and very long vehicle so beautifully camouflaged as to be invisible at more than twenty paces.

General Zimmermann and his ADC, Captain Warburg, were at that moment inside the truck. Their mood appeared to match the permanent twilight of the woods. Zimmermann had one of those high-foreheaded, lean and aquiline and intelligent faces which so rarely betray any emotion, but there was no lack of emotion now, no lack of anxiety and impatience as he removed his cap and ran his hand through his thinning grey hair. He said to the radio-operator seated behind the big transceiver:

'No word yet? Nothing?'

'Nothing, sir.'

'You are in constant touch with Captain Neufeld's camp?'

'Every minute, sir.'

'And his operator is keeping a continuous radio watch?'

'All the time, sir. Nothing. Just nothing.'

Zimmermann turned and descended the steps, followed by Warburg. He walked, head down, until he was out of earshot of the truck, then said: 'Damn it! Damn it! God damn it all!'

'You're as sure as that, sir.' Warburg was tall, good-looking, flaxen-haired and thirty, and his face at the moment reflected a nice balance of apprehension and unhappiness. 'That they're coming?'

'It's in my bones, boy. One way or another it's coming, coming for all of us.'

'You can't be *sure*, sir,' Warburg protested.

'True enough.' Zimmermann sighed. 'I can't be sure. But

I'm sure of this. If they do come, if the 11th Army Group can't break through from the north, if we can't wipe out those damned Partisans in the Zenica Cage—'

Warburg waited for him to continue, but Zimmermann seemed lost in reverie. Apparently apropos of nothing, Warburg said: 'I'd like to see Germany again, sir. Just once more.'

'Wouldn't we all, my boy, wouldn't we all.' Zimmermann walked slowly to the edge of the wood and stopped. For a long time he gazed out over the bridge at Neretva. Then he shook his head, turned and was almost at once lost to sight in the dark depths of the forest.

The pine fire in the great fireplace in the drawing-room in Termoli was burning low. Jensen threw on some more logs, straightened, poured two drinks and handed one to Mallory.

Jensen said: 'Well?'

'That's the plan?' No hint of his incredulity, of his near-despair, showed in Mallory's impassive face. 'That's *all* of the plan?'

'Yes.'

'Your health.' Mallory paused. 'And mine.' After an even longer pause he said reflectively: 'It should be interesting to watch Dusty Miller's reactions when he hears about this little lot this evening.'

As Mallory had said, Miller's reactions were interesting, even if wholly predictable. Some six hours later, clad now, like Mallory and Andrea, in British Army uniform, Miller listened in visibly growing horror as Jensen outlined what he considered should be their proposed course of action in the next twenty-four hours or so. When he had finished, Jensen looked directly at Miller and said: 'Well? Feasible?'

'Feasible?' Miller was aghast. 'It's suicidal!'

'Andrea?'

Andrea shrugged, lifted his hands palms upwards and said nothing.

Jensen nodded and said: 'I'm sorry, but I'm fresh out of

options. We'd better go. The others are waiting at the airstrip.'

Andrea and Miller left the room, began to walk down
the long passage-way. Mallory hesitated in the doorway,
momentarily blocking it, then turned to face Jensen who was
watching him with a surprised lift of the eyebrows.

Mallory said in a low voice: 'Let me tell Andrea, at least.'

Jensen looked at him for a considering moment or two,
shook his head briefly and brushed by into the corridor.

Twenty minutes later, without a further word being
spoken, the four men arrived at the Termoli airstrip to find
Vukalovic and two sergeants waiting for them: the third,
Reynolds, was already at the controls of his Wellington,
one of two standing at the end of the airstrip, propellers
already turning. Ten minutes later both planes were airborne, Vukalovic in one, Mallory, Miller, Andrea, and the
three sergeants in the other, each plane bound for its separate destination.

Jensen, alone on the tarmac, watched both planes climbing, his straining eyes following them until they disappeared
into the overcast darkness of the moonless sky above. Then,
just as General Zimmermann had done that afternoon, he
shook his head in slow finality, turned and walked heavily
away.

III

FRIDAY 0030-0200

Sergeant Reynolds, Mallory reflected, certainly knew how to
handle a plane, especially this one. Although his eyes showed
him to be always watchful and alert, he was precise, com-
petent, calm and relaxed in everything he did. No less com-
petent was Groves: the poor light and cramped confines of
his tiny plotting-table clearly didn't worry him at all and as
an air navigator he was quite clearly as experienced as he

was proficient. Mallory peered forward through the wind-screen, saw the white-capped waters of the Adriatic rushing by less than a hundred feet beneath their fuselage, and turned to Groves.

'The flight-plan calls for us to fly as low as this?'

'Yes. The Germans have radar installations on some of the outlying islands off the Yugoslav coast. We start climbing when we reach Dalmatia.'

Mallory nodded his thanks, turned to watch Reynolds again. He said, curiously: 'Captain Jensen was right about you. As a pilot. How on earth does a Marine Commando come to learn to drive one of those things?'

'I've had plenty of practice,' Reynolds said. 'Three years in the RAF, two of them as sergeant-pilot in a Wellington bomber squadron. One day in Egypt I took a Lysander up without permission. People did it all the time—but the crate I'd picked had a defective fuel gauge.'

'You were grounded?'

'With great speed.' He grinned. 'There were no objections when I applied for a service transfer. I think they felt I wasn't somehow quite right for the RAF.'

Mallory looked at Groves. 'And you?'

Groves smiled broadly. 'I was his navigator in that old crate. We were fired on the same day.'

Mallory said consideringly: 'Well, I should think that might be rather useful.'

'What's useful?' Reynolds asked.

'The fact that you're used to this feeling of disgrace. It'll enable you to act your part all the better when the time comes. If the time comes.'

Reynolds said carefully: 'I'm not quite sure—'

'Before we jump, I want you—all of you—to remove every distinguishing badge or emblem of rank on your clothes.' He gestured to Andrea and Miller at the rear of the flight-deck to indicate that they were included as well, then looked at Reynolds again. 'Sergeants' stripes, regimental flashes, medal ribbons—the lot.'

'Why the hell should I?' Reynolds, Mallory thought, had the lowest boiling-point he'd come across in quite some time. 'I *earned* those stripes, those ribbons, that flash. I don't see—'

Mallory smiled. 'Disobeying an officer on active service?'

'Don't be so damned touchy,' Reynolds said.

'Don't be so damned touchy, *sir.*'

'Don't be so damned touchy, *sir.*' Reynolds suddenly grinned. 'OK, so who's got the scissors?'

'You see,' Mallory explained, 'the last thing we want to happen is to fall into enemy hands.'

'Amen,' Miller intoned.

'But if we're to get the information we want we're going to have to operate close to or even inside their lines. We might get caught. So we have our cover story.'

Groves said quietly: 'Are we permitted to know just what that cover story is, sir?'

'Of course you are,' Mallory said in exasperation. He went on earnestly: 'Don't you realize that, on a mission like this, survival depends on one thing and one thing only —complete and mutual trust? As soon as we start having secrets from each other—we're finished.'

In the deep gloom at the rear of the flight-deck, Andrea and Miller glanced at each other and exchanged their wearily cynical smiles.

As Mallory left the flight-deck for the fuselage, his right hand brushed Miller's shoulder. After about two minutes Miller yawned, stretched and made his way aft. Mallory was waiting towards the rear of the fuselage. He had two pieces of folded paper in his hand, one of which he opened and showed to Miller, snapping on a flash-light at the same time. Miller stared at it for some moments, then lifted an eyebrow.

'And what is this supposed to be?'

'It's the triggering mechanism for a 1,500-pound submersible mine. Learn it by heart.'

Miller looked at it without expression, then glanced at the other paper Mallory held.

'And what have you there?'

Mallory showed him. It was a large-scale map, the central

feature of which appeared to be a winding lake with a very long eastern arm which bent abruptly at right-angles into a very short southern arm, which in turn ended abruptly at what appeared to be a dam wall. Beneath the dam, a river flowed away through a winding gorge.

Mallory said: 'What does it look like to you? Show them both to Andrea and tell him to destroy them.'

Mallory left Miller engrossed in his homework and moved forward again to the flight-deck. He bent over Groves's chart table.

'Still on course?'

'Yes, sir. We're just clearing the southern tip of the island of Hvar. You can see a few lights on the mainland ahead.' Mallory followed the pointing hand, located a few clusters of lights, then reached out a hand to steady himself as the Wellington started to climb sharply. He glanced at Reynolds.

'Climbing now, sir. There's some pretty lofty stuff ahead. We should pick up the Partisan landing lights in about half an hour.'

'Thirty-three minutes,' Groves said. 'One-twenty, near enough.'

For almost half an hour Mallory remained on a jump-seat in the flight-deck, just looking ahead. After a few minutes Andrea disappeared and did not reappear. Miller did not return. Groves nagivated, Reynolds flew, Saunders listened in to his portable transceiver and nobody talked at all. At one-fifteen Mallory rose, touched Saunders on the shoulders, told him to pack up his gear and headed aft. He found Andrea and a thoroughly miserable-looking Miller with their parachute snap-catches already clipped on to the jumping wire. Andrea had the door pulled back and was throwing out tiny pieces of shredded paper which swirled away in the slipstream. Mallory shivered in the suddenly intense cold. Andrea grinned, beckoned him to the open doorway and pointed downwards. He yelled in Mallory's ear: 'There's a lot of snow down there.'

There was indeed a lot of snow down there. Mallory understood now Jensen's insistence on not landing a plane in those parts. The terrain below was rugged in the extreme,

consisting almost entirely of a succession of deep and winding valleys and steep-sided mountains. Maybe half of the
landscape below was covered in dense forests of pine trees:
all of it was covered in what appeared to be a very heavy
blanket of snow. Mallory drew back into the comparative
shelter of the Wellington's fuselage and glanced at his
watch.

'One-sixteen.' Like Andrea, he had to shout.

'Your watch is a little fast, maybe?' Miller bawled unhappily. Mallory shook his head, Miller shook his. A bell
rang and Mallory made his way to the flight-deck, passing
Saunders going the other way. As Mallory entered, Reynolds
looked briefly over his shoulder, then pointed directly ahead.
Mallory bent over his shoulder and peered forwards and
downwards. He nodded.

The three lights, in the form of an elongated V, were still
some miles ahead, but quite unmistakable, Mallory turned,
touched Groves on the shoulder and pointed aft. Groves rose
and left. Mallory said to Reynolds: 'Where are the red and
green jumping lights?'

Reynolds indicated them.

'Press the red light. How long?'

'Thirty seconds. About.'

Mallory looked ahead again. The lights were less than half
as distant as they had been when first he'd looked. He said
to Reynolds: 'Automatic pilot. Close the fuel switches.'

'Close the—for the petrol that's left—'

'Shut off the bloody tanks! And get aft. Five seconds.'

Reynolds did as he was told. Mallory waited, briefly made
a last check of the landing lights ahead, pressed the green
light button, rose and made his way swiftly aft. By the time
he reached the jump door, even Reynolds, the last of the
first five, was gone. Mallory clipped on his snap-catch,
braced his hands round the edge of the doorway and launched
himself out into the bitter Bosnian night.

The sudden jarring impact from the parachute harness
made him look quickly upwards: the concave circle of a
fully open parachute was a reassuring spectacle. He glanced
downwards and saw the equally reassuring spectacle of an-

other five open parachutes, two of which were swaying quite wildly across the sky—just as was his own. There were some things, he reflected, about which he, Andrea and Miller had a great deal to learn. Controlling parachute descents was one of those things.

He looked up and to the east to see if he could locate the Wellington, but it was no longer visible. Suddenly, as he looked and listened, both engines, almost in perfect unison, cut out. Long seconds passed when the only sound was the rush of the wind in his ears, then there came an explosively metallic sound as the bomber crashed either into the ground or into some unseen mountainside ahead. There was no fire or none that he could see: just the crash, then silence. For the first time that night, the moon broke through.

Andrea landed heavily on an uneven piece of ground, rolled over twice, rose rather experimentally to his feet, discovered he was still intact, pressed the quick-release button of his parachute, then automatically, instinctively—Andrea had a built-in computer for assuring survival—swung through a complete 360° circle. But no immediate danger threatened, or none that he could see. Andrea made a more leisurely survey of their landing spot.

They had, he thought grimly, been most damnably lucky. Another hundred yards to the south and they'd have spent the rest of the night, and for all he knew, the rest of the war, clinging to the tops of the most impossibly tall pine trees he had ever seen. As it was, luck had been with them and they had landed in a narrow clearing which abutted closely on the rocky scarp of a mountainside.

Or rather, all but one. Perhaps fifty yards from where Andrea had landed, an apex of the forest elbowed its way into the clearing. The outermost tree in this apex had come between one of the parachutists and terra firma. Andrea's eyebrows lifted in quizzical astonishment, then he broke into an ambling run.

The parachutist who had come to grief was dangling from the lowermost bough of the pine. He had his hands twisted in the shrouds, his legs bent, knees and ankles close together in the classic landing position, his feet perhaps thirty inches from the ground. His eyes were screwed tightly shut. Corporal Miller seemed acutely unhappy.

Andrea came up and touched him on the shoulder, gently. Miller opened his eyes and glanced at Andrea, who pointed downwards. Miller followed his glance and lowered his legs, which were then four inches from the ground. Andrea produced a knife, sliced through the shreds and Miller completed the remainder of his journey. He straightened his jacket, his face splendidly impassive, and lifted an enquiring elbow. Andrea, his face equally impassive, pointed down the clearing. Three of the other four parachutists had already landed safely: the fourth, Mallory, was just touching down.

Two minutes later, just as all six were coming together some little distance away from the most easterly landing flare, a shout announced the appearance of a young soldier running towards them from the edge of the forest. The parachutists' guns came up and were almost immediately lowered again: this was no occasion for guns. The soldier was trailing his by the barrel, excitedly waving his free hand in greeting. He was dressed in a faded and tattered near-uniform that had been pillaged from a variety of armies, had long flowing hair, a cast to his right eye and a straggling ginger beard. That he was welcoming them, was beyond doubt. Repeating some incomprehensible greeting over and over again, he shook hands all round and then a second time, the huge grin on his face reflecting his delight.

Within thirty seconds he'd been joined by at least a dozen others, all bearded, all dressed in the same nondescript uniforms, no two of which were alike, all in the same almost festive mood. Then, as at a signal almost, they fell silent and drew slightly apart as the man who was obviously their leader appeared from the edge of the forest. He bore little resemblance to his men. He differed in that he was completely shaven and wore a uniform, a British battledress, which appeared to be all of one piece. He differed in that he was not smiling: he had about him the air of one who was seldom if ever given to smiling. He also differed from the others in that he was a hawk-faced giant of a man, at least six feet four inches in height, carrying no fewer than four wicked-looking Bowie-type knives in his belt—an excess of armament that on another man might have looked incongruous or even comical but which on this man provoked no mirth at all. His face was dark and sombre and when he spoke it was in English, slow and stilted, but precise.

'Good evening.' He looked round questioningly. 'I am Captain Droshny.'

Mallory took a step forward. 'Captain Mallory.'

'Welcome to Yugoslavia, Captain Mallory—Partisan Yugoslavia.' Droshny nodded towards the dying flare, his face twitched in what may have been an attempt at a smile, but he made no move to shake hands. 'As you can see, we were expecting you.'

'Your lights were a great help,' Mallory acknowledged.

'Thank you.' Droshny stared away to the east, then back to Mallory, shaking his head. 'A pity about the plane.'

'All war is a pity.'

Droshny nodded. 'Come. Our headquarters is close by.'

No more was said. Droshny, leading, moved at once into the shelter of the forest. Mallory, behind him, was intrigued by the footprints, clearly visible in the now bright moonlight, left by Droshny in the deep snow. They were, thought Mallory, most peculiar. Each sole left three V-shaped marks, the heel one: the right-hand side of the leading V on the right sole had a clearly defined break in it. Unconsciously, Mallory filed away this little oddity in his mind. There was no reason why he should have done so other than that the Mallorys of this world always observe and record the unusual. It helps them to stay alive.

The slope steepened, the snow deepened and the pale moonlight filtered thinly down through the spreading, snow-laden branches of the pines. The light wind was from the east: the cold was intense. For almost ten minutes no voice was heard, then Droshny's came, softly but clearly and imperative in its staccato urgency.

'Be still.' He pointed dramatically upward. 'Be still! Listen!'

They stopped, looked upward and listened intently. At least, Mallory and his men looked upward and listened intently, but the Yugoslavs had other things on their minds: swiftly, efficiently and simultaneously, without either spoken or gestured command being given, they rammed the muzzles of their machine-guns and rifles into the sides and backs of the six parachutists with a force and uncompromising authority that rendered any accompanying orders quite superfluous.

The six men reacted as might have been expected. Reynolds, Groves and Saunders, who were rather less accustomed to the vicissitudes of fate than their three older companions, registered a very similar combination of startled anger and open-mouthed astonishment. Mallory looked thoughtful. Miller lifted a quizzical eyebrow. Andrea, predictably, registered nothing at all: he was too busy exhibiting his usual reaction to physical violence.

His right hand, which he had instantly lifted half-way to his shoulder in an apparent token of surrender, clamped down on the barrel of the rifle of the guard to his left, forcing it away from him, while his left elbow jabbed viciously into the solar plexus of the guard to his left, who gasped in pain and staggered back a couple of paces. Andrea, with both hands now on the rifle of the other guard, wrenched it effortlessly free, lifted it high and brought the barrel down in one continuous blur of movement. The guard collapsed as if a bridge had fallen on him. The winded guard to the left, still bent and whooping in agony, was trying to line up his rifle when the butt of Andrea's rifle struck him in the face: he made a brief coughing sound and fell senseless to the forest floor.

It took all of the three seconds that this action had lasted for the Yugoslavs to release themselves from their momentary thrall of incredulity. Half-a-dozen soldiers flung themselves on Andrea, bearing him to the ground. In the furious, rolling struggle that followed, Andrea laid about him in his usual willing fashion, but when one of the Yugoslavs started pounding him on the head with the barrel of a pistol, Andrea opted for discretion and lay still. With two guns in his back and four hands on either arm Andrea was dragged to his feet: two of his captors already looked very much the worse for wear.

Droshny, his eyes bleak and bitter, came up to Andrea, unsheathed one of his knives and thrust its point against Andrea's throat with a force savage enough to break the skin and draw blood that trickled on to the gleaming blade. For a moment it seemed that Droshny would push the knife home to the hilt, then his eyes moved sideways and downwards to look at the two huddled men lying in the snow. He nodded to the nearest man.

'How are they?'

A young Yugoslav dropped to his knees, looked first at the man who had been struck by the rifle-barrel, touched his head briefly, examined the second man, then stood up. In the filtered moonlight, his face was unnaturally pale.

'Josef is dead. I think his neck is broken. And his brother —he's breathing—but his jaw seems to be—' The voice trailed away uncertainly.

Droshny transferred his gaze back to Andrea. His lips drew back, he smiled the way a wolf smiles and leaned a little harder on the knife.

'I *should* kill you now. I *will* kill you later.' He sheathed his knife, held up his clawed hands in front of Andrea's face, and shouted: 'Personally. With those hands.'

'With those hands.' Slowly, meaningfully, Andrea examined the four pairs of hands pinioning his arms, then looked contemptuously at Droshny. He said: 'Your courage terrifies me.'

There was a brief and unbelieving silence. The three young sergeants stared at the tableau before them with faces reflecting various degrees of consternation and incredulity. Mallory and Miller looked on impassively. For a moment or two, Droshny looked as if he hadn't heard aright, then his face twisted in savage anger as he struck Andrea backhanded across the face. Immediately a trickle of blood appeared at the right-hand corner of Andrea's mouth but Andrea himself remained unmoving, his face without expression.

Droshny's eyes narrowed. Andrea smiled again, briefly. Droshny struck again, this time with the back of the other hand. The effect was as before, with the exception that this time the trickle of blood came from the left-hand corner of the mouth. Andrea smiled again but to look into his eyes was to look into an open grave. Droshny wheeled and walked away, then halted as he approached Mallory.

'You *are* the leader of those men, Captain Mallory?'

'I am.'

'You're a very—*silent* leader, Captain?'

'What am I to say to a man who turns his guns on his friends and allies?' Mallory looked at him dispassionately. 'I'll talk to your commanding officer, not to a madman.'

Droshny's face darkened. He stepped forward, his arm lifted to strike. Very quickly, but so smoothly and calmly that the movement seemed unhurried, and totally ignoring the two rifle-muzzles pressing into his side, Mallory lifted his Luger and pointed it at Droshny's face. The click of the Luger safety-catch being released came like a hammer-blow in the suddenly unnatural intensity of silence.

And unnatural intensity of silence there was. Except for one little movement, so slow as to be almost imperceptible, both Partisans and parachutists had frozen into a tableau that would have done credit to the frieze on an Ionic temple. The three sergeants, like most of the Partisans, registered astonished incredulity. The two men guarding Mallory looked at Droshny with questioning eyes. Droshny looked at Mallory as if he were mad. Andrea wasn't looking at anyone, while Miller wore that look of world-weary detachment which only he could achieve. But it was Miller who made that one little movement, a movement that now came to an end with his thumb resting on his Schmeisser's safety-release. After a moment or two he removed his thumb: there would come a time for Schmeissers, but this wasn't it.

Droshny lowered his hand in a curious slow-motion gesture and took two paces backwards. His face was still dark with anger, the dark eyes cruel and unforgiving, but he had himself well in hand. He said: 'Don't you know we have to take precautions? Till we are satisfied with your identity?'

'How should I know that?' Mallory nodded at Andrea.
'Next time you tell your men to take precautions with my
friend here, you might warn them to stand a little farther
back. He reacted the only way he knows how. And I know
why.'

'You can explain later. Hand over your guns.'

'No.' Mallory returned the Luger to its holster.

'Are you mad? I can take them from you.'

'That's so,' Mallory said reasonably. 'But you'd have to
kill us first, wouldn't you? I don't think you'd remain a
captain very long, my friend.'

Speculation replaced anger in Droshny's eyes. He gave a
sharp order in Serbo-Croat and again his soldiers levelled
their guns at Mallory and his five companions. But they
made no attempt to remove the prisoners' guns. Droshny
turned, gestured and started moving up the steeply-sloping
forest floor again. Droshny wasn't, Mallory reflected, a man
likely to be given to taking too many chances.

For twenty minutes they scrambled awkwardly up the slippery hillside. A voice called out from the darkness ahead
and Droshny answered without breaking step. They passed
by two sentries armed with machine-carbines and, within a
minute, were in Droshny's HQ.

It was a moderately-sized military encampment—if a wide
circle of rough-hewn adze-cut cabins could be called an
encampment—set in one of those very deep hollows in the
forest floor that Mallory was to find so characteristic of the
Bosnian area. From the base of this hollow grew two con-
centric rings of pines far taller and more massive than anything to be found in western Europe, massive pines whose
massive branches interlocked eighty to a hundred feet above
the ground, forming a snow-shrouded canopy of such impenetrable density that there wasn't even a dusting of snow
on the hard-packed earth of the camp compound: by the
same token, the same canopy also effectively prevented any
upward escape of light: there was no attempt at any black-
out in several illuminated cabin windows and there were
even some oil-lamps suspended on outside hooks to illumin-

ate the compound itself. Droshny stopped and said to Mallory:

'You come with me. The rest of you stay here.'

He led Mallory towards the door of the largest hut in the compound. Andrea, unbidden, slipped off his pack and sat on it, and the others, after various degrees of hesitation, did the same. Their guards looked them over uncertainly, then withdrew to form a ragged but watchful semi-circle. Reynolds turned to Andrea, the expression on his face registering a complete absence of admiration and goodwill.

'You're crazy.' Reynolds's voice came in a low, furious whisper. 'Crazy as a loon. You could have got yourself killed. You could have got all of us killed. What are you, shell-shocked or something?'

Andrea did not reply. He lit one of his obnoxious cigars and regarded Reynolds with mild speculation or as near an approach to mildness as it was possible for him to achieve.

'Crazy isn't half the word for it.' Groves, if anything, was even more heated than Reynolds. 'Or didn't you *know* that was a Partisan you killed? Don't you *know* what that means? Don't you *know* people like that must always take precautions?'

Whether he knew or not, Andrea wasn't saying. He puffed at his cigar and transferred his peaceable gaze from Reynolds to Groves.

Miller said soothingly: 'Now, now. Don't be like that. Maybe Andrea *was* a mite hasty but—'

'God help us all,' Reynolds said fervently. He looked at his fellow-sergeants in despair. 'A thousand miles from home and help and saddled with a trigger-happy bunch of has-beens.' He turned back to Miller and mimicked: ' "Don't be like that." '

Miller assumed his wounded expression and looked away.

The room was large and bare and comfortless. The only concession to comfort was a pine fire crackling in a rough hearth-place. The only furniture consisted of a cracked deal table, two chairs and a bench.

Those things Mallory noted only subconsciously. He didn't even register when he heard Droshny say: 'Captain Mallory. This is my commanding officer.' He seemed to be too busy staring at the man seated behind the table.

The man was short, stocky and in his mid-thirties. The deep lines around eyes and mouth could have been caused by weather or humour or both: just at that moment he was smiling slightly. He was dressed in the uniform of a captain in the German Army and wore an Iron Cross at his throat.

IV

FRIDAY 0200-0330

The German captain leaned back in his chair and steepled his fingers. He had the air of a man enjoying the passing moment.

'Hauptmann Neufeld, Captain Mallory.' He looked at the places on Mallory's uniform where the missing insignia should have been. 'Or so I assume. You are surprised to see me?'

'I am *delighted* to meet you, Hauptmann Neufeld.' Mallory's astonishment had given way to the beginnings of a long, slow smile and now he sighed in deep relief. 'You just can't imagine *how* delighted.' Still smiling, he turned to Droshny, and at once the smile gave way to an expression of consternation. 'But who *are* you? Who is this man, Hauptmann Neufeld? Who in the name of God are those men out there? They must be—they must be—'

Droshny interrupted heavily: 'One of his men killed one of my men tonight.'

'What!' Neufeld, the smile now in turn vanishing from his face, stood abruptly: the backs of his legs sent his chair crashing to the floor. Mallory ignored him, looked again at Droshny.

'*Who are you*? For God's sake, tell me!'

Droshny said slowly: 'They call us Cetniks.'

'Cetniks? Cetniks? What on earth are Cetniks?'

'You will forgive me, Captain, if I smile in weary disbelief.' Neufeld was back on balance again, and his face had assumed a curiously wary impassivity, an expression in which only the eyes were alive: things, Mallory reflected, unpleasant things could happen to people misguided enough to underrate Hauptmann Neufeld. 'You? The leader of a special mission to this country and you haven't been well enough briefed to know that the Cetniks are our Yugoslav allies?'

'Allies? Ah!' Mallory's face cleared in understanding. 'Traitors? Yugoslav Quislings? Is that it?'

A subterranean rumble came from Droshny's throat and he moved towards Mallory, his right hand closing round the haft of a knife. Neufeld halted him with a sharp word of command and a brief downward-chopping motion of his hand.

'And what do you mean by a special mission?' Mallory demanded. He looked at each man in turn and smiled in wry understanding. 'Oh, we're special mission all right, but not in the way you think. At least, not in the way I think you think.'

'No?' Neufeld's eyebrow-raising technique, Mallory reflected, was almost on a par with Miller's. 'Then why do you think we were expecting you?'

'God only knows,' Mallory said frankly. 'We thought the Partisans were. That's why Droshny's man was killed, I'm afraid.'

'That's why Droshny's man—' Neufeld regarded Mallory with his warily impassive eyes, picked up his chair and sat down thoughtfully. 'I think, perhaps, you had better explain yourself.'

As befitted a man who had adventured far and wide in the West End of London, Miller was in the habit of using a napkin when at meals, and he was using one now, tucked into the top of his tunic, as he sat on his rucksack in the compound of Neufeld's camp and fastidiously consumed some indeterminate goulash from a mess-tin. The three sergeants, seated near by, briefly observed this spectacle with open disbelief, then resumed a low-voiced conversation. Andrea, puffing the inevitable nostril-wrinkling cigar and totally ignoring half-a-dozen watchful and understandably apprehensive guards, strolled unconcernedly about the compound, poisoning the air wherever he went. Clearly through the frozen night air came the distant sound of someone singing a low-voiced accompaniment to what appeared to be guitar music. As Andrea completed his circuit of the compound, Miller looked up and nodded in the direction of the music.

'Who's the soloist?'

Andrea shrugged. 'Radio, maybe.'

'They want to buy a new radio. My trained ear—'

'Listen.' Reynolds's interrupting whisper was tense and urgent. 'We've been talking.'

Miller performed some fancy work with his napkin and said kindly: 'Don't. Think of the grieving mothers and sweethearts you'd leave behind you.'

'What do you mean?'

'About making a break for it is what I mean,' Miller said. 'Some other time, perhaps?'

'Why not now?' Groves was belligerent. 'They're off guard—'

'Are they now.' Miller sighed. 'So young, so young. Take another look. You don't think Andrea *likes* exercise, do you?'

The three sergeants took another look, furtively, surreptitiously, then glanced interrogatively at Andrea.

'Five dark windows,' Andrea said. 'Behind them, five dark men. With five dark machine-guns.'

Reynolds nodded and looked away.

'Well, now.' Neufeld, Mallory noted, had a great propensity for steepling his fingers: Mallory had once known a hanging judge with exactly the same propensity. 'This *is* a most remarkably odd story you have to tell us, my dear Captain Mallory.'

'It is,' Mallory agreed. 'It would have to be, wouldn't it, to account for the remarkably odd position in which we find ourselves at this moment.'

'A point, a point.' Slowly, deliberately, Neufeld ticked off other points on his fingers. 'You have for some months, you claim, been running a penicillin and drug-running ring in the south of Italy. As an Allied liaison officer you found no difficulty in obtaining supplies from American Army and Air Force bases.'

'We found a little difficulty towards the end,' Mallory admitted.

'I'm coming to that. Those supplies, you also claim, were funnelled through to the Wehrmacht.'

'I wish you wouldn't keep using the word "claim" in that tone of voice,' Mallory said irritably. 'Check with Field-Marshal Kesselring's Chief of Military Intelligence in Padua.'

'With pleasure.' Neufeld picked up a phone, spoke briefly in German and replaced the receiver.

Mallory said in surprise: 'You have a direct line to the outside world? From *this* place?'

'I have a direct line to a hut fifty yards away where we have a very powerful radio transmitter. So. You further claim that you were caught, court-martialled and were awaiting the confirmation of your death sentence. Right?'

'If your espionage system in Italy is all we hear it is, you'll know about it to-morrow,' Mallory said drily.

'Quite, quite. You then broke free, killed your guards and overheard agents in the briefing-room being briefed on a mission to Bosnia.' He did some more finger-steepling. 'You may be telling the truth at that. What did you say their mission was?'

'"I didn't say. I didn't really pay attention. It had something to do with locating missing British mission leaders and trying to break your espionage set-up. I'm not sure. We had more important things to think about.'

'I'm sure you had,' Neufeld said distastefully. 'Such as your skins. What happened to your epaulettes, Captain? The medal ribbons? The buttons?'

'You've obviously never attended a British court-martial, Hauptmann Neufeld.'

Neufeld said mildly: 'You could have ripped them off yourself.'

'And then, I suppose, emptied three-quarters of the fuel from the tanks before we stole the plane?'

'Your tanks were only a quarter full?' Mallory nodded. 'And your plane crashed without catching fire?'

'We didn't mean to crash,' Mallory said in a weary patience. 'We meant to land. But we were out of fuel—and, as we know now, at the wrong place.'

Neufeld said absently: 'Whenever the Partisans put up landing flares we try a few ourselves—*and* we knew that you—or someone—were coming. No petrol, eh?' Again Neufeld spoke briefly on the telephone, then turned back to Mallory. 'All very satisfactory—if true. There just remains to explain the death of Captain Droshny's man here.'

'I'm sorry about that. It was a ghastly blunder. But surely you can understand. The last thing we wanted was to land among you, to make direct contact with you. We've heard what happens to British parachutists dropping over German territory.'

Neufeld steepled his fingers again. 'There is a state of war. Proceed.'

'Our intention was to land in Partisan territory, slip across the lines and give ourselves up. When Droshny turned his guns on us we thought the Partisans were on to us, that they had been notified that we'd stolen the plane. And that could mean only one thing for us.'

'Wait outside. Captain Droshny and I will join you in a moment.'

Mallory left. Andrea, Miller and the three sergeants were sitting patiently on their rucksacks. From the distance there still came the sound of distant music. For a moment Mallory cocked his head to listen to it, then walked across to join the others. Miller patted his lips delicately with his napkin and looked up at Mallory.

'Had a cosy chat?'

'I spun him a yarn. The one we talked about in the plane.' He looked at the three sergeants. 'Any of you speak German?'

All three shook their heads.

'Fine. Forget you speak English too. If you're questioned you know nothing.'

'If I'm not questioned,' Reynolds said bitterly, 'I still don't know anything.'

'All the better,' Mallory said encouragingly. 'Then you can never tell anything, can you?'

He broke off and turned round as Neufeld and Droshny appeared in the doorway. Neufeld advanced and said: 'While we're waiting for some confirmation, a little food and wine, perhaps.' As Mallory had done, he cocked his head and listened to the singing. 'But first of all, you must meet our minstrel boy.'

'We'll settle for just the food and wine,' Andrea said.

'Your priorities are wrong. You'll see. Come.'

The dining-hall, if it could be dignified by such a name, was about forty yards away. Neufeld opened the door to reveal a crude and makeshift hut with two rickety trestle tables and four benches set on the earthen floor. At the far end of the room the inevitable pine fire burnt in the inevitable stone hearth-place. Close to the fire, at the end of the farther table, three men—obviously, from their high-collared coats and guns propped by their sides, some kind of temporarily off-duty guards—were drinking coffee and listening to the quiet singing coming from a figure seated on the ground by the fire.

The singer was dressed in a tattered anorak type jacket, an even more incredibly tattered pair of trousers and a pair of knee boots that gaped open at almost every possible seam. There was little to be seen of his face other than a mass of dark hair and a large pair of rimmed dark spectacles.

Beside him, apparently asleep with her head on his shoulder, sat a girl. She was clad in a high-collared British Army great-coat in an advanced state of dilapidation, so long that it completely covered her tucked-in legs. The uncombed platinum hair spread over her shoulders would have done justice to any Scandinavian, but the broad cheekbones, dark eyebrows and long dark lashes lowered over very pale cheeks were unmistakably Slavonic.

Neufeld advanced across the room and stopped by the fireside. He bent over the singer and said: 'Petar, I want you to meet some friends.'

Petar lowered his guitar, looked up, then turned and touched the girl on the arm. Instantly, the girl's head lifted and her eyes, great dark sooty eyes, opened wide. She had the look, almost, of a hunted animal. She glanced around her, almost wildly, then jumped quickly to her feet, dwarfed by the greatcoat which reached almost to her ankles, then reached down to help the guitarist to his feet. As he did so, he stumbled: he was obviously blind.

'This is Maria,' Neufeld said. 'Maria, this is Captain Mallory.'

'Captain Mallory.' Her voice was soft and a little husky: she spoke in almost accentless English. 'You are English, Captain Mallory?'

It was hardly, Mallory thought, the time or the place for proclaiming his New Zealand ancestry. He smiled. 'Well, sort of.'

Maria smiled in turn. 'I've always wanted to meet an Englishman.' She stepped forward towards Mallory's outstretched hand, brushed it aside and struck him, open-handed and with all her strength, across the face.

'Maria!' Neufeld stared at her. 'He's on our side.'

'An Englishman *and* a traitor!' She lifted her hand again but the swinging arm was suddenly arrested in Andrea's grip. She struggled briefly, futilely, then subsided, dark eyes glowing in an angry face. Andrea lifted his free hand and rubbed his own cheek in fond recollection.

He said admiringly: 'By heavens, she reminds me of my own Maria,' then grinned at Mallory. 'Very handy with their hands, those Yugoslavs.'

Mallory rubbed his cheek ruefully with his hand and turned to Neufeld. 'Perhaps Petar—that's his name—'

'No.' Neufeld shook his head definitely. 'Later. Let's eat now.' He led the way across to the table at the far end of the room, gestured the others to seats, sat down himself and went on: 'I'm sorry. That was my fault. I should have known better.'

Miller said delicately: 'Is she—um—all right?'

'A wild animal, you think?'

'She'd make a rather dangerous pet, wouldn't you say?'

'She's a graduate of the University of Belgrade. Languages. With honours, I'm told. Some time after graduation she returned to her home in the Bosnian mountains. She found her parents and two small brothers butchered. She—well, she's been like this ever since.'

Mallory shifted in his seat and looked at the girl. Her eyes, dark and unmoving and unwinking, were fixed on him and their expression was less than encouraging. Mallory turned back to Neufeld.

'Who did it? To her parents, I mean.'

'The Partisans,' Droshny said savagely. 'Damn their black souls, the Partisans. Maria's people were our people. Cetniks.'

'And the singer?' Mallory asked.

'Her elder brother.' Neufeld shook his head. 'Blind from birth. Wherever they go, she leads him by the hand. She is his eyes: she is his life.'

They sat in silence until food and wine were brought in. If an army marched on its stomach, Mallory thought, this one wasn't going to get very far: he had heard that the food situation with the Partisans was close to desperate, but, if this were a representative sample, the Cetniks and Germans appeared to be in little better case. Unenthusiastically, he spooned—it would have been impossible to use a fork—a little of the greyish stew, a stew in which little oddments of indefinable meat floated forlornly in a mushy gravy of obscure origin, glanced across at Andrea and marvelled at the gastronomic fortitude that lay behind the already almost empty plate. Miller averted his eyes from the plate before him and delicately sipped the rough red wine. The three sergeants, so far, hadn't even looked at their food: they were too occupied in looking at the girl by the fireside. Neufeld saw their interest, and smiled.

'I do agree, gentlemen, that I've never seen a more beautiful girl and heaven knows what she'd look like if she had a wash. But she's not for you, gentlemen. She's not for any man. She's wed already.' He looked at the questioning faces and shook his head. 'Not to any man. To an ideal— if you can call death an ideal. The death of the Partisans.'

'Charming,' Miller murmured. There was no other comment, for there was none to make. They ate in a silence broken only by the soft singing from the fireside, the voice was melodious enough, but the guitar sounded sadly out of tune. Andrea pushed away his empty plate, looked irritably at the blind musician and turned to Neufeld.

'What's that he's singing?'

'An old Bosnian love-song, I've been told. Very old and very sad. In English you have it too.' He snapped his fingers, 'Yes, that's it. "The girl I left behind me".'

'Tell him to sing something else,' Andrea muttered. Neufeld looked at him, puzzled, then looked away as a German sergeant entered and bent to whisper in his ear. Neufeld nodded and the sergeant left.

'So.' Neufeld was thoughtful. 'A radio report from the patrol that found your plane. The tanks *were* empty. I hardly think we need await confirmation from Padua, do you, Captain Mallory?'

'I don't understand.'

'No matter. Tell me, have you ever heard of a General Vukalovic?'

'General which?'

'Vukalovic.'

'He's not on our side,' Miller said positively. 'Not with a name like that.'

'You must be the only people in Yugoslavia who *don't* know him. Everybody else does. Partisans, Cetniks, Germans, Bulgarians, everyone. He is one of their national heroes.'

'Pass the wine,' Andrea said.

'You'd do better to listen.' Neufeld's tone was sharp. 'Vukalovic commands almost a division of Partisan infantry who have been trapped in a loop of the Neretva river for almost three months. Like the men he leads. Vukalovic is insane. They have no shelter, none. They are short of weapons, have almost no ammunition left and are close to starvation. Their army is dressed in rags. They are finished.'

'Then why don't they escape?' Mallory asked.

'Escape is impossible. The precipices of the Neretva cut them off to the east. To the north and west are impenetrable mountains. The only conceivable way out is to the south, over the bridge at Neretva. And we have two armoured divisions waiting there.'

'No gorges?' Mallory asked. 'No passes through the mountains?'

'Two. Blocked by our best combat troops.'

'Then why don't they give up?' Miller asked reasonably. 'Has no one told them the rules of war?'

'They're insane, I tell you,' Neufeld said. 'Quite insane.'

At that precise moment in time, Vukalovic and his Partisans were proving to some other Germans just how extraordinary their degree of insanity was.

The Western Gap was a narrow, tortuous, boulder-strewn and precipitously walled gorge that afforded the only passage through the impassable mountains that shut off the Zenica Cage to the east. For three months now German infantry units—units which had recently included an increasing number of highly-skilled Alpine troops—had been trying to force the pass: for three months they had been bloodily repulsed. But the Germans never gave up trying and on this intensely cold night of fitful moonlight and gently, intermittently falling snow, they were trying again.

The Germans carried out their attack with the coldly professional skill and economy of movement born of long and harsh experience. They advanced up the gorge in three fairly even and judiciously spaced lines: the combination of white snow-suits, of the utilization of every scrap of cover and of confining their brief forward rushes to those moments when the moon was temporarily obscured made it almost impossible to see them. There was, however, no difficulty in locating them: they had obviously ammunition and to spare for machine-pistols and rifles alike and the fire-flashes from those muzzles were almost continuous. Almost as continuous, but some distance behind them, the sharp flat cracks of fixed mountain pieces pin-pointed the source of the creeping artillery barrage that preceded the Germans up the boulder-strewn slope of that narrow defile.

The Yugoslav Partisans waited at the head of the gorge, entrenched behind a redoubt of boulders, hastily piled stones and splintered tree-trunks that had been shattered by German artillery fire. Although the snow was deep and the east wind full of little knives, few of the Partisans wore greatcoats. They were clad in an extraordinary variety of uniforms, uniforms that had belonged in the past to members of British, German, Italian, Bulgarian and Yugoslav armies: the one identifying feature that all had in common was a red star sewn on to the right-hand side of their forage caps. The uniforms, for the most part, were thin and tattered, offering little protection against the piercing cold, so that the men shivered almost continuously. An astonishing proportion of them appeared to be wounded: there were splinted legs, arms in slings and bandaged heads everywhere. But the most common characteristic among this rag-tag collection of defenders was their pinched and emaciated faces, faces where the deeply etched lines of starvation were matched only by the calm and absolute determination of men who have no longer anything to lose.

Near the centre of the group of defenders, two men stood in the shelter of the thick bole of one of the few pines still left standing. The silvered black hair, the deeply trenched —and now even more exhausted—face of General Vukalovic was unmistakable. But the dark eyes glowed as brightly as ever as he bent forward to accept a cigarette and light from the officer sharing his shelter, a swarthy, hook-nosed man with at least half of his black hair concealed under a blood-stained bandage. Vukalovic smiled.

'Of course I'm insane, my dear Stephan. You're insane— or you would have abandoned this position weeks ago. We're all insane. Didn't you know?'

'I know this.' Major Stephan rubbed the back of his hand across a week-old growth of beard. 'Your parachute landing, an hour ago. That was insane. Why, you—' He broke off as a rifle fired only feet away, moved to where a thin youngster, not more than seventeen years of age, was peering down into the white gloom of the gorge over the sights of a Lee-Enfield. 'Did you get him?'

The boy twisted and looked up. A child. Vukalovic thought despairingly, no more than a child: he should still have been at school. The boy said: 'I'm not sure, sir.'

'How many shells have you left. Count them.'

'I don't have to. Seven.'

'Don't fire till you are sure.' Stephan turned back to Vukalovic. 'God above, General, you were almost blown into German hands.'

'I'd have been worse off without the parachute,' Vukalovic said mildly.

'There's so little time.' Stephan struck a clenched fist against a palm. 'So little time left. You were crazy to come back. They need you far more—' He stopped abruptly, listened for a fraction of a second, threw himself at Vukalovic and brought them both crashing heavily to the ground as a whining mortar shell buried itself among loose rocks a few feet away, exploding on impact. Close by, a man screamed in agony. A second mortar shell landed, then a third and a fourth, all within thirty feet of one another.

'They've got the range now, damn them.' Stephan rose quickly to his feet and peered down the gorge. For long seconds he could see nothing, for a band of dark cloud had crossed the face of the moon: then the moon broke through and he could see the enemy all too clearly. Because of some almost certainly prearranged signal, they were no longer making any attempt to seek cover: they were pounding straight up the slope with all the speed they could muster, machine-carbines and rifles at the ready in their hands—and as soon as the moon broke through they squeezed the triggers of those guns. Stephan threw himself behind the shelter of a boulder.

'Now!' he shouted. 'Now!'

The first ragged Partisan fusillade lasted for only a few seconds, then a black shadow fell over the valley. The firing ceased.

'Keep firing,' Vukalovic shouted. 'Don't stop now. They're closing in.' He loosed off a burst from his own machine-pistol and said to Stephan, 'They know what they are about, our friends down there.'

'They should.' Stephan armed a stick grenade and spun it down the hill. 'Look at all the practice we've given them.'

The moon broke through again. The leading German infantry were no more than twenty-five yards away. Both sides exchanged hand-grenades, fired at point-blank range. Some German soldiers fell, but many more came on, flinging themselves on the redoubt. Matters became temporarily confused. Here and there bitter hand-to-hand fighting developed. Men shouted at each other, cursed each other, killed each other. But the redoubt remained unbroken. Suddenly, dark heavy clouds again rolled over the moon, darkness flooded the gorge and everything slowly fell quiet. In the distance the thunder of artillery and mortar fire fell away to a muted rumble, then finally died.

'A trap?' Vukalovic said softly to Stephan. 'You think they will come again?'

'Not tonight.' Stephan was positive. 'They're brave men, but—'

'But not insane?'

'But not insane.'

Blood poured down over Stephan's face from a re-opened wound in his face, but he was smiling. He rose to his feet and turned as a burly sergeant came up and delivered a sketchy salute.

'They've gone, Major. We lost seven of ours this time, and fourteen wounded.'

'Set pickets two hundred metres down,' Stephan said. 'He turned to Vukalovic. 'You heard, sir? Seven dead. Fourteen hurt.'

'Leaving how many?'

'Two hundred. Perhaps two hundred and five.'

'Out of four hundred.' Vukalovic's mouth twisted. 'Dear God, out of four hundred.'

'And sixty of those are wounded.'

'At least you can get them down to the hospital now.'

'There is no hospital,' Stephan said heavily. 'I didn't have time to tell you. It was bombed this morning. Both doctors killed. All our medical supplies—poof! Like that.'

'Gone? All gone?' Vukalovic paused for a long moment. 'I'll have some sent up from HQ. The walking wounded can make their own way to HQ.'

'The wounded won't leave, sir. Not any more.'

Vukalovic nodded in understanding and went on: 'How much ammunition?'

'Two days. Three, if we're careful.'

'Sixty wounded.' Vukalovic shook his head in slow disbelief. 'No medical help whatsoever for them. Ammunition almost gone. No food. No shelter. And they won't leave. Are they insane, too?'

'Yes, sir.'

'I'm going down to the river,' Vukalovic said. 'To see Colonel Lazlo at HQ.'

'Yes, sir.' Stephan smiled faintly. 'I doubt if you'll find his mental equilibrium any better than mine.'

'I don't suppose I will,' Vukalovic said.

Stephan saluted and turned away, mopping blood from his face, walked a few short swaying steps then knelt down to comfort a badly wounded man. Vukalovic looked after him expressionlessly, shaking his head: then he, too, turned and left.

Mallory finished his meal and lit a cigarette. He said. 'So what's going to happen to the Partisans in the Zenica Cage, as you call it?'

'They're going to break out,' Neufeld said. 'At least, they're going to try to.'

'But you've said yourself that's impossible.'

'Nothing is too impossible for those mad Partisans to try. I wish to heaven,' Neufeld said bitterly, 'that we were fighting a normal war against normal people, like the British or Americans. Anyway, we've had information—reliable information—that an attempted break-out is imminent. Trouble is, there are those two passes—they might even try to force the bridge at Neretva—and we don't know where the break-out is coming.'

C E

'This is very interesting.' Andrea looked sourly at the blind musician who was still giving his rendering of the same old Bosnian love-song. 'Can we get some sleep now?'

'Not tonight, I'm afraid.' Neufeld exchanged a smile with Droshny. '*You* are going to find out for us where this break-out is coming.'

'We are?' Miller drained his glass and reached for the bottle. 'Infectious stuff, this insanity.'

Neufeld might not have heard him. 'Partisan HQ is about ten kilometres from here. You are going to report there as the bona-fide British mission that has lost its way. Then, when you've found out their plans, you tell them that you are going to their main HQ at Drvar, which of course, you don't. You come back here instead. What could be simpler?'

'Miller's right,' Mallory said with conviction. 'You *are* mad.'

'I'm beginning to think there's altogether too much talk of this madness.' Neufeld smiled. 'You would prefer, perhaps, that Captain Droshny here turned you over to his men. I assure you, they are most unhappy about their—ah—late comrade.'

'You can't ask us to do this!' Mallory was hard-faced in anger. 'The Partisans are bound to get a radio message about us. Sooner or later. And then—well, you know what then. You just can't ask this of us.'

'I can and I will.' Neufeld looked at Mallory and his five companions without enthusiasm. 'It so happens that I don't care for dope-peddlers and drug-runners.'

'I don't think your opinion will carry much weight in certain circles,' Mallory said.

'And that means?'

'Kesselring's Director of Military Intelligence isn't going to like this at all.'

'If you don't come back, they'll never know. If you do—' Neufeld smiled and touched the Iron Cross at his throat—'they'll probably give me an oak leaf to this.'

'Likeable type, isn't he?' Miller said to no one in particular.

'Come, then.' Neufeld rose from the table. 'Petar?'

The blind singer nodded, slung his guitar over his shoulder and rose to his feet, his sister rising with him.

'What's this, then?' Mallory asked.

'Guides.'

'*Those* two?'

'Well,' Neufeld said reasonably, 'you can't very well find your own way there, can you? Petar and his sister—well, his sister—know Bosnia better than the foxes.'

'But won't the Partisans—' Mallory began, but Neufeld interrupted.

'You don't know your Bosnia. These two wander wherever they like and no one will turn them from their door. The Bosnians believe, and God knows with sufficient reason, that they are accursed and have the evil eye on them. This is a land of superstition, Captain Mallory.'

'But—but how will they know where to take us?'

'They'll know.' Neufeld nodded to Droshny, who talked rapidly to Maria in Serbo-Croat: she in turn spoke to Petar, who made some strange noises in his throat.

'That's an odd language,' Miller observed.

'He's got a speech impediment,' Neufeld said shortly. 'He was born with it. He can sing, but not talk—it's not unknown. Do you wonder people think they are cursed?' He turned to Mallory. 'Wait outside with your men.'

Mallory nodded, gestured to the others to precede him. Neufeld, he noted, was immediately engaged in a short, low-voiced discussion with Droshny, who nodded, summoned one of his Cetniks and dispatched him on some errand. Once outside, Mallory moved with Andrea slightly apart from the others and murmured something in his ear, inaudible to all but Andrea, whose nodded acquiescence was almost imperceptible.

Neufeld and Droshny emerged from the hut, followed by Maria who was leading Petar by the hand. As they approached Mallory's group, Andrea walked casually towards them, smoking the inevitable noxious cigar. He planted himself in front of a puzzled Neufeld and arrogantly blew smoke into his face.

'I don't think I care for you very much, Hauptmann Neufeld,' Andrea announced. He looked at Droshny. 'Nor for the cutlery salesman here.'

Neufeld's face immediately darkened, became tight in anger. But he brought himself quickly under control and said with restraint: 'Your opinion of me is of no concern to me.' He nodded to Droshny. 'But do not cross Captain Droshny's path, my friend. He is a Bosnian and a proud one—and the best man in the Balkans with a knife.'

'The best man—' Andrea broke off with a roar of laughter, and blew smoke into Droshny's face. 'A knife-grinder in a comic opera.'

Droshny's disbelief was total but of brief duration. He bared his teeth in a fashion that would have done justice to any Bosnian wolf, swept a wickedly-curved knife from his belt and threw himself on Andrea, the gleaming blade hooking viciously upwards, but Andrea, whose prudence was exceeded only by the extraordinary speed with which he could move his vast bulk, was no longer there when the knife arrived. But his hand was. It caught Droshny's knife wrist as it flashed upwards and almost at once the two big men crashed heavily to the ground, rolling over and over in the snow while they fought for possession of the knife.

So unexpectedly, so wholly incredible the speed with which the fight had developed from nowhere that, for a few seconds, no one moved. The three young sergeants, Neufeld and the Cetniks registered nothing but utter astonishment. Mallory, who was standing close behind the wide-eyed girl, rubbed his chin thoughtfully while Miller, delicately tapping the ash off the end of his cigarette, regarded the scene with a sort of weary interest.

Almost at the same instant, Reynolds, Groves and two Cetniks flung themselves upon the struggling pair on the ground and tried to pull them apart. Not until Saunders and Neufeld lent a hand did they succeed. Droshny and Andrea were pulled to their feet, the former with contorted face and hatred in his eyes, Andrea calmly resuming the smoking of the cigar which he'd somehow picked up after they had been separated.

'You madman!' Reynolds said savagely to Andrea. 'You crazy maniac. You—you're a bloody psychopath. You'll get us all killed.'

'That wouldn't surprise me at all,' Neufeld said thoughtfully. 'Come. Let us have no more of this foolishness.'

He led the way from the compound, and as he did so they were joined by a group of half-a-dozen Cetniks, whose apparent leader was the youth with the straggling ginger beard and cast to his eye, the first of the Cetniks to greet them when they had landed.

'Who are they and what are they for?' Mallory demanded of Neufeld. 'They're not coming with us.'

'Escort,' Neufeld explained. 'For the first seven kilometres only.'

'Escorts? What would we want with escorts? We're in no danger from you, nor, according to what you say, will we be from the Yugoslav Partisans.'

'We're not worried about you,' Neufeld said drily. 'We're worried about the vehicle that is going to take you most of the way there. Vehicles are very few and very precious in this part of Bosnia—and there are many Partisan patrols about.'

Twenty minutes later, in a now moonless night and with snow falling, they reached a road, a road which was little more than a winding track running through a forested valley floor. Waiting for them there was one of the strangest four-wheeled contraptions Mallory or his companions had ever seen, an incredibly ancient and battered truck which at first sight, from the vast clouds of smoke emanating from it, appeared to be on fire. It was, in fact, a very much pre-war wood-burning truck, of a type at one time common in the Balkans. Miller regarded the smoke-shrouded truck in astonishment and turned to Neufeld.

'You call this a vehicle?'

'You call it what you like. Unless you'd rather walk.'

'Ten kilometres? I'll take my chance on asphyxiation.' Miller climbed in, followed by the others, till only Neufeld and Droshny remained outside.

Neufeld said: 'I shall expect you back before noon.'

'If we ever come back,' Mallory said. 'If a radio message has come through—'

'You can't make an omelette without breaking eggs,' Neufeld said indifferently.

With a great rattling and shaking and emission of smoke and steam, all accompanied by much red-eyed coughing from the canvas-covered rear, the truck jerked uncertainly into motion and moved off slowly along the valley floor, Neufeld and Droshny gazing after it. Neufeld shook his head. 'Such clever little men.'

'Such *very* clever little men,' Droshny agreed. 'But I want the big one, Captain.'

Neufeld clapped him on the shoulder. 'You shall have him, my friend. Well, they're out of sight. Time for you to go.'

Droshny nodded and whistled shrilly between his fingers. There came the distant whirr of an engine starter, and soon an elderly Fiat emerged from behind a clump of pines and approached along the hard-packed snow of the road, its chains clanking violently, and stopped beside the two men. Droshny climbed into the front passenger seat and the Fiat moved off in the wake of the truck.

V

FRIDAY 0330-0500

For the fourteen people jammed on the narrow side benches under the canvas-hooped roof, the journey could hardly be called pleasurable. There were no cushions on the seats just as there appeared to be a total absence of springs on the vehicle, and the torn and badly fitting hood admitted large quantities of icy night air and eye-smarting smoke in about equal proportions. At least, Mallory thought, it all helped considerably to keep them awake.

Andrea was sitting directly opposite him, seemingly oblivious of the thick choking atmosphere inside the truck, a fact hardly surprising considering that the penetrating power and the pungency of the smoke from the truck was of a lower order altogether than that emanating from the black cheroot clamped between Andrea's teeth. Andrea glanced idly across and caught Mallory's eye. Mallory nodded once, a millimetric motion of the head that would have gone unremarked by even the most suspicious. Andrea dropped his eyes until his gaze rested on Mallory's right hand, lying loosely on his knee. Mallory sat back and sighed, and as he did his right hand slipped until his thumb was pointing directly at the floor. Andrea puffed out another Vesuvian cloud of acrid smoke and looked away indifferently.

For some kilometres the smoke-enshrouded truck clattered and screeched its way along the valley floor, then swung off to the left on to an even narrower track, and began to climb. Less than two minutes later, with Droshny sitting impassively in the front passenger seat, the pursuing Fiat made a similar turn off.

The slope was now so steep and the spinning driving wheels losing so much traction on the frozen surface of the track that the ancient wood-burning truck was reduced to little more than walking pace. Inside the truck, Andrea and Mallory were as watchful as ever, but Miller and the three sergeants seemed to be dozing off, whether through exhaustion or incipient asphyxiation it was difficult to say. Maria and Petar, hand in hand, appeared to be asleep. The Cetniks, on the other hand, could hardly have been more wide awake, and were making it clear for the first time that the rents and holes in the canvas cover had not been caused by accident: Droshny's six men were now kneeling on the benches with the muzzles of their machine-pistols thrust through the apertures in the canvas. It was clear that the truck was now moving into Partisan territory, or, at least, what passed for no-man's-land in that wild and rugged territory.

The Cetnik farthest forward in the truck suddenly withdrew his face from a gap in the canvas and rapped the butt of his gun against the driver's cab. The truck wheezed to a grateful halt, the ginger-bearded Cetnik jumped down, checked swiftly for any signs of ambush, then gestured the others to disembark, the repeatedly urgent movements of his

hand making it clear that he was less than enamoured of
the idea of hanging around that place for a moment longer
than necessity demanded. One by one Mallory and his companions jumped down on to the frozen snow. Reynolds
guided the blind singer down to the ground, then reached up
a hand to help Maria as she clambered over the tail-board.
Wordlessly, she struck his hand aside and leapt nimbly to
the ground: Reynolds stared at her in hurt astonishment.
The truck, Mallory observed, had stopped opposite a small
clearing in the forest. Backing and filling and issuing denser
clouds of smoke than ever, it used this space to turn around
in a remarkably short space of time and clanked its way off
down the forest path at a considerably higher speed than it
had made the ascent. The Cetniks gazed impassively from
the back of the departing truck, made no gesture of farewell.

Maria took Petar's hand, looked coldly at Mallory, jerked
her head and set off up a tiny footpath leading at right-angles
from the track. Mallory shrugged and set off, followed by the
three sergeants. For a moment or two Andrea and Miller
remained where they were, gazing thoughtfully at the corner
round which the truck had just disappeared. Then they, too,
set off, talking in low tones to each other.

The ancient wood-burning truck did not maintain its initial
impetus for any lengthy period of time. Less than four
hundred yards after rounding the corner which blocked
it from the view of Mallory and his companions it braked
to a halt. Two Cetniks, the ginger-bearded leader of the
escort and another black-bearded man, jumped over the tail-
board and moved at once into the protective covering of the
forest. The truck rattled off once more, its belching smoke
hanging heavily in the freezing night air.

A kilometre farther down the track, an almost identical scene
was taking place. The Fiat slid to a halt, Droshny scrambled
from the passenger's seat and vanished among the pines.
The Fiat reversed quickly and moved off down the track.

The track up through the heavily wooded slope was very
narrow, very winding: the snow was no longer hard-packed,

but soft and deep and making for very hard going. The moon was quite gone now, the snow, gusted into their faces by the east wind, was becoming steadily heavier and the cold was intense. The path frequently arrived at a V-shaped branch but Maria, in the lead with her brother, never hesitated: she knew, or appeared to know, exactly where she was going. Several times she slipped in the deep snow, on the last occasion so heavily that she brought her brother down with her. When it happened yet again, Reynolds moved forward and took the girl by the arm to help her. She struck out savagely and drew her arm away. Reynolds stared at her in astonishment, then turned to Mallory.

'What the devil's the matter with—I mean, I was only trying to help—'

'Leave her alone,' Mallory said. 'You're one of them.'

'I'm one of—'

'You're wearing a British uniform. That's all the poor kid understands. Leave her be.'

Reynolds shook his head uncomprehendingly. He hitched his pack more securely on his shoulders, glanced back down the trail, made to move on, then glanced backwards again. He caught Mallory by the arm and pointed.

Andrea had already fallen thirty yards behind. Weighed down by his rucksack and Schmeisser and weight of years, he was very obviously making heavy weather of the climb and was falling steadily behind by the second. At a gesture and word from Mallory the rest of the party halted and peered back down through the driving snow, waiting for Andrea to make up on them. By this time Andrea was beginning to stumble almost drunkenly and clutched at his right side as if in pain. Reynolds looked at Groves: they both looked at Saunders: all three slowly shook their heads. Andrea came up with them and a spasm of pain flickered across his face.

'I'm sorry.' The voice was gasping and hoarse. 'I'll be all right in a moment.'

Saunders hesitated, then advanced towards Andrea. He smiled apologetically, then reached out a hand to indicate the rucksack and Schmeisser.

'Come on, Dad. Hand them over.'

For the minutest fraction of a second a flicker of menace, more imagined than seen, touched Andrea's face, then he shrugged off his rucksack and wearily handed it over. Saunders accepted it and tentatively indicated the Schmeisser.

'Thanks.' Andrea smiled wanly. 'But I'd feel lost without it.'

Uncertainly, they resumed their climb, looking back frequently to check on Andrea's progress. Their doubts were well-founded. Within thirty seconds Andrea had stopped, his eyes screwed up and bent almost double in pain. He said, gaspingly: 'I must rest . . . Go on. I'll catch up with you.'

Miller said solicitously: 'I'll stay with you.'

'I don't need anybody to stay with me,' Andrea said surlily. 'I can look after myself.'

Miller said nothing. He looked at Mallory and jerked his head in an uphill direction. Mallory nodded, once, and gestured to the girl. Reluctantly, they moved off, leaving Andrea and Miller behind. Twice, Reynolds looked back over his shoulder, his expression an odd mixture of worry and exasperation: then he shrugged his shoulders and bent his back to the hill.

Andrea, scowling blackly and still clutching his ribs, remained bent double until the last of the party had rounded the nearest uphill corner, then straightened effortlessly, tested the wind with a wetted forefinger, established that it was moving up-trail, produced a cigar, lit it and puffed in deep and obvious contentment. His recovery was quite astonishing, but it didn't appear to astonish Miller, who grinned and nodded downhill. Andrea grinned in return, made a courteous gesture of precedence.

Thirty yards down-trail, at a position which gave them an uninterrupted view of almost a hundred yards of the track below them they moved into the cover of the bole of a giant pine. For about two minutes they stood there, staring downhill and listening intently, then suddenly Andrea nodded, stooped and carefully laid his cigar in a sheltered dried patch of ground behind the bole of the pine.

They exchanged no words: there was need of none. Miller crawled round to the downhill-facing front of the pine and carefully arranged himself in a spread-eagled position in the deep snow, both arms outflung, his apparently sightless face turned up to the falling snow. Behind the pine, Andrea reversed his grip on his Schmeisser, holding it by the barrel, produced a knife from the recesses of his clothing and stuck it in his belt. Both men remained as motionless as if they had died there and frozen solid over the long and bitter Yugoslav winter.

Probably because his spread-eagled form was sunk so deeply in the soft snow as to conceal most of his body, Miller saw the two Cetniks coming quite some time before they saw him. At first they were no more than two shapeless and vaguely ghostlike forms gradually materializing from the falling snow: as they drew nearer, he identified them as the Cetnik escort leader and one of his men.

They were less than thirty yards away before they saw Miller. They stopped, stared, remained motionless for at least five seconds, looked at each other, unslung their machine-pistols and broke into a stumbling uphill run. Miller closed his eyes. He didn't require them any more, his ears gave him all the information he wanted, the closing sound of crunching footsteps in the snow, the abrupt cessation of those, the heavy breathing as a man bent over him.

Miller waited until he could actually feel the man's breath in his face, then opened his eyes. Not twelve inches from his own were the eyes of the ginger-bearded Cetnik. Miller's outflung arms curved upwards and inwards, his sinewy fingers hooked deeply into the throat of the startled man above him.

Andrea's Schmeisser had already reached the limit of its backswing as he stepped soundlessly round the bole of the pine. The black-bearded Cetnik was just beginning to move to help his friend when he caught sight of Andrea from the corner of one eye, and flung up both arms to protect himself. A pair of straws would have served him as well. Andrea grimaced at the sheer physical shock of the impact, dropped the Schmeisser, pulled out his knife and fell upon the other Cetnik still struggling desperately in Miller's stranglehold.

Miller rose to his feet and he and Andrea stared down at the two dead men. Miller looked in puzzlement at the ginger-bearded man, then suddenly stooped, caught the beard and tugged. It came away in his hand, revealing beneath it a clean-shaven face and a scar which ran from the corner of a lip to the chin.

Andrea and Miller exchanged speculative glances, but neither made comment. They dragged the dead men some little way off the path into the concealment of some undergrowth. Andrea picked up a dead branch and swept away the drag-marks in the snow and, by the base of the pine, all traces of the encounter: inside the hour, he knew, the brush-marks he had made would have vanished under a fresh covering of snow. He picked up his cigar and threw the branch deep into the woods. Without a backward glance, the two men began to walk briskly up the hill.

Had they given this backward glance, it was barely possible that they might have caught a glimpse of a face peering round the trunk of a tree farther downhill. Droshny had arrived at the bend in the track just in time to see Andrea complete his brushing operations and throw the branch away: what the meaning of this might be he couldn't guess.

He waited until Andrea and Miller had disappeared from his sight, waited another two minutes for good measure and safety, then hurried up the track, the expression on his swarthy brigand's face nicely balanced between puzzlement and suspicion. He reached the pine where the two Cetniks had been ambushed, briefly quartered the area, then followed the line of brush-marks leading into the woods, the puzzlement on his face giving way first to pure suspicion, then the suspicion to complete certainty.

He parted the bushes and peered down at the two Cetniks lying half-buried in a snow-filled gully with that curiously huddled shapelessness that only the dead can achieve. After a few moments he straightened, turned and looked uphill in the direction in which Andrea and Miller had vanished: his face was not pleasant to look upon.

Andrea and Miller made good time up the hill. As they

approached one of the innumerable bends in the trail they heard up ahead the sound of a softly-played guitar, curiously muffled and softened in tone by the falling snow. Andrea slowed up, threw away his cigar, bent forward and clutched his ribs. Solicitously, Miller took his arm.

The main party, they saw, was less than thirty yards ahead. They, too, were making slow time: the depth of snow and the increasing slope of the track made any quicker movement impossible. Reynolds glanced back—Reynolds was spending a great deal of his time in looking over his shoulder, he appeared to be in a highly apprehensive state—caught sight of Andrea and Miller and called out to Mallory who halted the party and waited for Andrea and Miller to make up with them. Mallory looked worriedly at Andrea.

'Getting worse?'

'How far to go?' Andrea asked hoarsely.

'Must be less than a mile.'

Andrea said nothing, he just stood there breathing heavily and wearing the stricken look of a sick man contemplating the prospect of another upward mile through deep snow. Saunders, already carrying two rucksacks, approached Andrea diffidently, tentatively. He said: 'It would help, you know, if—'

'I know.' Andrea smiled painfully, unslung his Schmeisser and handed it to Saunders. 'Thanks, son.'

Petar was still softly plucking the strings of his guitar, an indescribably eerie sound in those dark and ghostly pine woods. Miller looked at him and said to Mallory: 'What's the music while we march for?'

'Petar's password, I should imagine.'

'Like Neufeld said? Nobody touches our singing Cetnik?'

'Something like that.'

They moved on up the trail. Mallory let the others pass by until he and Andrea were bringing up the rear. Mallory glanced incuriously at Andrea, his face registering no more than a mild concern for the condition of his friend. Andrea caught his glance and nodded fractionally: Mallory looked away.

Fifteen minutes later they were halted, at gun-point, by

three men, all armed with machine-pistols, who simply appeared to have materialized from nowhere, a surprise so complete that not even Andrea could have done anything about it—even if he had had his gun. Reynolds looked urgently at Mallory, who smiled and shook his head.

'It's all right. Partisans—look at the red star on their forage caps. Just outposts guarding one of the main trails.'

And so it proved. Maria talked briefly to one of the soldiers, who listened, nodded and set off up the path, gesturing to the party to follow him. The other two Partisans remained behind, both men crossing themselves as Petar again strummed gently on his guitar. Neufeld, Mallory reflected, hadn't exaggerated about the degree of awed respect and fear in which the blind singer and his sister were held.

They came to Partisan HQ inside another ten minutes, an HQ curiously similar in appearance and choice of location to Hauptmann Neufold's camp: the same rough circle of crude huts set deep in the same *jamba*—depression—with similar massive pines towering high above. The guide spoke to Maria and she turned coldly to Mallory, the disdain on her face making it very plain how much against the grain it went for her to speak to him at all.

'We are to go to the guest hut. You are to report to the commandant. This soldier will show you.'

The guide beckoned in confirmation. Mallory followed him across the compound to a fairly large, fairly well-lit hut. The guide knocked, opened the door and waved Mallory inside, he himself following.

The commandant was a tall, lean, dark man with that aquiline, aristocratic face so common among the Bosnian mountainmen. He advanced towards Mallory with outstretched hand and smiled.

'Major Broznik, and at your service. Late, late hours, but as you see we are still up and around. Although I must say I did expect you before this.'

'I don't know what you're talking about.'

'You don't know—you *are* Captain Mallory, are you not?'

'I've never heard of him.' Mallory gazed steadily at Broznik, glanced briefly sideways at the guide, then looked back to Broznik again. Broznik frowned for a moment, then his face cleared. He spoke to the guide, who turned and left. Mallory put out his hand.

'Captain Mallory, at your service. I'm sorry about that, Major Broznik, but I insist we must talk alone.'

'You trust no one? Not even in *my* camp?'

'No one.'

'Not even your own men?'

'I don't trust them not to make mistakes. I don't trust myself not to make mistakes. I don't trust *you* not to make mistakes.'

'Please?' Broznik's voice was as cold as his eyes.

'Did you ever have two of your men disappear, one with ginger hair, the other with black, the ginger-haired man with a cast to his eye and a scar running from mouth to chin?'

Broznik came closer. 'What do you know about those men?'

'Did you? Know them, I mean?'

Broznik nodded and said slowly: 'They were lost in action. Last month.'

'You found their bodies?'

'No.'

'There were no bodies to be found. They had deserted— gone over to the Cetniks.'

'But they *were* Cetniks—converted to our cause.'

'They'd been re-converted. They followed us tonight. On the orders of Captain Droshny. I had them killed.'

'You—had—them—killed?'

'Think, man,' Mallory said wearily. 'If they had arrived here—which they no doubt intended to do a discreet interval after our arrival—we wouldn't have recognized them and you'd have welcomed them back as escaped prisoners. They'd have reported our every movement. Even if we had recognized them after they had arrived here and done something about it, you may have *other* Cetniks here who would have reported back to their masters that we had done away with their watch-dogs. So we disposed of them very quietly, no fuss, in a very remote place, then hid them.'

'There are no Cetniks in my command, Captain Mallory.'

Mallory said drily: 'It takes a very clever farmer, Major, to see two bad apples on the top of the barrel and be quite certain that there are none lower down. No chances. None. Ever.' Mallory smiled to remove any offence from his words and went on briskly: 'Now, Major, there's some information that Hauptmann Neufeld wants.'

To say that the guest hut hardly deserved so hospitable a title would have been a very considerable understatement. As a shelter for some of the less-regarded domesticated animals it might have been barely acceptable: as an overnight accommodation for human beings it was conspicuously lacking in what our modern effete European societies regard as the minimum essentials for civilized living. Even the Spartans of ancient Greece would have considered it as too much of a good thing. One rickety trestle table, one bench, a dying fire and lots of hard-packed earthen floor. It fell short of being a home from home.

There were six people in the hut, three standing, one sitting, two stretched out on the lumpy floor. Petar, for once without his sister, sat on the floor, silent guitar clasped in his hands, gazing sightlessly into the fading embers. Andrea, stretched in apparently luxurious ease in a sleeping-bag, peacefully puffed at what, judging from the frequent suffering glances cast in his direction, appeared to be a more than normally obnoxious cigar. Miller, similarly reclining, was reading what appeared to be a slender volume of poetry. Reynolds and Groves, unable to sleep, stood idly by the solitary window, gazing out abstractedly into the dimly-lit compound: they turned as Saunders removed his radio transmitter from its casing and made for the door.

With some bitterness Saunders said: 'Sleep well.'

'Sleep well?' Reynolds raised an eyebrow. 'And where are you going?'

'Radio hut across there. Message to Termoli. Mustn't spoil your beauty sleep when I'm transmitting.'

Saunders left. Groves went and sat by the table, cradling a weary head in his hands. Reynolds remained by the window, watched Saunders cross the compound and enter a darkened hut on the far side. Soon a light appeared in the window as Saunders lit a lamp.

Reynolds's eyes moved in response to the sudden appearance of an oblong of light across the compound. The door to Major Broznik's hut had opened and Mallory stood momentarily framed there, carrying what appeared to be a sheet of paper in his hand. Then the door closed and Mallory moved off in the direction of the radio hut.

Reynolds suddenly became very watchful, very still. Mallory had taken less than a dozen steps when a dark figure detached itself from the even darker shadow of a hut and confronted him. Quite automatically, Reynolds's hand reached for the Luger at his belt, then slowly withdrew. Whatever this confrontation signified for Mallory it certainly wasn't danger, for Maria, Reynolds knew, did not carry a gun. And unquestionably it was Maria who was now in such apparent close conversation with Mallory.

Bewildered now, Reynolds pressed his face close against the glass. For almost two minutes he stared at this astonishing spectacle of the girl who had slapped Mallory with such venom, who had lost no opportunity of displaying an animosity bordering on hatred, now talking to him not only animatedly but also clearly very amicably. So total was Reynold's baffled incomprehension at this inexplicable turn of events that his mind moved into a trance-like state, a spell that was abruptly snapped when he saw Mallory put a reassuring arm around her shoulder and pat her in a way that might have been comforting or affectionate or both but which in any event clearly evoked no resentment on the part of the girl. This was still inexplicable: but the only interpretation that could be put upon it was an uncompromisingly sinister one. Reynolds whirled round and silently and urgently beckoned Groves to the window. Groves rose quickly, moved to the window and looked out, but by the time he had done so there was no longer any sign of Maria: Mallory was alone, walking across the compound towards the radio hut, the paper still in his hand. Groves glanced questioningly at Reynolds.

'They were together,' Reynolds whispered. 'Mallory and Maria. I saw them! They were talking?'

'What? You sure?'

'God's my witness. I *saw* them, man. He even had his arm around—Get away from this window—Maria's coming.'

Without haste, so as to arouse no comment from Andrea or Miller, they turned and walked unconcernedly towards the table and sat down. Seconds later, Maria entered and, without looking at or speaking to anyone, crossed to the fire, sat by Petar and took his hand. A minute or so later Mallory entered, and sat on a palliasse beside Andrea, who removed his cigar and glanced at him in mild enquiry. Mallory casually checked to see that he wasn't under observation, then nodded. Andrea returned to the contemplation of his cigar.

Reynolds looked uncertainly at Groves, then said to Mallory: 'Shouldn't we be setting a guard, sir?'

'A guard?' Mallory was amused. 'Whatever for? This is a Partisan camp, Sergeant. Friends, you know. And, as you've seen, they have their own excellent guard system.'

'You never know—'

'*I* know. Get some sleep.'

Reynolds went on doggedly: 'Saunders is alone over there. I don't like—'

'He's coding and sending a short message for me. A few minutes, that's all.'

'But—'

'Shut up,' Andrea said. 'You heard the captain?'

Reynolds was by now thoroughly unhappy and uneasy, an unease which showed through in his instantly antagonistic irritation.

'Shut up? Why should I shut up? I don't take orders from you. And while we're telling each other what to do, you might put out that damned stinking cigar.'

Miller wearily lowered his book of verse.

'I quite agree about the damned cigar, young fellow. But do bear in mind that you are talking to a ranking colonel in the army.'

Miller reverted to his book. For a few moments Reynolds and Groves stared open-mouthed at each other, then Reynolds stood up and looked at Andrea.

'I'm extremely sorry, sir. I—I didn't realize—'

Andrea waved him to silence with a magnanimous hand and resumed his communion with his cigar. The minutes passed in silence. Maria, before the fire, had her head on Petar's shoulder, but otherwise had not moved: she appeared to be asleep. Miller shook his head in rapt admiration of what appeared to be one of the more esoteric manifestations of the poetic muse, closed his book reluctantly and slid down into his sleeping-bag. Andrea ground out his cigar and did the same. Mallory seemed to be already asleep. Groves lay down and Reynolds, leaning over the table, rested his forehead on his arms. For five minutes, perhaps longer, Reynolds remained like this, uneasily dozing off, then he lifted his head, sat up with a jerk, glanced at his watch, crossed to Mallory and shook him by the shoulder. Mallory stirred.

'Twenty minutes,' Reynolds said urgently. 'Twenty minutes and Saunders isn't back yet.'

'All right, so it's twenty minutes,' Mallory said patiently. 'He could take that long to make contact, far less transmit the message.'

'Yes, sir. Permission to check, sir?'

Mallory nodded wearily and closed his eyes. Reynolds picked up his Schmeisser, left the hut and closed the door softly behind him. He released the safety-catch on his gun and ran across the compound.

The light still burned in the radio hut. Reynolds tried to peer through the window but the frost of that bitter night had made it completely opaque. Reynolds moved around to the door. It was slightly ajar. He set his finger to the trigger and opened the door in the fashion in which all Commandos were trained to open doors—with a violent kick of his right foot.

There was no one in the radio hut, no one, that is, who could bring him to any harm. Slowly, Reynolds lowered his gun and walked in in a hesitant, almost dream-like fashion, his face masked in shock.

Saunders was leaning tiredly over the transmitting table, his head resting on it at an unnatural angle, both arms dangling limply towards the ground. The hilt of a knife protruded between his shoulder-blades: Reynolds noted, almost subconsciously, that there was no trace of blood: death had been instantaneous. The transmitter itself lay on the floor, a twisted and mangled mass of metal that was obviously smashed beyond repair. Tentatively, not knowing why he did so, he reached out and touched the dead man on the shoulder: Saunders seemed to stir, his cheek slid along the table and he toppled to one side, falling heavily across the battered remains of the transmitter. Reynolds stooped low over him. Grey parchment now, where a bronzed tan had been, sightless, faded eyes uselessly guarding a mind now flown. Reynolds swore briefly, bitterly, straightened and ran from the hut.

Everyone in the guest hut was asleep, or appeared to be. Reynolds crossed to where Mallory lay, dropped to one knee and shook him roughly by the shoulder. Mallory stirred, opened weary eyes and propped himself up on one elbow. He gave Reynolds a look of unenthusiastic enquiry.

'Among friends, you said!' Reynolds voice was low, vicious, almost a hissing sound. 'Safe, you said. Saunders will be all right, you said. You *knew*, you said. You bloody well knew.'

Mallory said nothing. He sat up abruptly on his palliasse, and the sleep was gone from his eyes. He said: 'Saunders?'

Reynolds said. 'I think you'd better come with me.'

In silence the two men left the hut, in silence they crossed the deserted compound and in silence they entered the radio hut. Mallory went no farther than the doorway. For what was probably no more than ten seconds but for what seemed to Reynolds to be an unconsciously long time, Mallory stared at the dead man and the smashed transmitter, his eyes bleak, his face registering no emotional reaction. Reynolds mistook the expression, or lack of it, for something else, and could suddenly no longer contain his pent-up fury.

'Well, aren't you bloody well going to do something about it instead of standing there all night?'

'Every dog's entitled to his one bite,' Mallory said mildly. 'But don't talk to me like that again. Do what, for instance?'

'Do what?' Reynolds visibly struggled for his self-control. 'Find the nice gentleman who did this.'

'Finding him will be very difficult.' Mallory considered. 'Impossible, I should say. If the killer came from the camp here, then he'll have gone to earth in the camp here. If he came from outside, he'll be a mile away by this time and putting more distance between himself and us every second. Go and wake Andrea and Miller and Groves and tell them to come here. Then go and tell Major Broznik what's happened.'

'I'll tell them what's happened,' Reynolds said bitterly. 'And I'll also tell them it never *would* have happened if you'd listened to me. But oh no, you wouldn't listen, would you?'

'So you were right and I was wrong. Now do as I ask you.'

Reynolds hesitated, a man obviously on the brink of outright revolt. Suspicion and defiance alternated in the angry face. Then some strange quality in the expression in Mallory's face tipped the balance for sanity and compliance and he nodded in sullen antagonism, turned and walked away.

Mallory waited until he had rounded the corner of the hut, brought out his torch and started, not very hopefully, to quarter the hard-packed snow outside the door of the radio hut. But almost at once he stopped, stooped, and brought the head of the torch close to the surface of the ground.

It was a very small portion of footprint indeed, only the front half of the sole of a right foot. The pattern showed two V-shaped marks, the leading V with a cleanly-cut break in it. Mallory, moving more quickly now, followed the direction indicated by the pointed toe-print and came across two more similar indentations, faint but unmistakable, before the frozen snow gave way to the frozen earth of the compound, ground so hard as to be incapable of registering any footprints at all. Mallory retraced his steps, carefully erasing all three prints with the toe of his boot and reached the radio hut only seconds before he was joined by Reynolds, Andrea, Miller and Groves. Major Broznik and several of his men joined them soon after.

They searched the interior of the radio hut for clues as to the killer's identity, but clues there were none. Inch by inch they searched the hard-packed snow surrounding the hut, with the same completely negative results. Reinforced, by this time, by perhaps sixty or seventy sleepy-eyed Partisan soldiers, they carried out a simultaneous search of all the buildings and of the woods surrounding the encampment: but neither the encampment nor the surrounding woods had any secrets to yield.

'We may as well call it off,' Mallory said finally. 'He's got clean away.'

'It looks that way,' Major Broznik agreed. He was deeply troubled and bitterly angry that such a thing should have happened in his encampment. 'We'd better double the guards for the rest of the night.'

'There's no need for that,' Mallory said. 'Our friend won't be back.'

'There's no need for that,' Reynolds mimicked savagely. 'There was no need for that for poor Saunders, you said. And where's Saunders now? Sleeping comfortably in his bed? Is he hell! No need—'

Andrea muttered warningly and took a step nearer Reynolds, but Mallory made a brief conciliatory movement of his right hand. He said: 'It's entirely up to you, of course, Major. I'm sorry that we have been responsible for giving you and your men so sleepless a night. See you in the morning.' He smiled wryly. 'Not that that's so far away.' He turned to go, found his way blocked by Sergeant Groves, a

Groves whose normally cheerful countenance now mirrored the tight hostility of Reynolds's.

'So he's got clear away, has he? Away to hell and gone. And that's the end of it, eh?'

Mallory looked at him consideringly. 'Well, no. I wouldn't quite say that. A little time. We'll find him.'

'A little time? Maybe even before he dies of old age?'

Andrea looked at Mallory. 'Twenty-four hours?'

'Less.'

Andrea nodded and he and Mallory turned and walked away towards the guest hut. Reynolds and Groves, with Miller slightly behind them, watched the two men as they went, then looked at each other, their faces still bleak and bitter.

'Aren't they a nice warm-hearted couple now? Completely broken up about old Saunders.' Groves shook his head. 'They don't care. They just don't care.'

'Oh, I wouldn't say that,' Miller said diffidently. 'It's just that they don't *seem* to care. Not at all the same thing.'

'Faces like wooden Indians,' Reynolds muttered. 'They never even said they were *sorry* that Saunders was killed.'

'Well,' Miller said patiently, 'it's a cliché, but different people react in different ways. Okay, so grief and anger is the natural reaction to this sort of thing, but if Mallory and Andrea spent their time in reacting in that fashion to all the things that have happened to *them* in their lifetimes, they'd have come apart at the seams years ago. So they don't react that way any more. They do things. Like they're going to do things to your friend's killer. Maybe you didn't get it, but you just heard a death sentence being passed.'

'How do *you* know?' Reynolds said uncertainly. He nodded in the direction of Mallory and Andrea who were just entering the guest hut. 'And how did *they* know? Without talking, I mean.'

'Telepathy.'

'What do you mean—"telepathy"?'

'It would take too long,' Miller said wearily. 'Ask me in the morning.'

VI

FRIDAY 0800-1000

Crowning the tops of the towering pines, the dense, interlock-
ing snow-laden branches formed an almost impenetrable
canopy that effectively screened Major Broznik's camp,
huddled at the foot of the *jamba*, from all but the most
fleeting glimpses of the sky above. Even at high noon on
a summer's day, it was never more than a twilit dusk
down below: on a morning such as this, an hour after
dawn with snow falling gently from an overcast sky, the
quality of light was such as to be hardly distinguishable
from a starlit midnight. The interior of the dining hut, where
Mallory and his company were at breakfast with Major
Broznik, was gloomy in the extreme, the darkness emphasized
rather than alleviated by the two smoking oil-lamps which
formed the only primitive means of illumination.

The atmosphere of gloom was significantly deepened by the
behaviour and expression of those seated round the breakfast
table. They ate in a moody silence, heads lowered, for the
most part not looking at one another: the events of
the previous night had clearly affected them all deeply but
none so deeply as Reynolds and Groves in whose faces was
still unmistakably reflected the shock caused by Saunders's
murder. They left their food untouched.

To complete the atmosphere of quiet desperation, it was
clear that the reservations held about the standard of the
Partisan early-morning cuisine were of a profound and
lasting nature. Served by two young *partisankas*—women
members of Marshal Tito's army—it consisted of *polenta*, a
highly unappetizing dish made from ground corn, and
raki, a Yugoslav spirit of unparalleled fierceness. Miller
spooned his breakfast with a marked lack of enthusiasm.

'Well,' he said to no one in particular, 'it makes a change,
I'll say that.'

'It's all we have,' Broznik said apologetically. He laid down his spoon and pushed his plate away from him. 'And even that I can't eat. Not this morning. Every entrance to the *jamba* is guarded, yet there was a killer loose in my camp last night. But maybe he *didn't* come in past the guards, maybe he was already inside. Think of it—a traitor in my own camp. And if there is, I can't even find him. I can't even believe it!'

Comment was superfluous, nothing could be said that hadn't been said already, nobody as much as looked in Broznik's direction: his acute discomfort, embarrassment and anger were apparent to everyone in his tone of voice. Andrea, who had already emptied his plate with apparent relish, looked at the two untouched plates in front of Reynolds and Groves and then enquiringly at the two sergeants themselves, who shook their heads. Andrea reached out, brought their plates before him and set to with every sign of undiminished appetite. Reynolds and Groves looked at him in shocked disbelief, possibly awed by the catholicity of Andrea's tastes, more probably astonished by the insensitivity of a man who could eat so heartily only a few hours after the death of one of his comrades. Miller, for his part, looked at Andrea in near horror, tried another tiny portion of his *polenta* and wrinkled his nose in delicate distaste. He laid down his spoon and looked morosely at Petar who, guitar slung over his shoulder, was awkwardly feeding himself.

Miller said irritably: 'Does he *always* wear that damned guitar?'

'Our lost one,' Broznik said softly. 'That's what we call him. Our poor blind lost one. Always he carries it or has it by his side. Always. Even when he sleeps—didn't you notice last night? That guitar means as much to him as life itself. Some weeks ago, one of our men, by way of a joke, tried to take it from him: Petar, blind though he is, almost killed him.'

'He must be stone tone deaf,' Miller said wonderingly. 'It's the most god-awful guitar I ever heard.'

Broznik smiled faintly. 'Agreed. But don't you understand? He can feel it. He can touch it. It's his own. It's the only thing left to him in the world, a dark and lonely and empty world. Our poor lost one.'

'He could at least tune it,' Miller muttered.

'You are a good man, my friend. You try to take our minds off what lies ahead this day. But no man can do that.' He turned to Mallory. 'Any more than you can hope to carry out your crazy scheme of rescuing your captured agents and breaking up the German counter-espionage network here. It is insanity. Insanity!'

Mallory waved a vague hand. 'Here you are. No food. No artillery. No transport. Hardly any guns—and practically no ammunition for those guns. No medical supplies. No tanks. No planes. No hope—and you keep on fighting. That makes you sane?'

'Touché.' Broznik smiled, pushed across the bottle of *raki*, waited until Mallory had filled his glass. 'To the madmen of this world.'

'I've just been talking to Major Stephan up at the Western Gap,' General Vukalovic said. 'He thinks we're all mad. Would you agree, Colonel Lazlo?'

The man lying prone beside Vukalovic lowered his binoculars. He was a burly, sun-tanned, thick-set, middle-aged man with a magnificent black moustache that had every appearance of being waxed. After a moment's consideration, he said: 'Without a doubt, sir.'

'Even you?' Vukalovic said protestingly. 'With a Czech father?'

'He came from the High Tatra,' Lazlo explained. 'They're all mad there.'

Vukalovic smiled, settled himself more comfortably on his elbows, peered downhill through the gap between two rocks, raised his binoculars and scanned the scene to the south of him, slowly raising his glasses as he did so.

Immediately in front of where he lay was a bare, rocky hillside, dropping gently downhill for a distance of about two hundred feet. Beyond its base it merged gradually into a long flat grassy plateau, no more than two hundred yards wide at its maximum, but stretching almost as far as the eye could see on both sides, on the right-hand side stretching away to the west, on the left curving away to the east, north-east and finally north.

Beyond the edge of the plateau, the land dropped abruptly to form the bank of a wide and swiftly flowing river, a river of that peculiarly Alpine greenish-white colour, green from the melting ice-water of spring, white from where it foamed over jagged rocks and overfalls in the bed of the river. Directly to the south of where Vukalovic and Lazlo lay, the river was spanned by a green-and-white-painted and very solidly-constructed cantilevered steel bridge. Beyond the river, the grassy bank on the far side rose in a very easy slope for a distance of about a hundred yards to the very regularly defined limit of a forest of giant pines which stretched away into the southern distance. Scattered through the very outermost of the pines were a few dully metallic objects, unmistakably tanks. In the farthest distance, beyond the river and beyond the pines, towering, jagged mountains dazzled in their brilliant covering of snow and above that again, but more to the south-east, an equally white and dazzling sun shone from an incongruously blue patch in an otherwise snow-cloud-covered sky.

Vukalovic lowered his binoculars and sighed.

'No idea at all how many tanks are across in the woods there?'

'I wish to heaven I knew.' Lazlo lifted his arms in a small, helpless gesture. 'Could be ten. Could be two hundred. We've no idea. We've sent scouts, of course, but they never came back. Maybe they were swept away trying to cross the Neretva.' He looked at Vukalovic, speculation in his eyes. 'Through the Zenica Gap, through the Western Gap or across that bridge there—you don't know where the attack is coming from, do you, sir?'

Vukalovic shook his head.

'But you expect it soon?'

'Very soon.' Vukalovic struck the rocky ground with a clenched fist. 'Is there *no* way of destroying that damned bridge?'

'There have been five RAF attacks,' Lazlo said heavily. 'To date, twenty-seven planes lost—there are two hundred AA guns along the Neretva and the nearest Messerschmitt station only ten minutes flying time away. The German radar picks up the British bombers crossing our coast—and the Messerschmitts are here, waiting, by the time they arrive. And don't forget that the bridge is set in rock on either side.'

'A direct hit or nothing?'

'A direct hit on a target seven metres wide from three thousand metres. It is impossible. And a target so camouflaged that you can hardly see it five hundred metres away on land. Doubly impossible.'

'And impossible for us,' Vukalovic said bleakly.

'Impossible for us. We made our last attempt two nights ago.'

'You made—I told you not to.'

'You *asked* us not to. But of course I, Colonel Lazlo, knew better. They started firing star-shells when our troops were halfway across the plateau, God knows how they knew they were coming. Then the searchlights—'

'Then the shrapnel shells,' Vukalovic finished. 'And the Oerlikons. Casualties?'

'We lost half a battalion.'

'Half a battalion! And tell me, my dear Lazlo, what would have happened in the unlikely event of your men reaching the bridge?'

'They had some amatol blocks, some hand-grenades—'

'No fireworks?' Vukalovic asked in heavy sarcasm. 'That might have helped. That bridge is built of steel set in reinforced concrete, man! You were mad even to try.'

'Yes, sir,' Lazlo looked away. 'Perhaps you ought to relieve me.'

'I think I should.' Vukalovic looked closely at the exhausted face. 'In fact I would. But for one thing.'

'One thing?'

'All my other regimental commanders are as mad as you are. And if the Germans do attack—maybe even tonight?'

'We stand here. We are Yugoslavs and we have no place to go. What else can we do?'

'What else? Two thousand men with pop-guns, most of them weak and starving and lacking ammunition, against what may perhaps be two first-line German armoured divisions. And you stand here. You could always surrender, you know.'

Lazlo smiled. 'With respect, General, this is no time for facetiousness.'

Vukalovic clapped his shoulder. 'I didn't think it funny, either. I'm going up to the dam, to the north-eastern re-doubt. I'll see if Colonel Janzy is as mad as you are. And Colonel?'

'Sir?'

'If the attack comes, I may give the order to retreat.'

'Retreat!'

'Not surrender. Retreat. Retreat to what, one hopes, may be victory.'

'I am sure the General knows what he is talking about.'

'The General isn't.' Oblivious to possible sniper fire from across the Neretva, Vukalovic stood up in readiness to go. 'Ever heard of a man called Captain Mallory. Keith Mallory, a New Zealander?'

'No.' Lazlo said promptly. He paused, then went on: 'Wait a minute, though. Fellow who used to climb mountains?'

'That's the one. But he has also, I'm given to under-stand, other accomplishments.' Vukalovic rubbed a stubbly chin. 'If all I hear about him is true, I think you could quite fairly call him a rather gifted individual.'

'And what about this gifted individual?' Lazlo asked curiously.

'Just this.' Vukalovic was suddenly very serious, even sombre. 'When all things are lost and there is no hope left, there is always, somewhere in the world, one man you can turn to. There may be only that one man. More often than not there *is* only that one man. But that one man is always there.' He paused reflectively. 'Or so they say.'

'Yes, sir,' Lazlo said politely. 'But about this Keith Mallory—'

'Before you sleep tonight, pray for him. I will.'

'Yes, sir. And about us? Shall I pray for us, too?'

'That,' said Vukalovic, 'wouldn't be at all a bad idea.'

The sides of the *jamba* leading upwards from Major Broznik's camp were very steep and very slippery and the ascending cavalcade of men and ponies were making very heavy going of it. Or most of them were. The escort of dark stocky Bosnian Partisans, to whom such terrain was part and parcel of existence, appeared quite unaffected by the climb: and it in no way appeared to interfere with Andrea's rhythmic puffing of his usual vile-smelling cigar. Reynolds noticed this, a fact which fed fresh fuel to the already dark doubts and torments in his mind.

He said sourly: 'You seem to have made a remarkable recovery in the night-time, Colonel Stavros, sir.'

'Andrea.' The cigar was removed. 'I have a heart condition. It comes and it goes.' The cigar was replaced.

'I'm sure it does,' Reynolds muttered. He glanced suspiciously, and for the twentieth time, over his shoulder. 'Where the hell is Mallory?'

'Where the hell is *Captain* Mallory,' Andrea chided.

'Well, where?'

'The leader of an expedition has many responsibilities,' Andrea said. 'Many things to attend to. Captain Mallory is probably attending to something at this very moment.'

'You can say that again,' Reynolds muttered.

'What was that?'

'Nothing.'

Captain Mallory was, as Andrea had so correctly guessed, attending to something at that precise moment. Back in Broznik's office, he and Broznik were bent over a map spread out on the trestle table. Broznik pointed to a spot near the northern limit of the map.

'I agree. This *is* the nearest possible landing strip for a plane. But it is very high up. At this time of year there will still be almost a metre of snow up there. There are other places, better places.'

'I don't doubt that for a moment.' Mallory said. 'Faraway

fields are always greener, maybe even faraway airfields. But I haven't the time to go to them.' He stabbed his forefinger on the map. 'I want a landing-strip here and only here by night-fall. I'd be most grateful if you'd send a rider to Konjic within the hour and have my request radioed immediately to your Partisan HQ at Drvar.'

Broznik said drily: 'You are accustomed to asking for instant miracles, Captain Mallory?'

'This doesn't call for miracles. Just a thousand men. The feet of a thousand men. A small price for seven thousand lives?' He handed Broznik a slip of paper. 'Wavelength and code. Have Konjic transmit it as soon as possible.' Mallory glanced at his watch. 'They have twenty minutes on me already. I'd better hurry.'

'I suppose you'd better,' Broznik said hurriedly. He hesitated, at a momentary loss for words, then went on awkwardly: 'Captain Mallory, I—I—'

'I know. Don't worry. The Mallorys of this world never make old bones anyway. We're too stupid.'

'Aren't we all, aren't we all?' Broznik gripped Mallory's hand. 'Tonight, I make a prayer for you.'

Mallory remained silent for a moment, then nodded.

'Make it a long one.'

The Bosnian scouts, now, like the remainder of the party, mounted on ponies, led the winding way down through the gentle slopes of the thickly-forested valley, followed by Andrea and Miller riding abreast, then by Petar, whose pony's bridle was in the hand of his sister. Reynolds and Groves, whether by accident or design, had fallen some little way behind and were talking in soft tones.

Groves said speculatively: 'I wonder what Mallory and the Major are talking about back there?'

Reynolds's mouth twisted in bitterness. 'It's perhaps as well we don't know.'

'You may be right at that. I just don't know.' Groves paused, went on almost pleadingly: 'Broznik is on the up-and-up. I'm sure of it. Being what he is, he *must* be.'

'That's as may be. Mallory too, eh?'

'*He* must be, too.'

'Must?' Reynolds was savage. 'God alive, man, I tell you I saw him with my own eyes.' He nodded towards Maria, some twenty yards ahead, and his face was cruel and hard. 'That girl hit him—and *how* she hit him—back in Neufeld's camp and the next thing I see is the two of them having a cosy little lovey-dovey chat outside Broznik's hut. Odd, isn't it? Soon after, Saunders was murdered. Coincidence, isn't it? I tell you, Groves, Mallory could have done it himself. The girl *could* have had time to do it before she met Mallory —except that it would have been physically impossible for her to drive a six-inch knife home to the hilt. But Mallory could have done it all right. He'd time enough—and opportunity enough—when he handed that damned message into the radio hut.'

Groves said protestingly: 'Why in God's name should he do that?'

'Because Broznik had given him some urgent information. Mallory *had* to make a show of passing this information back to Italy. But maybe sending that message was the last thing he wanted. Maybe he stopped it in the only way he knew how—and smashed the transmitter to make sure no one else could send a message. Maybe that's why he stopped me from mounting a guard or going to see Saunders—to prevent me from discovering the fact that Saunders was already dead—in which case, of course, because of the time factor, suspicion would have automatically fallen on him.'

'You're imagining things.' Despite his discomfort, Groves was reluctantly impressed by Reynold's reasoning.

'You think so? That knife in Saunders's back—did I imagine that too?'

Within half an hour, Mallory had rejoined the party. He jogged past Reynolds and Groves, who studiously ignored him, past Maria and Petar, who did the same, and took up position behind Andrea and Miller.

It was in this order, for almost an hour, that they

passed through the heavily-wooded Bosnian valleys. Occasionally, they came to clearings in the pines, clearings that
had once been the site of human habitation, small villages or
hamlets. But now there were no humans, no habitations, for
the villages had ceased to exist. The clearings were all the
same, chillingly and depressingly the same. Where the hard-
working but happy Bosnians had once lived in their simple
but sturdy homes, there were now only the charred and
blackened remains of what had once been thriving com-
munities, the air still heavy with the acrid smell of ancient
smoke, the sweet-sour stench of corruption and death, mute
testimony to the no-quarter viciousness and total ruthlessness
of the war between the Germans and the Partisan Yugoslavs.
Occasionally, here and there, still stood a few small,
stone-built houses which had not been worth the expenditure
of bombs or shells or mortars or petrol: but few of the
larger buildings had escaped complete destruction. Churches
and schools appeared to have been the primary targets: on
one occasion, as evidenced by some charred steel equipment
that could have come only from an operating theatre, they
passed by a small cottage hospital that had been so razed to
the ground that no part of the resulting ruins was more
than three feet high. Mallory wondered what would have
happened to the patients occupying the hospital at the
time: but he no longer wondered at the hundreds of
thousands of Yugoslavs—350,000 had been the figure quoted
by Captain Jensen, but, taking women and children into
account, the number must have been at least a million
—who had rallied under the banner of Marshal Tito.
Patriotism apart, the burning desire for liberation and
revenge apart, there was no place else left for them to
go. They were a people, Mallory realized, with literally
nothing left, with nothing to lose but their lives which they
apparently held of small account, but with everything
to gain by the destruction of the enemy: were he a
German soldier, Mallory reflected, he would not have felt
particularly happy about the prospect of a posting to Yugoslavia. It was a war which the Wehrmacht could never win,

which the soldiers of no Western European country could
ever have won, for the peoples of the high mountains are
virtually indestructible.

The Bosnian scouts, Mallory observed, looked neither to
left nor right as they passed through the lifeless shattered
villages of their countrymen, most of whom were now almost
certainly dead. They didn't _have_ to look, he realized: they
had their memories, and even their memories would be
too much for them. If it were possible to feel pity for an
enemy, then Mallory at that moment felt pity for the
Germans.

By and by they emerged from the narrow winding
mountain track on to a narrow, but comparatively wide
road, wide enough, at least, for single-file vehicular traffic.
The Bosnian scout in the lead threw up his hand and halted
his pony.

'Unofficial no-man's-land, it would seem,' Mallory said. 'I
think this is where they turfed us off the truck this
morning.'

Mallory's guess appeared to be correct. The Partisans
wheeled their horses, smiled widely, waved, shouted some
unintelligible words of farewell and urged their horses back
the way they had come.

With Mallory and Andrea in the lead and the two sergeants
bringing up the rear, the seven remaining members of the
party moved off down the track. The snow had stopped
now, the clouds above had cleared away and the sunlight
was filtering down between the now thinning pines. Suddenly Andrea, who had been peering to his left, reached
out and touched Mallory on the arm. Mallory followed the
direction of Andrea's pointing hand. Downhill, the pines
petered out less than a hundred yards away and through the
trees could be glimpsed some distant object, a startling
green in colour. Mallory swung round in his saddle.

'Down there. I want to take a look. _Don't_ move below the
tree-line.'

The ponies picked their delicate sure-footed way down the
steep and slippery slope. About ten yards from the tree-line
and at a signal from Mallory, the riders dismounted and

advanced cautiously on foot, moving from the cover of one pine to the next. The last few feet they covered on hands and knees, then finally stretched out flat in the partial concealment of the boles of the lowermost pines. Mallory brought out his binoculars, cleared the cold-clouded lenses and brought them to his eyes.

The snow-line, he saw, petered out some three or four hundred yards below them. Below that again was a mixture of fissured and eroded rock-faces and brown earth and beyond that again a belt of sparse and discouraged-looking grass. Along the lower reaches of this belt of grass ran a tarmacadam road, a road which struck Mallory as being, for that area, in remarkably good condition: the road was more or less exactly paralleled, at a distance of about a hundred yards, by a single-track and extremely narrow-gauge railway: a grass-grown and rusted line that looked as if it hadn't been used for many years. Just beyond the line the land dropped in a precipitous cliff to a narrow winding lake, the farther margin of which was marked by far more towering precipices leading up without break and with hardly any variation in angle to rugged snow-capped mountains.

From where he lay Mallory was directly overlooking a right-angled bend in the lake, a lake which was almost incredibly beautiful. In the bright clear sparkling sunlight of that spring morning it glittered and gleamed like the purest of emeralds. The smooth surface was occasionally ruffled by errant catspaws of wind, catspaws which had the effect of deepening the emerald colour to an almost translucent aquamarine. The lake itself was nowhere much more than a quarter of a mile in width, but obviously miles in length: the long right-hand arm, twisting and turning between the mountains, stretched to the east almost as far as the eye could see: to the left, the short southern arm, hemmed in by increasingly vertical walls which finally appeared almost to meet overhead, ended against the concrete ramparts of a dam. But what caught and held the attention of the watchers was the incredible mirrored gleam of the far mountains in that equally incredible emerald mirror.

'Well, now,' Miller murmured, 'that *is* nice.' Andrea gave him a long expressionless look, then turned his attention to the lake again.

Groves's interest momentarily overcame his animosity.

'What lake is that, sir?'

Mallory lowered the binoculars. 'Haven't the faintest idea. Maria?' She made no answer. 'Maria! What—lake—is —that?'

'That's the Neretva dam,' she said sullenly. 'The biggest in Yugoslavia.'

'It's important, then?'

'It is important. Whoever controls that controls Central Yugoslavia.'

'And the Germans control it, I suppose?'

'They control it. *We* control it.' There was more than a hint of triumph in her smile. 'We—the Germans—have got it completely sealed off. Cliffs on both sides. To the east there—the upper end—they have a boom across a gorge only ten yards wide. And that boom is patrolled night and day. So is the dam wall itself. The only way in is by a set of steps—ladders, rather—fixed to the cliff face just below the dam.'

Mallory said drily: 'Very interesting information—for a parachute brigade. But we've other and more urgent fish to fry. Come on.' He glanced at Miller, who nodded and began to ease his way back up the slope, followed by the two sergeants, Maria and Petar. Mallory and Andrea lingered for a few moments longer.

'I wonder what it's like,' Mallory murmured.

'What's what like?' Andrea asked.

'The other side of the dam.'

'And the ladder let into the cliff?'

'And the ladder let into the cliff.'

From where General Vukalovic lay, high on a cliff-top on the right-hand or western side of the Neretva gorge, he had an excellent view of the ladder let into the cliff: he had, in fact, an excellent view of the entire outer face of the dam wall and of the gorge which began at the foot of the wall and extended southwards for almost a mile before vanishing from sight round an abrupt right-hand corner.

The dam wall itself was quite narrow, not much more than thirty yards in width, but very deep, stretching down in a slightly V-formation from between overhanging cliff-faces to the greenish-white torrent of water foaming from the outlet pipes at the base. On top of the dam, at the eastern end and on a slight eminence, were the control station and two small huts, one of which, judging from the clearly visible soldiers patrolling the top of the wall, was almost certainly a guard-room. Above those buildings the walls of the gorge rose quite vertically for about thirty feet, then jutted out in a terrifying overhang.

From the control-room, a zig-zag, green-painted iron ladder, secured by brackets to the rock-face, led down to the floor of the gorge. From the base of the ladder a narrow path extended down the gorge for a distance of about a hundred yards, ending abruptly at a spot where some ancient landslide had gouged a huge scar into the side of the gorge. From here a bridge spanned the river to another path on the right-hand bank.

As bridges go, it wasn't much, an obviously very elderly and rickety wooden swing bridge which looked as if its own weight would be enough to carry it into the torrent at any moment: what was even worse, it seemed, at first glance, as if its site had been deliberately picked by someone with an unhinged mind, for it lay directly below an enormous boulder some forty feet up the landslide, a boulder so clearly in a highly precarious state of balance that none but the most foolhardy would have lingered in the crossing of the bridge. In point of fact, no other site would have been possible.

From the western edge of the bridge, the narrow, boulder-strewn path followed the line of the river, passing by what looked like an extremely hazardous ford, and finally curving away from sight with the river.

General Vukalovic lowered his binoculars, turned to the man at his side and smiled.

'All quiet on the eastern front, eh, Colonel Janzy?'

'All quiet on the eastern front,' Janzy agreed. He was a small, puckish, humorous-looking character with a youthful face and incongruous white hair. He twisted round and gazed to the north. 'But not so quiet on the northern front, I'm afraid.'

The smile faded from Vukalovic's face as he turned, lifted his binoculars again and gazed to the north. Less than three miles away and clearly visible in the morning sunlight, lay the heavily wooded Zenica Gap, for weeks a hotly contested strip of territory between Vukalovic's northern defensive forces, under the command of Colonel Janzy, and units of the invading German 11th Army Corps. At that moment frequent puffs of smoke could be seen, to the left a thick column of smoke spiralled up to form a dark pall against the now cloudless blue of the sky, while the distant rattle of small-arms fire, punctuated by the occasional heavier boom of artillery, was almost incessant. Vukalovic lowered his glasses and looked thoughtfully at Janzy.

'The softening-up before the main attack?'

'What else? The final assault.'

'How many tanks?'

'It's difficult to be sure. Collating reports, my staff estimate a hundred and fifty.'

'One hundred and fifty!'

'That's what they make it—and at least fifty of those are Tiger tanks.'

'Let's hope to heaven your staff can't count.' Vukalovic rubbed a weary hand across his bloodshot eyes: he'd had no sleep during the night just gone, no sleep during the night previous to that. 'Let's go and see how many *we* can count.'

Maria and Petar led the way now, with Reynolds and Groves, clearly in no mood for other company, bringing up the rear almost fifty yards behind. Mallory, Andrea and Miller rode abreast along the narrow road. Andrea looked at Mallory, his eyes speculative.

'Saunders's death? Any idea?'

Mallory shook his head. 'Ask me something else.'

'The message you'd given him to send. What was it?'

'A report of our safe arrival in Broznik's camp. Nothing more.'

'A psycho,' Miller announced. 'The handy man with the knife, I mean. Only a psycho would kill for that reason.'

'Maybe he didn't kill for that reason,' Mallory said mildly. 'Maybe he thought it was some other kind of message.'

'Some other kind of message?' Miller lifted an eyebrow in the way that only he knew how. 'Now what kind—' He caught Andrea's eye, broke off and changed his mind about saying anything more. Both he and Andrea gazed curiously at Mallory who seemed to have fallen into a mood of intense introspection.

Whatever its reason, the period of deep preoccupation did not last for long. With the air of a man who has just arrived at a conclusion about something, Mallory lifted his head and called to Maria to stop, at the same time reining in his own pony. Together they waited until Reynolds and Groves had made up on them.

'There are a good number of options open to us,' Mallory said, 'but for better or worse this is what I have decided to do.' He smiled faintly. 'For better, I think, if for no other reason than that this is the course of action that will get us out of here fastest. I've talked to Major Broznik and found out what I wanted. He tells me—'

'Got your information for Neufeld, then, have you?' If Reynolds was attempting to mask the contempt in his voice he made a singularly poor job of it.

'The hell with Neufeld,' Mallory said without heat. 'Partisan spies have discovered where the four captured Allied agents are being held.'

'They have?' Reynolds said. 'Then why don't the Partisans do something about it?'

'For a good enough reason. The agents are held deep in German territory. In an impregnable block-house high up in the mountains.'

'And what are *we* going to do about the Allied agents held in this impregnable block-house?'

'Simple.' Mallory corrected himself. 'Well, in theory

it's simple. We take them out of there and make our break tonight.'

Reynolds and Groves stared at Mallory, then at each other in frank disbelief and consternation. Andrea and Miller carefully avoided looking at each other or at anyone else.

'You're mad!' Reynolds spoke with total conviction.

'You're mad, *sir*,' Andrea said reprovingly.

Reynolds looked uncomprehendingly at Andrea, then turned back to Mallory again.

'You must be!' he insisted. 'Break? Break for where, in heaven's name?'

'For home. For Italy.'

'Italy!' It took Reynolds all of ten seconds to digest this startling piece of information, then he went on sarcastically: 'We're going to fly there, I suppose?'

'Well, it's a long swim across the Adriatic, even for a fit youngster like you. How else?'

'Flying?' Groves seemed slightly dazed.

'Flying. Not ten kilometres from here is a high—a very high mountain plateau, mostly in Partisan hands. There'll be a plane there at nine o'clock tonight.'

In the fashion of people who have failed to grasp something they have just heard, Groves repeated the statement in the form of a question. 'There'll be a plane there at nine o'clock tonight? You've just arranged this?'

'How could I? We've no radio.'

Reynolds's distrustful face splendidly complemented the scepticism in his voice. 'But *how* can you be sure—well, at nine o'clock?'

'Because, starting at six o'clock this evening, there'll be a Wellington bomber over the airstrip every three hours for the next week if necessary.'

Mallory kneed his pony and the party moved on, Reynolds and Groves taking up their usual position well to the rear of the others. For some time Reynolds, his expression alternating between hostility and speculation, stared fixedly at Mallory's back: then he turned to Groves.

'Well, well, well. Isn't that very convenient indeed. We

just *happen* to be sent to Broznik's camp. He just *happens* to know where the four agents are held. It just *happens* that an airplane will be over a certain airfield at a certain time—and it also so happens that I know for an absolute certainty that there are no airfields up in the high plateau. Still think everything clean and above-board?'

It was quite obvious from the unhappy expression on Groves's face that he thought nothing of the kind. He said: 'What in God's name are we going to do?'

'Watch our backs.'

Fifty yards ahead of them Miller cleared his throat and said delicately to Mallory: 'Reynolds seems to have lost some of his—um—earlier confidence in you, sir.'

Mallory said drily: 'It's not surprising. He thinks I stuck that knife in Saunders's back.'

This time Andrea and Miller did exchange glances, their faces registering expressions as close to pure consternation as either of those poker-faced individuals was capable of achieving.

VII

FRIDAY 1000-1200

Half a mile from Neufeld's camp they were met by Captain Droshny and some half-dozen of his Cetniks. Droshny's welcome was noticeably lacking in cordiality but at least he managed, at what unknown cost, to maintain some semblance of inoffensive neutrality.

'So you came back?'

'As you can see,' Mallory agreed.

Droshny looked at the ponies. 'And travelling in comfort.'

'A present from our good friend Major Broznik.' Mallory grinned. 'He thinks we're heading for Konjic on them.'

Droshny didn't appear to care very much what Major Broznik had thought. He jerked his head, wheeled his horse and set off at a fast trot for Neufeld's camp.

When they had dismounted inside the compound, Droshny immediately led Mallory into Neufeld's hut. Neufeld's welcome, like Droshny's, was something less than ecstatic, but at least he succeeded in imparting a shade more benevolence to his neutrality. His face held, also, just a hint of surprise, a reaction which he explained at once.

'Candidly, Captain, I did not expect to see you again. There were so many—ah—imponderables. However, I am delighted to see you—you would not have returned without the information I wanted. Now then, Captain Mallory, to business.'

Mallory eyed Neufeld without enthusiasm. 'You're not a very business-like partner, I'm afraid.'

'I'm not?' Neufeld said politely. 'In what way?'

'Business partners don't tell lies to each other. Sure you said Vukalovic's troops are massing. So they are indeed. But not, as you said, to break out. Instead, they're massing to defend themselves against the final German attack, the assault that is to crush them once and for all, and this assault they believe to be imminent.'

'Well, now, you surely didn't expect me to give away our military secrets—which you might, I say just might, have relayed to the enemy—before you had proved yourselves,' Neufeld said reasonably. 'You're not that naïve. About this proposed attack. Who gave you the information.'

'Major Broznik.' Mallory smiled in recollection. 'He was very expansive.'

Neufeld leaned forward, his tension reflected in the sudden stillness of his face, in the way his unblinking eyes held Mallory's. 'And did they say where they expected this attack to come?'

'I only know the name. The bridge at Neretva.'

Neufeld sank back into his chair, exhaled a long soundless sigh of relief and smiled to rob his next words of any offence. 'My friend, if you weren't British, a deserter, a renegade and a dope-peddler, you'd get the Iron Cross for this. By the way,' he went on, as if by casual afterthought, 'you've been cleared from Padua. The bridge at Neretva? You're sure of this?'

Mallory said irritably: 'If you doubt my word—'

'Of course not, of course not. Just a manner of speaking.' Neufeld paused for a few moments, then said softly: 'The bridge at Neretva.' The way he spoke them, the words sounded almost like a litany.

Droshny said softly: 'This fits in with all we suspected.'

'Never mind what you suspected,' Mallory said rudely. 'To *my* business now, if you don't mind. We have done well, you would say? We have fulfilled your request, got the precise information you wanted?' Neufeld nodded. 'Then get us the hell out of here. Fly us deep into some German-held territory. Into Austria or Germany itself, if you like—the farther away from here the better. You know what will happen to us if we ever again fall into British or Yugoslav hands?'

'It's not hard to guess,' Neufeld said almost cheerfully. 'But you misjudge us, my friend. Your departure to a place of safety has already been arranged. A certain Chief of Military Intelligence in northern Italy would very much like to make your personal acquaintance. He has reason to believe that you can be of great help to him.'

Mallory nodded his understanding.

General Vukalovic trained his binoculars on the Zenica Gap, a narrow and heavily-wooded valley floor lying between the bases of two high and steep-shouldered mountains, mountains almost identical in both shape and height.

The German 11th Army Corps tanks among the pines were not difficult to locate, for the Germans had made no attempt either to camouflage or conceal them, measure enough, Vukalovic thought grimly, of the Germans' total confidence in themselves and in the outcome of the battle that lay ahead. He could clearly see soldiers working on some stationary vehicles: other tanks were backing and filling and manœuvring into position as if making ready to take up battle formation for the actual attack: the deep rumbling roar of the heavy engines of Tiger tanks was almost incessant.

Vukalovic lowered his glasses, jotted down a few more pencil marks on a sheet of paper already almost covered with similar pencil marks, performed a few exercises in addition, laid paper and pencil aside with a sigh and turned to Colonel Janzy, who was similarly engaged.

Vukalovic said wryly: 'My apologies to your staff, Colonel. They can count just as well as I can.'

For once, Captain Jensen's piratical swagger and flashing, confident smile were not very much in evidence: at that moment, in fact, they were totally absent. It would have been impossible for a face of Jensen's generous proportions ever to assume an actually haggard appearance, but the set, grim face displayed unmistakable signs of strain and anxiety and sleeplessness as he paced up and down the 5th Army Operations Headquarters in Termoli in Italy.

He did not pace alone. Beside him, matching him step for step, a burly grey-haired officer in the uniform of a lieutenant-general in the British Army accompanied him backwards and forwards, the expression on his face an exact replica of that on Jensen's As they came to the farther end of the room, the General stopped and glanced interrogatively at a head-phone-wearing sergeant seated in front of a large RCA transceiver. The sergeant slowly shook his head. The two men resumed their pacing.

The General said abruptly: 'Time is running out. You do appreciate, Jensen, that once you launch a major offensive you can't possibly stop it?'

'I appreciate it,' Jensen said heavily. 'What are the latest reconnaissance reports, sir?'

'There is no shortage of reports, but God alone knows what to make of them all.' The General sounded bitter. 'There's intense activity all along the Gustav Line, involving—as far as we can make out—two Panzer divisions, one German infantry division, one Austrian infantry division and two Jaeger battalions—their crack Alpine troops. They're not mounting an offensive, that's for sure—in the first place, there's no possibility of their making an offensive from the area in which they are manœuvring and in the second place if they *were* contemplating an offensive they'd take damn good care to keep all their preparations secret.'

'All this activity, then? If they're not planning an attack.'

The General sighed. 'Informed opinion has it that they're making all preparations for a lightning pull-out. Informed opinion! All that concerns me is that those blasted divisions are still in the Gustav Line. Jensen, *what has gone wrong*?'

Jensen lifted his shoulders in a gesture of helplessness. 'It was arranged for a radio rendezvous every two hours from four a.m.—'

'There have been no contacts whatsoever.'

Jensen said nothing.

The General looked at him, almost speculatively. 'The best in Southern Europe, you said.'

'Yes, I did say that.'

The General's unspoken doubts as to the quality of the agents Jensen had selected for operation Force 10 would have been considerably heightened if he had been at that moment present with those agents in the guest hut in Hauptmann Neufeld's camp in Bosnia. They were exhibiting none of the harmony, understanding and implicit mutual trust which one would have expected to find among a team of agents rated as the best in the business. There was, instead, tension and anger in the air, an air of suspicion and mistrust so heavy as to be almost palpable. Reynolds, confronting Mallory, had his anger barely under control.

'I want to know now!' Reynolds almost shouted the words.

'Keep your voice down,' Andrea said sharply.

'I want to know now,' Reynolds repeated. This time his voice was little more than a whisper, but none the less demanding and insistent for that.

'You'll be told when the time comes.' As always, Mallory's voice was calm and neutral and devoid of heat. 'Not till then. What you don't know, you can't tell.'

Reynolds clenched his fists and advanced a step. 'Are you damn well insinuating that—'

Mallory said with restraint: 'I'm insinuating nothing. I was right, back in Termoli, Sergeant. You're no better than a ticking time-bomb.'

'Maybe.' Reynolds's fury was out of control now. 'But at least there's something honest about a bomb.'

'Repeat that remark,' Andrea said quietly.

'What?'

'Repeat it.'

'Look, Andrea—'

'Colonel Stavros, sonny.'

'Sir.'

'Repeat it and I'll guarantee you a minimum of five years for insubordination in the field.'

'Yes, sir.' Reynolds's physical effort to bring himself under control was apparent to everyone. 'But *why* should he *not* tell us his plans for this afternoon and at the same time let us all know that we'll be leaving from this Ivenici place tonight?'

'Because our plans are something the Germans can do something about,' Andreas said patiently. 'If they find out. If one of us talked under duress. But they can't do anything about Ivenici—that's in Partisan hands.'

Miller pacifically changed the subject. He said to Mallory: 'Seven thousand feet up, you say. The snow must be thigh-deep up there. How in God's name does anyone hope to clear all that lot away?'

'I don't know,' Mallory said vaguely. 'I suspect somebody will think of something.'

And, seven thousand feet up on the Ivenici plateau, somebody had indeed thought of something.

The Ivenici plateau was a wilderness in white, a bleak and desolate and, for many months of the year, a bitterly cold and howling and hostile wilderness, totally inimical to human life totally intolerant of human presence. The plateau was bounded to the west by a five-hundred-foot-high cliff-face, quite vertical in some parts, fractured and fissured in others. Scattered along its length were numerous frozen waterfalls and occasional lines of pine trees, impossibly growing on impossibly narrow ledges, their frozen branches drooped and laden with the frozen snow of six long months gone by. To the east the plateau was bounded

by nothing but an abrupt and sharply defined line marking
the top of another cliff-face which dropped away per-
pendicularly into the valleys below.

The plateau itself consisted of a smooth, absolutely level,
unbroken expanse of snow, snow which at that height of
2,000 metres and in the brilliant sunshine gave off a glare
and dazzling reflection which was positively hurtful to the
eyes. In length, it was perhaps half a mile: in width, nowhere more than a hundred yards. At its southern end, the
plateau rose sharply to merge with the cliff-face which
here tailed off and ran into the ground.

On this prominence stood two tents, both white, one small,
the other a large marquee. Outside the small tent stood
two men, talking. The taller and older man, wearing a heavy
greatcoat and a pair of smoked glasses, was Colonel Vis, the
commandant of a Sarajevo-based brigade of Partisans:
the younger, slighter figure was his adjutant, a Captain
Vlanovich. Both men were gazing out over the length of
the plateau.

Captain Vlanovich said unhappily: 'There must be easier
ways of doing this, sir.'

'You name it, Boris, my boy, and I'll do it.' Both in
appearance and voice Colonel Vis gave the impression of
immense calm and competence. 'Bull-dozers, I agree, would
help. So would snow-ploughs. But you will agree that to
drive either of them up vertical cliff-faces in order to reach
here would call for considerable skill on the part of the
drivers. Besides, what's an army for, if not for marching?'

'Yes, sir,' Vlanovich said, dutifully and doubtfully.

Both men gazed out over the length of the plateau to the
north.

To the north, and beyond, for all around a score of
encircling mountain peaks, some dark and jagged and
sombre, others rounded and snow-capped and rose-coloured,
soared up into the cloudless washed-out pale blue of the
sky. It was an immensely impressive sight.

Even more impressive was the spectacle taking place on
the plateau itself. A solid phalanx of a thousand uniformed
soldiers, perhaps half in the buff grey of the Yugoslav

army, the rest in a motley array of other countries'
uniforms, were moving, at a snail-pace, across the virgin
snow.

The phalanx was fifty people wide but only twenty
deep, each line of fifty linked arm-in-arm, heads and
shoulders bowed forward as they laboriously trudged at a
painfully slow pace through the snow. That the pace was
so slow was no matter for wonder, the leading line of
men were ploughing their way through waist-deep snow, and
already the signs of strain and exhaustion were showing
in their faces. It was killingly hard work, work which, at that
altitude, doubled the pulse rate, made a man fight for every
gasping breath, turned a man's legs into leaden and agonized
limbs where only the pain could convince him that they
were still part of him.

And not only men. After the first five lines of soldiers,
there were almost as many women and girls in the remainder
of the phalanx as there were men, although everyone was
so muffled against the freezing cold and biting winds of
those high altitudes that it was impossible almost to tell
man from woman. The last two lines of the phalanx were
composed entirely of *partisankas* and it was significantly
ominous of the murderous labour still to come that even
they were sinking knee-deep in the snow.

It was a fantastic sight, but a sight that was far from
unique in wartime Yugoslavia. The airfields of the low-
lands, completely dominated by the armoured divisions of
the Wehrmacht, were permanently barred to the Yugoslavs
and it was thus that the Partisans constructed many of their
airstrips in the mountains. In snow of this depth and in
areas completely inaccessible to powered mechanical aids,
there was no other way open to them.

Colonel Vis looked away and turned to Captain Vlanovich.

'Well, Boris, my boy, do you think you're up here for the
winter sports? Get the food and soup kitchens organized.
We'll use up a whole week's rations of hot food and hot soup
in this one day.'

'Yes, sir.' Vlanovich cocked his head, then removed his

ear-flapped fur cap the better to listen to the newly-begun sound of distant explosions to the north. 'What on earth is that?'

Vis said musingly: 'Sound does carry far in our pure Yugoslavian mountain air, does it not?'

'Sir? Please?'

'That, my boy,' Vis said with considerable satisfaction, 'is the Messerschmitt fighter base at Novo Derventa getting the biggest plastering of its lifetime.'

'Sir?'

Vis sighed in long-suffering patience. 'I'll make a soldier of you some day. Messerschmitts, Boris, are fighters, carrying all sorts of nasty cannons and machine-guns. What, at this moment, is the finest fighter target in Yugoslavia?'

'What is—' Vlanovich broke off and looked again at the trudging phalanx. 'Oh!'

' "Oh," indeed. The British Air Force have diverted six of their best Lancaster heavy bomber squadrons from the Italian front just to attend to our friends at Novo Derventa.' He in turn removed his cap, the better to listen. 'Hard at work, aren't they? By the time they're finished there won't be a Messerschmitt able to take off from that field for a week. If, that is to say, there are any left to take off.'

'If I might venture a remark, sir?'

'You may so venture, Captain Vlanovich.'

'There are other fighter bases.'

'True.' Vis pointed upwards. 'See anything?'

Vlanovich craned his neck, shielded his eyes against the brilliant sun, gazed into the empty blue sky and shook his head.

'Neither do I,' Vis agreed. 'But at seven thousand metres —and with their crews even colder than we are—squadrons of Beaufighters will be keeping relief patrol up there until dark.'

'Who—who *is* he, sir? Who can ask for all our soldiers down here, for squadrons of bombers and fighters?'

'Fellow called Captain Mallory, I believe.'

'A *captain*? Like me?'

'A captain. I doubt, Boris,' Vis went on kindly, 'whether he's quite like you. But it's not the rank that counts. It's the name. Mallory.'

'Never heard of him.'

'You will, my boy, you will.'

'But—but this man Mallory. What does he want all this *for*?'

'Ask him when you see him tonight.'

'When I—he's coming here tonight?'

'Tonight. If,' Vis added sombrely, 'he lives that long.'

Neufeld, followed by Droshny, walked briskly and confidently into his radio hut, a bleak, ramshackle lean-to furnished with a table, two chairs, a large portable transceiver and nothing else. The German corporal seated before the radio looked up enquiringly at their entrance.

'The Seventh Armoured Corps HQ at the Neretva bridge,' Neufeld ordered. He seemed in excellent spirits. 'I wish to speak to General Zimmermann personally.'

The corporal nodded acknowledgment, put through the call-sign and was answered within seconds. He listened briefly, looked up at Neufeld. 'The General is coming now, sir.'

Neufeld reached out a hand for the ear-phones, took them and nodded towards the door. The corporal rose and left the hut while Neufeld took the vacated seat and adjusted the head-phones to his satisfaction. After a few seconds he automatically straightened in his seat as a voice came crackling over the ear-phones.

'Hauptmann Neufeld here, Herr General. The Englishmen have returned. Their information is that the Partisan division in the Zenica Cage is expecting a full-scale attack from the south across the Neretva bridge.'

'Are they now?' General Zimmermann, comfortably seated in a swivel chair in the back of the radio truck parked on the tree-line due south of the Neretva bridge, made no attempt to conceal the satisfaction in his voice. The canvas hood of the truck was rolled back and he removed his peaked cap the better to enjoy the pale spring sunshine. 'Interesting, very interesting. Anything else.'

'Yes,' Neufeld's voice crackled metallically over the loud-speaker. 'They've asked to be flown to sanctuary. Deep behind our lines, even to Germany. They feel—ah—unsafe here.'

'Well, well, well. Is that how they feel.' Zimmermann paused, considered, then continued. 'You are fully informed of the situation, Hauptmann Neufeld? You are aware of the delicate balance of—um—niceties involved?'

'Yes, Herr General.'

'This calls for a moment's thought. Wait.'

Zimmermann swung idly to and fro in his swivel chair as he pondered his decision. He gazed thoughtfully but almost unseeingly to the north, across the meadows bordering the south bank of the Neretva, the river spanned by the iron bridge, then the meadows on the far side rising steeply to the rocky redoubt which served as the first line of defence for Colonel Lazlo's Partisan defenders. To the east, as he turned, he could look up the green-white rushing waters of the Neretva, the meadows on either side of it narrowing until, curving north, they disappeared suddenly at the mouth of the cliff-sided gorge from which the Neretva emerged. Another quarter turn and he was gazing into the pine forest to the south, a pine forest which at first seemed innocuous enough and empty of life—until, that was, one's eyes became accustomed to the gloom and scores of large rectangular shapes, effectively screened from both observation from the air and from the northern bank of the Neretva by camouflage canvas, camouflage nets and huge piles of dead branches. The sight of those camouflaged spearheads of his two Panzer divisions somehow helped Zimmermann to make up his mind. He picked up the microphone.

'Hauptmann Neufeld? I have decided on a course of action and you will please carry out the following instructions precisely . . .'

Droshny removed the duplicate pair of ear-phones that he

had been wearing and said doubtfully to Neufeld: 'Isn't the General asking rather a lot of us?'

Neufeld shook his head reassuringly. 'General Zimmermann *always* knows what he is doing. His psychological assessment of the Captain Mallorys of this world is invariably a hundred per cent right.'

'I hope so.' Droshny was unconvinced. 'For our sakes, I hope so.'

They left the hut. Neufeld said to the radio-operator: 'Captain Mallory in my office, please. And Sergeant Baer.'

Mallory arrived in the office to find Neufeld, Droshny and Baer already there. Neufeld was brief and business-like.

'We've decided on a ski-plane to fly you out—they're the only planes that can land in those damned mountains. You'll have time for a few hours sleep—we don't leave till four. Any questions?'

'Where's the landing-strip?'

'A clearing. A kilometre from here. Anything else?'

'Nothing. Just get us out of here, that's all.'

'You need have no worry on that score,' Neufeld said emphatically. 'My one ambition is to see you safely on your way. Frankly, Mallory, you're just an embarrassment to me and the sooner you're on your way the better.'

Mallory nodded and left. Neufeld turned to Baer and said: 'I have a little task for you, Sergeant Baer. Little but very important. Listen carefully.'

Mallory left Neufeld's hut, his face pensive, and walked slowly across the compound. As he approached the guest hut, Andrea emerged and passed wordlessly by, wreathed in cigar smoke and scowling. Mallory entered the hut where Petar was again playing the Yugoslavian version of 'The girl I left behind me.' It seemed to be his favourite song. Mallory glanced at Maria, Reynolds and Groves, all sitting silently by, then at Miller who was reclining in his sleeping-bag with his volume of poetry.

Mallory nodded toward the doorway. 'Something's upset our friend.'

Miller grinned and nodded in turn towards Petar. 'He's playing Andrea's tune again.'

Mallory smiled briefly and turned to Maria. 'Tell him to stop playing. We're pulling out late this afternoon and we all need all the sleep we can get.'

'We can sleep in the plane,' Reynolds said sullenly. 'We can sleep when we arrived at our destination—wherever that may be.'

'No, sleep now.'

'Why now?'

'Why now?' Mallory's unfocused eyes gazed into the far distance. He said in a quiet voice: 'For now is all the time there may be.'

Reynolds looked at him strangely. For the first time that day his face was empty of hostility and suspicion. There was puzzled speculation in his eyes, and wonder and the first faint beginnings of understanding.

On the Ivenici plateau, the phalanx moved on, but they moved no more like human beings. They stumbled along now in the advanced stages of exhaustion, automatons, no more, zombies resurrected from the dead, their faces twisted with pain and unimaginable fatigue, their limbs on fire and their minds benumbed. Every few seconds someone stumbled and fell and could not get up again and had to be carried to join scores of others already lying in an almost comatose condition by the side of the primitive runway, where *partisankas* did their best to revive their frozen and exhausted bodies with mugs of hot soup and liberal doses of *raki*.

Captain Vlanovich turned to Colonel Vis. His face was distressed, his voice low and deeply earnest.

'This is madness, Colonel, madness! It's—it's impossible, you can see it's impossible. We'll never—look, sir, two hundred and fifty dropped out in the first two hours. The altitude, the cold, sheer physical exhaustion. It's madness.'

'All war is madness,' Vis said calmly. 'Get on the radio. We require five hundred more men.'

VIII

FRIDAY 1500-2115

Now it had come, Mallory knew. He looked at Andrea and Miller and Reynolds and Groves and knew that they knew it too. In their faces he could see very clearly reflected what lay at the very surface of his own mind, the explosive tension, the hair-trigger alertness straining to be translated into equally explosive action. Always it came, this moment of truth that stripped men bare and showed them for what they were. He wondered how Reynolds and Groves would be: he suspected they might acquit themselves well. It never occurred to him to wonder about Miller and Andrea, for he knew them too well: Miller, when all seemed lost, was a man above himself, while the normally easy-going, almost lethargic Andrea was transformed into an unrecognizable human being, an impossible combination of an icily calculating mind and berserker fighting machine entirely without the remotest parallel in Mallory's knowledge or experience. When Mallory spoke his voice was as calmly impersonal as ever.

'We're due to leave at four. It's now three. With any luck we'll catch them napping. Is everything clear?'

Reynolds said wonderingly, almost unbelievingly: 'You mean if anything goes wrong we're to shoot our way out?'

'You're to shoot and shoot to kill. That, Sergeant, is an order.'

'Honest to God,' Reynolds said, 'I just don't know what's going on.' The expression on his face clearly indicated that he had given up all attempts to understand what was going on.

Mallory and Andrea left the hut and walked casually across the compound towards Neufeld's hut. Mallory said: 'They're on to us, you know.'

'I know. Where are Petar and Maria?'

118

'Asleep, perhaps? They left the hut a couple of hours ago. We'll collect them later.'

'Later may be too late . . . They are in great peril, my Keith.'

'What can a man do, Andrea? I've thought of nothing else in the past ten hours. It's a crucifying risk to have to take, but I have to take it. They are expendable, Andrea. You know what it would mean if I showed my hand now.'

'I know what it would mean,' Andrea said heavily. 'The end of everything.'

They entered Neufeld's hut without benefit of knocking. Neufeld, sitting behind his desk with Droshny by his side, looked up in irritated surprise and glanced at his watch.

He said curtly: 'Four o'clock, I said, not three.'

'Our mistake,' Mallory apologized. He closed the door. 'Please do not be foolish.'

Neufeld and Droshny were not foolish, few people would have been while staring down the muzzles of two Lugers with perforated silencers screwed to the end: they just sat there, immobile, the shock slowly draining from their faces. There was a long pause then Neufeld spoke, the words coming almost haltingly.

'I have been seriously guilty of underestimating—'

'Be quiet. Broznik's spies have discovered the whereabouts of the four captured Allied agents. We know roughly where they are. You know precisely where they are. You will take us there. Now.'

'You're mad,' Neufeld said with conviction.

'We don't require you to tell us that.' Andrea walked round behind Neufeld and Droshny, removed their pistols from their holsters, ejected the shells and replaced the pistols. He then crossed to a corner of the hut, picked up two Schmeisser machine-pistols, emptied them, walked back round to the front of the table and placed the Schmeissers on its top, one in front of Neufeld, one in front of Droshny.

'There you are, gentlemen,' Andrea said affably. 'Armed to the teeth.'

Droshny said viciously: 'Suppose we decide not to come with you?'

Andrea's affability vanished. He walked unhurriedly round the table and rammed the Luger's silencer with such force against Droshny's teeth that he gasped in pain. 'Please—' Andrea's voice was almost beseeching—'*please* don't tempt me.'

Droshny didn't tempt him. Mallory moved to the window and peered out over the compound. There were, he saw, at least a dozen Cetniks within thirty feet of Neufeld's hut, all of them armed. Across the other side of the compound he could see that the door to the stables was open indicating that Miller and the two sergeants were in position.

'You will walk across the compound to the stables,' Mallory said. 'You will talk to nobody, warn nobody, make no signals. We will follow about ten yards behind.'

'Ten yards behind. What's to prevent us making a break for it. You wouldn't dare hold a gun on us out there.'

'That's so,' Mallory agreed. 'From the moment you open this door you'll be covered by three Schmeissers from the stables. If you try anything—*anything*—you'll be cut to pieces. That's why we're keeping well behind you—we don't want to be cut to pieces too.'

At a gesture from Andrea, Neufeld and Droshny slung their empty Schmeissers in angry silence. Mallory looked at them consideringly and said: 'I think you'd better do something about your expressions. They're a dead giveaway that something is wrong. If you open that door with faces like that, Miller will cut you down before you reach the bottom step. Please try to believe me.'

They believed him and by the time Mallory opened the door had managed to arrange their features into a near enough imitation of normality. They went down the steps and set off across the compound to the stables. When they had reached half-way Andrea and Mallory left Neufeld's hut and followed them. One or two glances of idle curiosity came their way, but clearly no one suspected that anything was amiss. The crossing to the stables was completely uneventful.

So also, two minutes later, was their departure from the camp. Neufeld and Droshny, as would have been proper and expected, rode together in the lead, Droshny in particular looking very warlike with his Schmeisser, pistol and the wickedly-curved knives at his waist. Behind them rode Andrea, who appeared to be having some trouble with the action of his Schmeisser, for he had it in his hands and was examining it closely: he certainly wasn't looking at either Droshny or Neufeld and the fact that the gun-barrel, which Andrea had sensibly pointed towards the ground, had only to be lifted a foot and the trigger pressed to riddle the two men ahead was a preposterous idea that would not have occurred to even the most suspicious. Behind Andrea, Mallory and Miller rode abreast: like Andrea, they appeared unconcerned, even slightly bored. Reynolds and Groves brought up the rear, almost but not quite attaining the degree of nonchalance of the other three: their still faces and restlessly darting eyes betrayed the strain they were under. But their anxiety was needless for all seven passed from the camp not only unmolested but without as much as even an enquiring glance being cast in their direction.

They rode for over two and a half hours, climbing nearly all the time, and a blood-red sun was setting among the thinning pines to the west when they came across a clearing set on, for once, a level stretch of ground. Neufeld and Droshny halted their ponies and waited until the others came up with them. Mallory reined in and gazed at the building in the middle of the clearing, a low, squat, immensely strong-looking blockhouse, with narrow, heavily barred windows and two chimneys, from one of which smoke was coming.

'This the place?' Mallory asked.

'Hardly a necessary question.' Neufeld's voice was dry, but the underlying resentment and anger unmistakable. 'You think I spent all this time leading you to the wrong place?'

'I wouldn't put it past you,' Mallory said. He examined the building more closely. 'A hospitable-looking place.'

'Yugoslav Army ammunition dumps were never intended as first-class hotels.'

'I dare say not,' Mallory agreed. At a signal from him they urged their ponies forward into the clearing, and as they did so two metal strips in the facing wall of the block-house slid back to reveal a pair of embrasures with machine-pistols protruding. Exposed as they were, the seven mounted men were completely at the mercy of those menacing muzzles.

'Your men keep a good watch,' Mallory acknowledged to Neufeld. 'You wouldn't require many men to guard and hold a place like this. How many are there?'

'Six,' Neufeld said reluctantly.

'Seven and you're a dead man,' Andrea warned.

'Six.'

As they approached, the guns—almost certainly because the men behind them had identified Neufeld and Droshny —were withdrawn, the embrasures closed, the heavy metal front door opened. A sergeant appeared in the doorway and saluted respectfully, his face registering a certain surprise.

'An unexpected pleasure, Hauptmann Neufeld,' the sergeant said. 'We had no radio message informing us of your arrival.'

'It's out of action for the moment.' Neufeld waved them inside but Andrea gallantly insisted on the German officer taking precedence, reinforcing his courtesy with a threatening hitch of his Schmeisser. Neufeld entered, followed by Droshny and the other five men.

The windows were so narrow that the burning oil-lamps were obviously a necessity, the illumination they afforded being almost doubled by a large log fire blazing in the hearth. Nothing could ever overcome the bleakness created by four rough-cut stone walls, but the room itself was surprisingly well furnished with a table, chairs, two arm-chairs and a sofa: there were even some pieces of carpet. Three doors led off from the room, one heavily barred. Including the sergeant who had welcomed them, there were three armed soldiers in the room. Mallory glanced at Neufeld who nodded, his face tight in suppressed anger.

Neufeld said to one of the guards: 'Bring out the prisoners.' The guard nodded, lifted a heavy key from the wall and headed for the barred door. The sergeant and the other guard were sliding the metal screens back across the embrasures. Andrea walked casually towards the nearest guard, then suddenly and violently shoved him against the sergeant. Both men cannoned into the guard who had just inserted the key into the door. The third man fell heavily to the ground: the other two, though staggering wildly, managed to retain a semblance of balance or at least remain on their feet. All three twisted round to stare at Andrea, anger and startled incomprehension in their faces, and all three remained very still, and wisely so. Faced with a Schmeisser machine-pistol at three paces, the wise man always remains still.

Mallory said to the sergeant: 'There are three other men. Where are they?'

There was no reply: the guard glared at him in defiance. Mallory repeated the question, this time in fluent German: the guard ignored him and looked questioning at Neufeld, whose lips were tight-shut in a mask of stone.

'Are you mad?' Neufeld demanded of the sergeant. 'Can't you see those men are killers? Tell him.'

'The night guards. They're asleep.' The sergeant pointed to a door. 'That one.'

'Open it. Tell them to walk out. Backwards and with their hands clasped behind their necks.'

'Do exactly as you're told,' Neufeld ordered.

The sergeant did exactly what he was told and so did the three guards who had been resting in the inner room, who walked out as they had been instructed, with obviously no thought of any resistance in their minds. Mallory turned to the guard with the key who had by this time picked himself up somewhat shakily from the floor, and nodded to the barred door.

'Open it.'

The guard opened it and pushed the door wide. Four British officers moved out slowly and uncertainly into the outer room. Long confinement indoors had made them very pale, but apart from this prison pallor and the fact that they were rather thin they were obviously unharmed. The man in the lead, with a major's insignia and a Sandhurst moustache —and, when he spoke, a Sandhurst accent—stopped abruptly and stared in disbelief at Mallory and his men.

'Good God above! What on earth are you chaps—'

'Please.' Mallory cut him short. 'I'm sorry, but later. Collect your coats, whatever warm gear you have, and wait outside.'

'But—but where are you taking us?'

'Home. Italy. Tonight. Please hurry!'

'Italy. You're talking—'

'Hurry!' Mallory glanced in some exasperation at his watch. 'We're late already.'

As quickly as their dazed condition would allow, the four officers collected what warm clothing they had and filed outside. Mallory turned to the sergeant again. 'You must have ponies here, a stable.'

'Round the back of the block-house,' the sergeant said promptly. He had obviously made a rapid readjustment to the new facts of life.

'Good lad,' Mallory said approvingly. He looked at Groves and Reynolds. 'We'll need two more ponies. Saddle them up, will you?'

The two sergeants left. Under the watchful guns of Mallory and Miller, Andrea searched each of the six guards in turn, found nothing, and ushered them all into the cell, turning the heavy key and hanging it up on the wall. Then, just as carefully, Andrea searched Neufeld and Droshny: Droshny's face, as Andrea carelessly flung his knives into a corner of the room, was thunderous.

Mallory looked at the two men and said: 'I'd shoot you if necessary. It's not. You won't be missed before morning.'

'They might not be missed for a good few mornings,' Miller pointed out.

'So they're over-weight anyway,' Mallory said indifferently. He smiled. 'I can't resist leaving you with a last little pleasant thought, Hauptmann Neufeld. Something to think about until someone comes and finds you.' He looked consideringly at Neufeld, who said nothing, then went on: 'About that information I gave you this morning, I mean.'

Neufeld looked at him guardedly. 'What about the information you gave me this morning?'

'Just this. It wasn't, I'm afraid, quite accurate. Vukalovic expects the attack from the *north*, through the Zenica Gap, not across the bridge at Neretva from the south. There are, we know, close on two hundred of your tanks massed in the woods just to the north of the Zenica Gap—but there won't be at two a.m. this morning when your attack is due to start. Not after I've got through to our Lancaster squadrons in Italy. Think of it, think of the target. Two hundred tanks bunched in a tiny trap a hundred and fifty yards wide and not more than three hundred yards long. The RAF will be there at 1.30. By two this morning there won't be a single tank left in commission.'

Neufeld looked at him for a long moment, his face very still, then said, slowly and softly: 'Damn you! Damn you! Damn you!'

'Damning is all you'll have for it,' Mallory said agreeably. 'By the time you are released—hopefully assuming that you will be released—it will be all over. See you after the war.'

Andrea locked the two men in a side room and hung the key up by the one to the cell. Then they went outside, locked the outer door, hung the key on a nail by the door, mounted their ponies—Groves and Reynolds had already two additional ones saddled—and started climbing once again, Mallory, map in hand, studying in the fading light of dusk the route they had to take.

Their route took them up alongside the perimeter of a pine forest. Not more than half a mile after leaving the block-house, Andrea reined in his pony, dismounted, lifted the pony's right foreleg and examined it carefully. He looked up at the others who had also reined in their ponies.

'There's a stone wedged under the hoof,' he announced. 'Looks bad—but not too bad. I'll have to cut it out. Don't wait for me—I'll catch you up in a few minutes.'

Mallory nodded, gave the signal to move on. Andrea produced a knife, lifted the hoof and made a great play of excavating the wedged stone. After a minute or so, he glanced up and saw that the rest of the party had vanished round a corner of the pine wood. Andrea put away his knife and led the pony, which quite obviously had no limp whatsoever into the shelter of the wood and tethered it there, then moved on foot some way down the hill towards the block-house. He sat down behind the bole of a convenient pine and removed his binoculars from their case.

He hadn't long to wait. The head and shoulders of a figure appeared in the clearing below peering out cautiously from behind the trunk of a tree. Andrea flat in the snow now and with the icy rims of the binoculars clamped hard against his eyes, had no difficulty at all in making an immediate identification: Sergeant Baer, moon-faced, rotund and about seventy pounds overweight for his unimpressive height, had an unmistakable physical presence which only the mentally incapacitated could easily forget.

Baer withdrew into the woods, then reappeared shortly afterwards leading a string of ponies, one of which carried a bulky covered object strapped to a pannier bag. Two of the following ponies had riders, both of whom had their hands tied to the pommels of their saddles. Petar and Maria, without a doubt. Behind them appeared four mounted soldiers. Sergeant Baer beckoned them to follow him across the clearing and within moments all had disappeared from sight behind the block-house. Andrea regarded the now empty clearing thoughtfully, lit a fresh cigar and made his way uphill towards his tethered pony.

Sergeant Baer dismounted, produced a key from his pocket, caught sight of the key suspended from the nail beside the door, replaced his own, took down the other, opened the door with it and passed inside. He glanced around, took down one of the keys hanging on the wall and opened a side door with it. Hauptmann Neufeld emerged, glanced at his watch and smiled.

'You have been very punctual, Sergeant Baer. You have the radio?'

'I have the radio. It's outside.'

'Good, good, good.' Neufeld looked at Droshny and smiled again. 'I think it's time for us to make our rendezvous with the Ivenici plateau.'

Sergeant Baer said respectfully: 'How can you be so sure that it is the Ivenici plateau, Hauptmann Neufeld?'

'How can I be so sure? Simple, my dear Baer. Because Maria—you have her with you?'

'But of course, Hauptmann Neufeld.'

'Because Maria told me. The Ivenici plateau it is.'

Night had fallen on the Ivenici plateau, but still the phalanx of exhausted soldiers was trudging out the landing-strip for the plane. The work was not by this time so cruelly and physically exacting, for the snow was now almost trampled and beaten hard and flat: but, even allowing for the rejuvenation given by the influx of another five hundred fresh soldiers, the overall level of utter weariness was such that the phalanx was in no better condition than its original members who had trudged out the first outline of the airstrip in the virgin snow.

The phalanx, too, had changed its shape. Instead of being fifty wide by twenty deep it was now twenty wide by fifty deep: having achieved a safe clearance for the wings of the aircraft, they were now trudging out what was to be as close as possible an iron-hard surface for the landing wheels.

A three-quarters moon, intensely white and luminous, rode low in the sky, with scattered bands of cloud coming drifting down slowly from the north. As the successive bands moved across the face of the moon, the black shadows swept lazily across the surface of the plateau: the phalanx, at one moment bathed in silvery moonlight, was at the next almost lost to sight in the darkness. It was a fantastic scene with a remarkably faery-like quality of eeriness and foreboding about it. In fact it was, as Colonel Vis had just unromantically mentioned to Captain Vlanovich, like something out of Dante's *Inferno*, only a hundred degrees colder. At least a hundred degrees, Vis had amended: he wasn't sure how hot it was in hell.

It was this scene which, at twenty minutes to nine in the evening, confronted Mallory and his men when they topped the brow of a hill and reined in their ponies just short of the edge of the precipice which abutted on the western edge of the Ivenici plateau. For at least two minutes they sat there on their ponies, not moving, not speaking, mesmerized by the other-world quality of a thousand men with bowed heads and bowed shoulders, shuffling exhaustedly across the level floor of the plain beneath, mesmerized because they all knew they were gazing at a unique spectacle which none of them had ever seen before and would never see again. Mallory finally broke free from the trance-like condition, looked at Miller and Andrea, and slowly shook his head in an expression of profound wonder conveying his disbelief, that his refusal to accept the reality of what his own eyes told him was real and actual beyond dispute. Miller and Andrea returned his look with almost identical negative motions of their own heads. Mallory wheeled his pony to the right and led the way along the cliff-face to the point where the cliff ran into the rising ground below.

Ten minutes later they were being greeted by Colonel Vis.

'I did not expect to see you, Captain Mallory.' Vis pumped his hand enthusiastically. 'Before God, I did not expect to see you. You—and your men—must have a remarkable capacity for survival.'

'Say that in a few hours,' Mallory said drily, 'and I would be very happy indeed to hear it.'

'But it's all over now. We expect the plane—' Vis glanced at his watch—'in exactly eight minutes. We have a bearing surface for it and there should be no difficulty in landing and taking off provided it doesn't hang around too long. You have done all that you came to do and achieved it magnificently. Luck has been on your side.'

'Say that in a few hours,' Mallory repeated.

'I'm sorry.' Vis could not conceal his puzzlement. 'You expect something to happen to the plane?'

'I don't expect anything to happen to the plane. But what's gone, what's past, is—was, rather—only the prologue.'

'The—the prologue?'

'Let me explain.'

Neufeld, Droshny and Sergeant Baer left their ponies tethered inside the woodline and walked up the slight eminence before them, Sergeant Baer making heavy weather of their uphill struggle through the snow because of the weight of the large portable transceiver strapped to his back. Near the summit they dropped to their hands and knees and crawled forward till they were within a few feet of the edge of the cliff overlooking the Ivenici plateau. Neufeld unslung his binoculars and then replaced them: the moon had just moved from behind a dark barred cloud highlighting every aspect of the scene below: the intensely sharp contrast afforded by black shadow and snow so deeply and gleamingly white as to be almost phosphorescent made the use of binoculars superfluous.

Clearly visible and to the right were Vis's command tents and, near by, some hastily erected soup kitchens. Outside the smallest of the tents could be seen a group of perhaps a dozen people, obviously, even at that distance, engaged in close conversation. Directly beneath where they lay, the three men could see the phalanx turning round at one end of the runway and beginning to trudge back slowly, so terribly slowly, so terribly tiredly, along the wide path already tramped out. As Mallory and his men had been, Neufeld, Droshny and Baer were momentarily caught and held by the weird and other-worldly dark grandeur of the spectacle below. Only by a conscious act of will could Neufeld bring himself to look away and return to the world of normality and reality.

'How very kind,' he murmured, 'of our Yugoslav friends to go to such lengths on our behalf.' He turned to Baer and indicated the transceiver. 'Get through to the General, will you?'

Baer unslung his transceiver, settled it firmly in the snow, extended the telescopic aerial, pre-set the frequency and cranked the handle. He made contact almost at once, talked briefly then handed the microphone and head-piece to Neufeld, who fitted on the phones and gazed down, still half mesmerized, at the thousand men and women moving antlike across the plain below. The head-phones cracked suddenly in his ears and the spell was broken.

'Herr General?'

'Ah. Hauptmann Neufeld.' In the ear-phones the General's

voice was faint but very clear, completely free from distortion or static. 'Now then. About my psychological assessment of the English mind?'

'You have mistaken your profession, Herr General. Everything has happened exactly as you forecast. You will be interested to know, sir, that the Royal Air Force is launching a saturation bombing attack on the Zenica Gap at precisely 1.30 a.m. this morning.'

'Well, well, well,' Zimmermann said thoughtfully. 'That is interesting. But hardly surprising.'

'No, sir.' Neufeld looked up as Droshny touched him on the shoulder and pointed to the north. 'One moment, sir.'

Neufeld removed the ear-phones and cocked his head in the direction of Droshny's pointing arm. He lifted his binoculars but there was nothing to be seen. But unquestionably there was something to be heard—the distant clamour of aircraft engines, closing. Neufeld readjusted the earphones.

'We have to give the English full marks for punctuality, sir. The plane is coming in now.'

'Excellent, excellent. Keep me informed.'

Neufeld eased off one ear-phone and gazed to the north. Still nothing to be seen, the moon was now temporarily behind a cloud, but the sound of the aircraft engines was unmistakably closer. Suddenly, somewhere down on the plateau, came three sharp blasts on a whistle. Immediately, the marching phalanx broke up, men and women stumbling off the runway into the deep snow on the eastern side of the plateau, leaving behind them, obviously by pre-arrangement, about eighty men who spaced themselves out on either side of the runway.

'They're organized, I'll say that for them,' Neufeld said admiringly.

Droshny smiled his wolf's smile. 'All the better for us, eh?'

'Everybody seems to be doing their best to help us tonight,' Neufeld agreed.

Overhead, the dark and obscuring band of cloud drifted away to the south and the white light of the moon raced across the plateau. Neufeld could immediately see the plane, less than half a mile away, its camouflaged shape sharply etched in the brilliant moonlight as it sank down towards the end of the runway. Another sharp blast of the whistle and at once the men lining both sides of the runway switched on hand-lamps—a superfluity, really, in those almost bright as day perfect landing conditions, but essential had the moon been hidden behind cloud.

'Touching down now,' Neufeld said into the microphone. 'It's a Wellington bomber.'

'Let's hope it makes a safe landing,' Zimmermann said.

'Let's hope so indeed, sir.'

The Wellington made a safe landing, a perfect landing considering the extremely difficult conditions. It slowed down quickly, then steadied its speed as it headed towards the end of the runway.

Neufeld said into the microphone: 'Safely down, Herr General, and rolling to rest.'

'Why doesn't it stop?' Droshny wondered.

'You can't accelerate a plane over snow as you can over a concrete runway,' Neufeld said. 'They'll require every yard of the runway for the take-off.'

Quite obviously, the pilot of the Wellington was of the same opinion. He was about fifty yards from the end of the runway when two groups of people broke from the hundreds lining the edge of the runway, one group heading for the already opened door in the side of the bomber, the other heading for the tail of the plane. Both groups reached the plane just as it rolled to a stop at the very end of the runway, a dozen men at once flinging themselves upon the tail unit and beginning to turn the Wellington through 180°.

Droshny was impressed. 'By heavens, they're not wasting much time, are they?'

'They can't afford to. If the plane stays there any time at all it'll start sinking in the snow.' Neufeld lifted his binoculars and spoke into the microphone.

'They're boarding now, Herr General. One, two, three . . . seven, eight, nine. Nine it is.' Neufeld sighed in relief and at the relief of tension. 'My warmest congratulations, Herr General. Nine it is, indeed.'

The plane was already facing the way it had come. The pilot stood on the brakes, revved the engines up to a crescendo, then twenty seconds after it had come to a halt the Wellington was on its way again, accelerating down the runway. The pilot took no chances, he waited till the very far end of the airstrip before lifting the Wellington off, but when he did it rose cleanly and easily and climbed steadily into the night sky.

'Airborne, Herr General,' Neufeld reported. 'Everything perfectly according to plan.' He covered the microphone, looked after the disappearing plane, then smiled at Droshny. 'I think we should wish them *bon voyage*, don't you?'

Mallory, one of the hundreds lining the perimeter of the airstrip, lowered his binoculars. 'And a very pleasant journey to them all.'

Colonel Vis shook his head sadly. 'All this work just to send five of my men on a holiday to Italy.'

'I dare say they needed a break,' Mallory said.

'The hell with them. How about us?' Reynolds demanded. In spite of the words, his face showed no anger, just a dazed and total bafflement. 'We should have been aboard that damned plane.'

'Ah. Well. I changed my mind.'

'Like hell you changed your mind,' Reynolds said bitterly.

Inside the fuselage of the Wellington, the moustached major surveyed his three fellow-escapees and the five Partisan soldiers, shook his head in disbelief and turned to the captain by his side.

'A rum do, what?'

'Very rum, indeed, sir,' said the captain. He looked curiously at the papers the major held in his hand. 'What have you there?'

'A map and papers that I'm to give to some bearded naval type when we land back in Italy. Odd fellow, that Mallory, what?'

'Very odd indeed, sir,' the captain agreed.

Mallory and his men, together with Vis and Vlanovich, had detached themselves from the crowd and were now standing outside Vis's command tent.

Mallory said to Vis: 'You have arranged for the ropes? We must leave at once.'

'What's all the desperate hurry, sir?' Groves asked. Like Reynolds, much of his resentment seemed to have gone to be replaced by a helpless bewilderment. 'All of a sudden, like, I mean?'

'Petar and Maria,' Mallory said grimly. 'They're the hurry.'

'What about Petar and Maria?' Reynolds asked suspiciously. 'Where do they come into this?'

'They're being held captive in the ammunition block-house. And when Neufeld and Droshny get back there—'

'Get back there,' Groves said dazedly. 'What do you mean, get back there. We—we left them locked up. And how in God's name do you know that Petar and Maria are being held in the block-house. How can they be? I mean, they weren't there when we left there—and that wasn't so long ago.'

'When Andrea's pony had a stone in its hoof on the way up here from the block-house, it didn't have a stone in its hoof. Andrea was keeping watch.'

'You see,' Miller explained, 'Andrea doesn't trust anyone.'

'He saw Sergeant Baer taking Petar and Maria there,' Mallory went on. 'Bound. Baer released Neufeld and Droshny and you can bet your last cent our precious pair were up on the cliff-side there checking that we really did fly out.'

'You don't tell us very much, do you, sir?' Reynolds said bitterly.

'I'll tell you this much,' Mallory said with certainty. 'If we don't get there soon, Maria and Petar are for the high jump. Neufeld and Droshny don't *know* yet, but by this time they must be pretty convinced that it was Maria who told me where those four agents were being kept. They've always known who we really were—Maria told them. Now they know who Maria is. Just before Droshny killed Saunders—'

'Droshny?' Reynolds's expression was that of a man who has almost given up all attempt to understand. 'Maria?'

'I made a miscalculation.' Mallory sounded tired. 'We all make miscalculations, but this was a bad one.' He smiled, but the smile didn't touch his eyes. 'You will recall that you had a few harsh words to say about Andrea here when he picked that fight with Droshny outside the dining hut in Neufeld's camp?'

'Sure I remember. It was one of the craziest—'

'You can apologize to Andrea at a later and more convenient time,' Mallory interrupted. 'Andrea provoked Droshny because I asked him to. I knew that Neufeld and Droshny were up to no good in the dining hut after we had left and I wanted a moment to ask Maria what they had been discussing. She told me that they intended to send a couple of Cetniks after us into Broznik's camp—suitably disguised, of course—to report on us. They were two of the men acting as our escort in that wood-burning truck. Andrea and Miller killed them.'

'Now you tell us,' Groves said almost mechanically. 'Andrea and Miller killed them.'

'What I didn't know was that Droshny was also following us. He saw Maria and myself together.' He looked at Reynolds. 'Just as you did. I didn't know at the time that he'd seen us, but I've known for some hours now. Maria has been as good as under sentence of death since this morning. But there was nothing I could do about it. Not until now. If I'd shown my hand, we'd have been finished.'

Reynolds shook his head. 'But you've just said that Maria betrayed us—'

'Maria,' Mallory said, 'is a top-flight British espionage agent. English father, Yugoslav mother. She was in this country even before the Germans came. As a student in Belgrade. She joined the Partisans, who trained her as a radio-operator, then arranged for her defection to the Cetniks. The Cetniks had captured a radio-operator from one of the first British missions. They—the Germans, rather—trained her to imitate this operator's hand—every radio-operator has his own unmistakable style—until their styles were quite indistinguishable. And her English, of course, was perfect. So then she was in direct contact with Allied Intelligence in both North Africa and Italy. The Germans thought they had us completely fooled: it was, in fact, the other way round.'

Miller said complainingly: 'You didn't tell me any of this, either.'

'I've so much on my mind. Anyway, she was notified direct of the arrival of the last four agents to be parachuted in. She, of course, told the Germans. And all those agents carried information reinforcing the German belief that a second front—a full-scale invasion—of Yugoslavia was imminent.'

Reynolds said slowly: 'They knew we were coming too?'

'Of course. They knew everything about us all along, what we really were. What they didn't know, of course, is that we knew they knew and though what they knew of us was true it was only part of the truth.'

Reynolds digested this. He said, hesitating: 'Sir?'

'Yes?'

'I could have been wrong about you, sir.'

'It happens,' Mallory agreed. 'From time to time, it happens. You were wrong, Sergeant, of course you were, but you were wrong from the very best motives. The fault is mine. Mine alone. But my hands were tied.' Mallory touched him on the shoulder. 'One of these days you might get round to forgiving me.'

'Petar?' Groves asked. 'He's not her brother?'

'Petar is Petar. No more. A front.'

'There's still an awful lot—' Reynolds began, but Mallory interrupted him.

'It'll have to wait. Colonel Vis, a map, please.' Captain Vlanovich brought one from the tent and Mallory shone a torch on it. 'Look. Here. The Neretva dam and the Zenica Cage. I told Neufeld that Broznik had told me that the Partisans believe that the attack is coming across the Neretva bridge from the south. But, as I've just said, Neufeld knew

—he knew even before we had arrived—who and what we *really* were. So he was convinced I was lying. He was convinced that I was convinced that the attack was coming through the Zenica Gap to the north here. Good reason for believing that, mind you: there are two hundred German tanks up there.'

Vis stared at him. 'Two hundred!'

'One hundred and ninety of them are made of plywood. So the only way Neufeld—and, no doubt, the German High Command—could ensure that this useful information got through to Italy was to allow us to stage this rescue bid. Which, of course, they very gladly did, assisting us in every possible way even to the extent of gladly collaborating with us in permitting themselves to be captured. They *knew*, of course, that we had no option left but to capture them and force them to lead us to the block-house—an arrangement they had ensured by previously seizing and hiding away the only other person who could have helped us in this—Maria. And, of course, knowing this in advance, they had arranged for Sergeant Baer to come and free them.'

'I see.' It was plain to everyone that Colonel Vis did not see at all. 'You mentioned an RAF saturation attack on the Zenica Gap. This, of course, will now be switched to the bridge?'

'No. You wouldn't have us break our word to the Wehrmacht, would you? As promised, the attack comes on the Zenica Gap. As a diversion. To convince them, in case they have any last doubts left in their minds, that we have been fooled. Besides, you know as well as I do that that bridge is immune to high-level air attack. It will have to be destroyed in some other way.'

'In what way?'

'We'll think of something. The night is young. Two last things, Colonel Vis. There'll be another Wellington in at midnight and a second at 3 a.m. Let them both go. The next in, at 6 a.m., hold it against our arrival. Well, our possible arrival. With any luck we'll be flying out before dawn.'

'With any luck,' Vis said sombrely.

'And radio General Vukalovic, will you? Tell him what I've told you, the exact situation. And tell him to begin intensive small-arms fire at one o'clock in the morning.'

'What are they supposed to fire at?'

'They can fire at the moon for all I care.' Mallory swung aboard his pony. 'Come on, let's be off.'

'The moon,' General Vukalovic agreed, 'is a fair-sized target, though rather a long way off. However, if that's what our friend wants, that's what he shall have.' Vukalovic paused for a moment, looked at Colonel Janzy who was sitting beside him on a fallen log in the woods to the south of the Zenica Gap, then spoke again into the radio mouthpiece.

'Anyway, many thanks, Colonel Vis. So the Neretva bridge it is. And you think it will be unhealthy for us to remain in the immediate vicinity of this area after 1 a.m. Don't worry, we won't be here.' Vukalovic removed the headphones and turned to Janzy. 'We pull out, quietly, at midnight. We leave a few men to make a lot of noise.'

'The ones who are going to fire at the moon?'

'The ones who are going to fire at the moon. Radio Colonel Lazlo at Neretva, will you? Tell him we'll be with him before the attack. Then radio Major Stephan. Tell him to leave just a holding force, pull out of the Western Gap and make his way to Colonel Lazlo's HQ.' Vukalovic paused for a thoughtful moment. 'We should be in for a few very interesting hours, don't you think?'

'Is there any chance in the world for this man Mallory?' Janzy's tone carried with it its own answer.

'Well, look at it this way,' Vukalovic said reasonably. 'Of course there's a chance. There has to be a chance. It is, after all, my dear Janzy, a question of options—and there are no other options left open to us.'

Janzy made no reply but nodded several times in slow succession as if Vukalovic had just said something profound.

IX

The pony-back ride downhill through the thickly wooded forests from the Ivenici plateau to the block-house took Mallory and his men barely a quarter of the time it had taken them to make the ascent. In the deep snow the going underfoot was treacherous to a degree, collision with the bole of a pine was always an imminent possibility and none of the five riders made any pretence towards being an experienced horseman, with the inevitable result that slips, stumbles and heavy falls were as frequent as they were painful. Not one of them escaped the indignity of involuntarily leaving his saddle and being thrown headlong into the deep snow, but it was the providential cushioning effect of that snow that was the saving of them, that and, more often, the sure-footed agility of their mountain ponies: whatever the reason or combination of reasons, bruises and winded falls there were in plenty, but broken bones, miraculously, there were none.

The block-house came in sight. Mallory raised a warning hand, slowing them down until they were about two hundred yards distant from their objective, where he reined in, dismounted and led his pony into a thick cluster of pines, followed by the others. Mallory tethered his horse and indicated to the others to do the same.

Miller said complainingly: 'I'm sick of this damned pony but I'm sicker still of walking through deep snow. Why don't we just ride on down there?'

'Because they'll have ponies tethered down there. They'll start whinnying if they hear or see or smell other ponies approaching.'

'They might start whinnying anyway.'

'And there'll be guards on watch,' Andrea pointed out. 'I

don't think, Corporal Miller, that we could make a very stealthy and unobtrusive approach on pony-back.'

'Guards. Guarding against what? As far as Neufeld and company are concerned, we're half-way over the Adriatic at this time.'

'Andrea's right,' Mallory said. 'Whatever else you may think about Neufeld, he's a first-class officer who takes no chances. There'll be guards.' He glanced up to the night sky where a narrow bar of cloud was just approaching the face of the moon. 'See that?'

'I see it,' Miller said miserably.

'Thirty seconds, I'd say. We make a run for the far gable end of the block-house—there are no embrasures there. And for God's sake, once we get there, keep dead quiet. If they hear anything, if they as much as suspect that we're outside, they'll bar the doors and use Petar and Maria as hostages. Then we'll just have to leave them.'

'You'd do that, sir?' Reynolds asked.

'I'd do that. I'd rather cut a hand off, but I'd do that. I've no choice, Sergeant.'

'Yes, sir. I understand.'

The dark bar of cloud passed over the moon. The five men broke from the concealment of the pines and pounded downhill through the deep clogging snow, heading for the farther gable-wall of the block-house. Thirty yards away, at a signal from Mallory, they slowed down lest the sound of their crunching, running footsteps be heard by any watchers who might be keeping guard by the embrasures and completed the remaining distance by walking as quickly and quietly as possible in single file, each man using the footprints left by the man in front of him.

They reached the blank gable-end undetected, with the moon still behind the cloud. Mallory did not pause to congratulate either himself or any of the others. He at once dropped to his hands and knees and crawled round the corner of the block-house, pressing close in to the stone wall.

Four feet from the corner came the first of the embrasures. Mallory did not bother to lower himself any deeper into the snow—the embrasures were so deeply recessed in the massive

stone walls that it would have been quite impossible for any
watcher to see anything at a lesser distance than six feet from
the embrasure. He concentrated, instead, on achieving as
minimal a degree of sound as was possible, and did so with
success, for he safely passed the embrasure without any
alarm being raised. The other four were equally successful
even although the moon broke from behind the cloud as
the last of them, Groves, was directly under the embrasure.
But he, too, remained undetected.

Mallory reached the door. He gestured to Miller, Reynolds
and Groves to remain prone where they were: he and
Andrea rose silently to their feet and pressed their ears
close again the door.

Immediately they heard Droshny's voice, thick with menace,
heavy with hatred.

'A traitress! That's what she is. A traitress to our cause.
Kill her now!'

'Why did you do it, Maria?' Neufeld's voice, in contrast
to Droshny's, was measured, calm, almost gentle.

'Why did she do it?' Droshny snarled. 'Money. That's
why she did it. What else?'

'Why?' Neufeld was quietly persistent. 'Did Captain
Mallory threaten to kill your brother?'

'Worse than that.' They had to strain to catch Maria's low
voice. 'He threatened to kill me. Who would have looked
after my blind brother then?'

'We waste time,' Droshny said impatiently. 'Let me
take them both outside.'

'No.' Neufeld's voice, still calm, admitted of no argument.
'A blind boy? A terrified girl? What are you, man?'

'A Cetnik!'

'And I'm an officer of the Wehrmacht.'

Andrea whispered in Mallory's ear: 'Any minute now and
someone's going to notice our foot-tracks in the snow.'

Mallory nodded, stood aside and made a small gesturing
motion of his hand. Mallory was under no illusions as to
their respective capabilities when it came to bursting open
doors leading into rooms filled with armed men. Andrea was

the best in the business—and proceeded to prove it in his usual violent and lethal fashion.

A twist of the door handle, a violent kick with the sole of the right foot and Andrea stood framed in the doorway. The wildly swinging door had still not reached the full limit of travel on its hinges when the room echoed to the flat staccato chatter of Andrea's Schmeisser: Mallory, peering over Andrea's shoulder through the swirling cordite smoke, saw two German soldiers, lethally cursed with over-fast reactions, slumping wearily to the floor. His own machine-pistol levelled, Mallory followed Andrea into the room.

There was no longer any call for Schmeissers. None of the other soldiers in the room was carrying any weapon at all while Neufeld and Droshny, their faces frozen into expressions of total incredulity, were clearly, even if only momentarily, incapable of any movement at all, far less being capable of the idea of offering any suicidal resistance.

Mallory said to Neufeld: 'You've just bought yourself your life.' He turned to Maria, nodded towards the door, waited until she had led her brother outside, then looked again at Neufeld and Droshny and said curtly: 'Your guns.'

Neufeld managed to speak, although his lips moved in a strangely mechanical fashion. 'What in the name of God—'

Mallory was in no mind for small talk. He lifted his Schmeisser. 'Your guns.'

Neufeld and Droshny, like men in a dream, removed their pistols and dropped them to the floor.

'The keys.' Droshny and Neufeld looked at him in almost uncomprehending silence. 'The keys,' Mallory repeated. 'Now. Or the keys won't be necessary.'

For several seconds the room was completely silent, then Neufeld stirred, turned to Droshny and nodded. Droshny scowled—as well as any man can scowl when his face is still overspread with an expression of baffled astonishment and homicidal fury—reached into his pocket and produced the keys. Miller took them, unlocked and opened wide the cell door wordlessly and with a motion of his machine-pistol invited Neufeld, Droshny, Baer and the other soldiers to

enter, waited until they had done so, swung shut the
door, locked it and pocketed the key. The room echoed
again as Andrea squeezed the trigger of his machine-
pistol and destroyed the radio beyond any hope of repair.
Five seconds later they were all outside, Mallory, the
last man to leave, locking the door and sending the key
spinning to fall yards away, buried from sight in the deep
snow.

Suddenly he caught sight of the number of ponies tethered
outside the block-house. Seven. Exactly the right number. He
ran across to the embrasure outside the cell window and
shouted: 'Our ponies are tethered two hundred yards uphill just inside the pines. Don't forget.' Then he ran quickly
back and ordered the other six to mount. Reynolds looked
at him in astonishment.

'You think of this, sir? At such a time?'

'I'd think of this at any time.' Mallory turned to Petar, who
had just awkwardly mounted his horse, then turned to
Maria. 'Tell him to take off his glasses.'

Maria looked at him in surprise, nodded in apparent
understanding and spoke to her brother, who looked at
her uncomprehendingly, then ducked his head obediently,
removed his dark glasses and thrust them deep inside his
tunic. Reynolds looked on in astonishment, then turned to
Mallory.

'I don't understand, sir.'

Mallory wheeled his pony and said curtly: 'It's not
necessary that you do.'

'I'm sorry, sir.'

Mallory turned his pony again and said, almost wearily:
'It's already eleven o'clock, boy, and almost already too
late for what we have to do.'

'Sir.' Reynolds was deeply if obscurely pleased that Mallory
should call him boy. 'I don't really want to know, sir.'

'You've asked. We'll have to go as quickly as our ponies
can take us. A blind man can't see obstructions, can't balance
himself according to the level of the terrain, can't anticipate
in advance how he should brace himself for an unexpectedly
sharp drop, can't lean in the saddle for a corner his pony

knows is coming. A blind man, in short, is a hundred times more liable to fall off in a downhill gallop than we are. It's enough that a blind man should be blind for life. It's too much that we should expose him to the risk of a heavy fall with his glasses on, to expose him to the risk of not only being blind but of having his eyes gouged out and being in agony for life.'

'I hadn't thought—I mean—I'm sorry, sir.'

'Stop apologizing, boy. It's really my turn, you know—to apologize to you. Keep an eye on him, will you?'

Colonel Lazlo, binoculars to his eyes, gazed down over the moonlit rocky slope below him towards the bridge at Neretva. On the southern bank of the river, in the meadows between the south bank and the beginning of the pine forest beyond, and, as far as Lazlo could ascertain, in the fringes of the pine forest itself, there was a disconcertingly ominous lack of movement, of any sign of life at all. Lazlo was pondering the disturbingly sinister significance of this unnatural peacefulness when a hand touched his shoulder. He twisted, looked up and recognized the figure of Major Stephan, commander of the Western Gap.

'Welcome, welcome. The General has advised me of your arrival. Your battalion with you?'

'What's left of it.' Stephan smiled without really smiling. 'Every man who could walk. And all those who couldn't.'

'God send we don't need them all tonight. The General has spoken to you of this man Mallory?' Major Stephan nodded, and Lazlo went on: 'If he fails? If the Germans cross the Neretva tonight—'

'So?" Stephan shrugged. 'We were all due to die tonight anyway.'

'A well-taken point,' Lazlo said approvingly. He lifted his binoculars and returned to his contemplation of the bridge at Neretva.

So far, and almost incredibly, neither Mallory nor any of the six galloping behind him had parted company with their ponies. Not even Petar. True, the incline of the slope was not nearly as steep as it had been from the Ivenici plateau down to the block-house, but Reynolds suspected it was because Mallory had imperceptibly succeeded in slowing down the pace of their earlier headlong gallop. Perhaps, Reynolds thought vaguely, it was because Mallory was subconsciously trying to protect the blind singer, who was riding almost abreast with him, guitar firmly strapped over his shoulder, reins abandoned and both hands clasped desperately to the pommel of his saddle. Unbidden, almost, Reynolds's thoughts strayed back to that scene inside the block-house. Moments later, he was urging his pony forwards until he had drawn alongside Mallory.

'Sir?'

'What is it?' Mallory sounded irritable.

'A word, sir. It's urgent. Really it is.'

Mallory threw up a hand and brought the company to a halt. He said curtly: 'Be quick.'

'Neufeld and Droshny, sir.' Reynolds paused in a moment's brief uncertainty, then continued. 'Do you reckon they know where you're going?'

'What's that to do with anything?'

'Please.'

'Yes, they do. Unless they're complete morons. And they're not.'

'It's a pity, sir,' Reynolds said reflectively, 'that you hadn't shot them after all.'

'Get to the point,' Mallory said impatiently.

'Yes, sir. You reckoned Sergeant Baer released them earlier on?'

'Of course.' Mallory was exercising all his restraint. 'Andrea saw them arrive. I've explained all this. They —Neufeld and Droshny—had to go up to the Ivenici plateau to check that we'd really gone.'

'I understand that, sir. So you knew that Baer was following us. How did he get into the block-house?'

Mallory's restraint vanished. He said in exasperation: 'Because I left both keys hanging outside.'

'Yes, sir. You were expecting him. But Sergeant Baer didn't

know you were expecting him—and even if he did he wouldn't be expecting to find keys so conveniently to hand.'

'Good God in heaven! Duplicates!' In bitter chagrin, Mallory smacked the fist of one hand into the palm of the other. 'Imbecile! Imbecile! Of *course* he would have his own keys!'

'And Droshny,' Miller said thoughtfully, 'may know a short-cut.'

'That's not all of it.' Mallory was completely back on balance again, outwardly composed, the relaxed calmness of the face the complete antithesis of his racing mind. 'Worse still, he may make straight for his camp radio and warn Zimmermann to pull his armoured divisions back from the Neretva. You've earned your passage tonight, Reynolds. Thanks, boy. How far to Neufeld's camp, do you think, Andrea?'

'A mile.' The words came over Andrea's shoulder, for Andrea, as always in situations which he knew called for the exercise of his highly specialized talents, was already on his way.

Five minutes later they were crouched at the edge of the forest less than twenty yards from the perimeter of Neufeld's camp. Quite a number of the huts had illuminated windows, music could be heard coming from the dining hut and several Cetnik soldiers vere moving about in the compound.

Reynolds whispered to Mallory: 'How do we go about it, sir?'

'We don't do anything at all. We just leave it to Andrea.'

Groves spoke, his voice low. 'One man? Andrea? We leave it to one man?'

Mallory sighed. 'Tell them, Corporal Miller.'

'I'd rather not. Well, if I have to. The fact is,' Miller went on kindly, 'Andrea is rather good at this sort of thing.'

'So are we,' Reynolds said. 'We're commandos. We've been trained for this sort of thing.'

'And very highly trained, no doubt,' said Miller approvingly. 'Another half-dozen years' experience and half a dozen of you might be just about able to cope with him.

Although I doubt it very much. Before the night is out, you'll learn—I don't mean to be insulting, Sergeants—that you are little lambs to Andrea's wolf.' Miller paused and went on sombrely: 'Like whoever happens to be inside that radio hut at this moment.'

'Like whoever happens—' Groves twisted round and looked behind him. 'Andrea? He's gone. I didn't see him go.'

'No one ever does,' Miller said. 'And those poor devils won't ever see him come.' He looked at Mallory. 'Time's a-wasting.'

Mallory glanced at the luminous hands of his watch. 'Eleven-thirty. Time *is* a-wasting.'

For almost a minute there was a silence broken only by the restless movements of the ponies tethered deep in the woods behind them, then Groves gave a muffled exclamation as Andrea materialized beside him. Mallory looked up and said: 'How many?'

Andrea held up two fingers and moved silently into the woods towards his pony. The others rose and followed him, Groves and Reynolds exchanging glances which indicated more clearly than any words could possibly have done that they could have been even more wrong about Andrea than they had ever been about Mallory.

At precisely the moment that Mallory and his companions were remounting their ponies in the woods fringing Neufeld's camp, a Wellington bomber came sinking down towards a well-lit airfield—the same airfield from which Mallory and his men had taken off less than twenty-four hours previously. Termoli, Italy. It made a perfect touch-down and as it taxied along the runway an army radio truck curved in on an interception course, turning to parallel the last hundred yards of the Wellington's run down. In the left-hand front seat and in the right-hand back seat of the truck sat two immediately recognizable figures: in the front, the piratical splendidly bearded figure of Captain Jensen, in the back the British lieutenant-general with whom Jensen had recently spent so much time in pacing the Termoli Operations Room.

Plane and truck came to a halt at the same moment. Jensen, displaying a surprising agility for one of his very considerable bulk, hopped nimbly to the ground and strode briskly across the tarmac and arrived at the Wellington just as its door opened and the first of the passengers, the moustached major, swung to the ground.

Jensen nodded to the papers clutched in the major's hand and said without preamble: 'Those for me?' The major blinked uncertainly, then nodded stiffly in return, clearly irked by this abrupt welcome for a man just returned from durance vile. Jensen took the papers without a further word, went back to his seat in the jeep, brought out a flash-light and studied the papers briefly. He twisted in his seat and said to the radio-operator seated beside the General: 'Flight plan as stated. Target as indicated. Now.' The radio-operator began to crank the handle.

Some fifty miles to the south-east, in the Foggia area, the buildings and runways of the RAF heavy bomber base echoed and reverberated to the thunder of scores of aircraft engines: at the dispersal area at the west end of the main runway several squadrons of Lancaster heavy bombers were lined up ready for take-off, obviously awaiting the signal to go. The signal was not long in coming.

Half-way down the airfield, but well to one side of the main runway, was parked a jeep identical to the one in which Jensen was sitting in Termoli. In the back seat a radio-operator was crouched over a radio, ear-phones to his head. He listened intently, then looked up and said matter-of-factly: 'Instructions as stated. Now. Now. Now.'

'Instructions as stated,' a captain in the front seat repeated. 'Now. Now. Now.' He reached for a wooden box, produced three Very pistols, aimed directly across the runway and fired each in turn. The brilliantly arcing flares burst into incandescent life, green, red and green again, before curving slowly back to earth. The thunder at the far end of the airfield mounted to a rumbling crescendo and the first of the Lancasters began to move. Within a few minutes the last of them had taken off and was lifting into the darkly hostile night skies of the Adriatic.

'I did say, I believe,' Jensen remarked conversationally and comfortably to the General in the back seat, 'that they are the best in the business. Our friends from Foggia are on their way.'

'The best in the business. Maybe. I don't know. What I do know is that those damned German and Austrian divisions are still in position in the Gustav Line. Zero hour for the assault on the Gustav Line is—' he glanced at his watch —'in exactly thirty hours.'

'Time enough,' Jensen said confidently.

'I wish I shared this blissful confidence.'

Jensen smiled cheerfully at him as the jeep moved off, then faced forward in his seat again. As he did, the smile vanished completely from his face and his fingers beat a drum tattoo on the seat beside him.

The moon had broken through again as Neufeld, Droshny and their men came galloping into camp and reined in ponies so covered with steam from their heaving flanks and distressed breathing as to have a weirdly insubstantial appearance in the pale moonlight. Neufeld swung from his pony and turned to Sergeant Baer.

'How many ponies left in the stables?'

'Twenty. About that.'

'Quickly. And as many men as there are ponies. Saddle up.'

Neufeld gestured to Droshny and together they ran towards the radio hut. The door, ominously enough on that icy night, was standing wide open. They were still ten feet short of the door when Neufeld shouted: 'The Neretva bridge at once. Tell General Zimmermann—'

He halted abruptly in the doorway, Droshny by his shoulder. For the second time that evening the faces of both men reflected their stunned disbelief, their total uncomprehending shock.

Only one small lamp burned in the radio hut, but that one small lamp was enough. Two men lay on the floor in grotesquely huddled positions, the one lying partially across the other: both were quite unmistakably dead. Beside them, with its face-plate ripped off and interior smashed, lay the mangled remains of what had once been a transmitter. Neufeld gazed at the scene for some time before shaking his head violently as if to break the shocked spell and turned to Droshny.

'The big one,' he said quietly. 'The big one did this.'

'The big one,' Droshny agreed. He was almost smiling. 'You will remember what you promised, Hauptmann Neufeld? The big one. He's for me.'

'You shall have him. Come. They can be only minutes ahead.' Both men turned and ran back to the compound where Sergeant Baer and a group of soldiers were already saddling up the ponies.

'Machine-pistols only,' Neufeld shouted. 'No rifles. It will be close-quarter work tonight. And Sergeant Baer?'

'Hauptmann Neufeld?'

'Inform the men that we will not be taking prisoners.'

As those of Neufeld and his men had been, the ponies of Mallory and his six companions were almost invisible in the dense clouds of steam rising from their sweat-soaked bodies: their lurching gait, which could not now even be called a trot, was token enough of the obvious fact that they had reached the limits of exhaustion. Mallory glanced at Andrea, who nodded and said: 'I agree. We'd make faster time on foot now.'

'I must be getting old,' Mallory said, and for a moment he sounded that way. 'I'm not thinking very well tonight, am I?'

'I do not understand.'

'Ponies. Neufeld and his men will have fresh ponies from the stables. We should have killed them—or at least driven them away.'

'Age is not the same thing as lack of sleep. It never occurred to me, either. A man cannot think of everything, my Keith.'

Andrea reined in his pony and was about to swing down when something on the slope below caught his attention. He pointed ahead.

A minute later they drew up alongside a very narrow-gauge railway line, of a type common in Central Yugoslavia. At this level the snow had petered out and the track, they could see, was over-grown and rusty, but for all that, apparently in fair enough mechanical condition: undoubtedly, it was the same track that had caught their eye when they had paused to examine the green waters of the Neretva dam on the way back from Major Broznik's camp that morning. But what simultaneously caught and held the attention of both Mallory and Miller was not the track itself, but a little siding leading on to the track—and a diminutive wood-burning locomotive that stood on the siding. The locomotive was practically a solid block of rust and looked as if it hadn't moved from its present position since the beginning of the war: in all probability, it hadn't.

Mallory produced a large-scale map from his tunic and flashed a torch on it. He said: 'No doubt of it, this is the track we saw this morning. It goes down along the Neretva for at least five miles before bearing off to the south.' He paused and went on thoughtfully: 'I wonder if we could get that thing moving.'

'What?' Miller looked at him in horror. 'It'll fall to pieces if you touch it—it's only the rust that's holding the damn thing together. And that gradient there!' He peered in dismay down the slope. 'What do you think our terminal velocity is going to be when we hit one of those monster pine trees a few miles down the track?'

'The ponies are finished,' Mallory said mildly, 'and you know how much you love walking.'

Miller looked at the locomotive with loathing. 'There must be some other way.'

'Shh!' Andrea cocked his head. 'They're coming. I can hear them coming.'

'Get the chocks away from those front wheels,' Miller shouted. He ran forward and after several violent and well-directed kicks which clearly took into no account the future state of his toes, succeeded in freeing the triangular block which was attached to the front of the locomotive by a chain: Reynolds, no less energetically, did the same for the other chock.

All of them, even Maria and Petar helping, flung all their weight against the rear of the locomotive. The locomotive remained where it was. They tried again, despairingly: the wheels refused to budge even a fraction of an inch. Groves said, with an odd mixture of urgency and diffidence: 'Sir, on a gradient like this, it would have been left with its brakes on.'

'Oh my God!' Mallory said in chagrin. 'Andrea. Quickly. Release the brake-lever.'

Andrea swung himself on to the footplate. He said complainingly: 'There are a dozen damned levers up here.'

'Well, open the dozen damned levers, then.' Mallory glanced anxiously back up the track. Maybe Andrea had heard something, maybe not: there was certainly no one in sight yet. But he knew that Neufeld and Droshny, who must have been released from the block-house only minutes after they had left there themselves and who knew those woods and paths better than they did, must be very close indeed by this time.

There was a considerable amount of metallic screeching and swearing coming from the cab and after perhaps half a minute Andrea said: 'That's the lot.'

'Shove,' Mallory ordered.

They shoved, heels jammed in the sleepers and backs to the locomotive, and this time the locomotive moved off so easily, albeit with a tortured squealing of rusted wheels, that most of those pushing were caught wholly by surprise and fell on their backs on the track. Moments later they were on their feet and running after the locomotive which was already perceptibly beginning to increase speed. Andrea reached down from the cab, swung Maria and Petar aboard in turn, then lent a helping hand to the others. The last, Groves, was reaching for the footplate when he suddenly braked, swung round, ran back to the ponies, unhitched the climbing ropes, flung them over his shoulder and chased after the locomotive again. Mallory reached down and helped him on to the footplate.

'It's not my day,' Mallory said sadly. 'Evening rather. First, I forget about Baer's duplicate keys. Then about the ponies. Then the brakes. Now the ropes. I wonder what I'll forget about next?'

'Perhaps about Neufeld and Droshny.' Reynolds's voice was carefully without expression.

'What about Neufeld and Droshny?'

Reynolds pointed back up the railway track with the barrel of his Schmeisser. 'Permission to fire, sir.'

Mallory swung round. Neufeld, Droshny and an indeterminate number of other pony-mounted soldiers had just appeared around a bend in the track and were hardly more than a hundred yards away.

'Permission to fire,' Mallory agreed. 'The rest of you get down.' He unslung and brought up his own Schmeisser just as Reynolds squeezed the trigger of his. For perhaps five seconds the closed metallic confines of the tiny cabin reverberated deafeningly to the crash of the two machine-pistols, then, at a nudge from Mallory, the two men stopped firing. There was no target left to fire at. Neufeld and his men had loosed off a few preliminary shots but immediately realized that the wildly swaying saddles of their ponies made an impossibly unsteady firing position as compared to the cab of the locomotive and had pulled their ponies off into the woods on either side of the track. But not all of them had pulled off in time: two men lay motionless and face down in the snow while their ponies still galloped down the track in the wake of the locomotive.

Miller rose, glanced worldlessly at the scene behind, then tapped Mallory on the arm. 'A small point occurs to me, sir. How do we stop this thing.' He gazed apprehensively through the cab window. 'Must be doing sixty already.'

'Well, we're doing at least twenty,' Mallory said agreeably. 'But fast enough to out-distance those ponies. Ask Andrea. He released the brake.'

'He released a dozen levers,' Miller corrected. 'Any one could have been the brake.'

'Well, you're not going to sit around doing nothing, are you?' Mallory asked reasonably. 'Find out how to stop the damn thing.'

Miller looked at him coldly and set about trying to find out how to stop the damn thing. Mallory turned as Reynolds touched him on the arm. 'Well?'

Reynolds had an arm round Maria to steady her on the now swaying platform. He whispered: 'They're going to get us, sir. They're going to get us for sure. Why don't we stop and leave those two, sir? Give them a chance to escape into the woods?'

'Thanks for the thought. But don't be mad. With us they have a chance—a small one to be sure, but a chance. Stay behind and they'll be butchered.'

The locomotive was no longer doing the twenty miles per hour Mallory had mentioned and if it hadn't approached the figure that Miller had so fearfully mentioned it was certainly going quickly enough to make it rattle and sway to what appeared to be the very limits of its stability. By this time the last of the trees to the right of the track had petered out, the darkened waters of the Neretva dam were clearly visible to the west and the railway track was now running very close indeed to the edge of what appeared to be a dangerously steep precipice. Mallory looked back into the cab. With the exception of Andrea, everyone now wore expressions of considerable apprehension on their faces. Mallory said: 'Found out how to stop this damn thing yet?'

'Easy.' Andrea indicated a lever. 'This handle here.'

'Okay, brakeman. I want to have a look.'

To the evident relief of most of the passengers in the cab, Andrea leaned back on the brake-lever. There was an eldritch screeching that set teeth on edge, clouds of sparks flew up past the sides of the cab as some wheels or other locked solid in the lines, then the locomotive eased slowly to a halt, both the intensity of sound from the squealing brakes and the number of sparks diminishing as it did so. Andrea, duty done, leaned out of the side of the cab with all the bored aplomb of the crack loco engineer: one had the feeling that all he really wanted in life that moment was a piece of oily waste and a whistle-cord to pull.

Mallory and Miller climbed down and ran to the edge of the cliff, less than twenty yards away. At least Mallory did. Miller made a much more cautious approach, inching forward the last few feet on hands and knees. He hitched one cautious eye over the edge of the precipice, screwed both eyes shut, looked away and just as cautiously inched his way back from the edge of the cliff: Miller claimed that he couldn't even stand on the bottom step of a ladder without succumbing to the overwhelming compulsion to throw himself into the abyss.

Mallory gazed down thoughtfully into the depths. They were, he saw, directly over the top of the dam wall, which, in the strangely shadowed half-light cast by the moon, seemed almost impossibly far below in the dizzying depths. The broad top of the dam wall was brightly lit by floodlights and patrolled by at least half a dozen German soldiers, jack-booted and helmeted. Beyond the dam, on the lower side, the ladder Maria had spoken of was invisible, but the frail-looking swing bridge, still menaced by the massive bulk of the boulder on the scree on the left bank, and farther down, the white water indicating what might or might not have been a possible—or passable—ford were plainly in sight. Mallory, momentarily abstracted in thought, gazed at the scene below for several moments, recalled that the pursuit must be again coming uncomfortably close and hurriedly made his way back to the locomotive. He said to Andrea: 'About a mile and a half, I should think. No more.' He turned to Maria. 'You know there's a ford—or what seems to be a ford—some way below the dam. Is there a way down?'

'For a mountain goat.'

'Don't insult him,' Miller said reprovingly.

'I don't understand.'

'Ignore him,' Mallory said. 'Just tell us when we get there.

Some five or six miles below the Neretva dam General

Zimmermann paced up and down the fringe of the pine forest bordering the meadow to the south of the bridge at Neretva. Beside him paced a colonel, one of his divisional commanders. To the south of them could just dimly be discerned the shapes of hundreds of men and scores of tanks and other vehicles, vehicles with all their protective camouflage now removed, each tank and vehicle surrounded by its coterie of attendants making last-minute and probably wholly unnecessary adjustments. The time for hiding was over. The waiting was coming to an end. Zimmermann glanced at his watch.

'Twelve-thirty. The first infantry battalions start moving across in fifteen minutes, and spread out along the north bank. The tanks at two o'clock.'

'Yes, sir.' The details had been arranged many hours ago, but somehow one always found it necessary to repeat the instructions and the acknowledgments. The colonel gazed to the north. 'I sometimes wonder if there's *anybody* at all across there.'

'It's not the north I'm worrying about,' Zimmermann said sombrely. 'It's the west.'

'The Allies? You—you think their air armadas will come soon? It's still in your bones, Herr General?'

'Still in my bones. It's coming soon. For me, for you, for all of us.' He shivered, then forced a smile. 'Some ill-mannered lout has just walked over my grave.'

X

SATURDAY 0040-0120

'We're coming up to it now,' Maria said. Blonde hair streaming in the passing wind, she peered out again through the cab window of the clanking, swaying locomotive, withdrew her head and turned to Mallory. 'About three hundred metres.'

Mallory glanced at Andrea. 'You heard, brakeman?'

'I heard.' Andrea leaned hard on the brake-lever. The

result was as before, a banshee shrieking of locked wheels on the rusty lines and a pyrotechnical display of sparks. The locomotive came to a juddering halt as Andrea looked out his cab window and observed a V-shaped gap in the edge of the cliff directly opposite where they had come to a stop. 'Within the yard, I should say?'

'Within the yard,' Mallory agreed. 'If you're unemployed after the war, there should always be a place for you in a shunter's yard.' He swung down to the side of the track, lent a helping hand to Maria and Petar, waited until Miller, Reynolds and Groves had jumped down, then said impatiently to Andrea: 'Well, hurry up, then.'

'Coming,' Andrea said peaceably. He pushed the handbrake all the way off, jumped down, and gave the locomotive a shove: the ancient vehicle at once moved off, gathering speed as it went. 'You never know,' Andrea said wistfully. 'It might hit somebody somewhere.'

They ran towards the cut in the edge of the cliff, a cut which obviously represented the beginning of some prehistoric landslide down to the bed of the Neretva, a maelstrom of white water far below, the boiling rapids resulting from scores of huge boulders which had slipped from this landslide in that distant aeon. By some exercise of the imagination, that scar in the side of the cliff-face might just perhaps have been called a gully, but it was in fact an almost perpendicular drop of scree and shale and small boulders, all of it treacherous and unstable to a frightening degree, the whole dangerous sweep broken only by a small ledge of jutting rock about half-way down. Miller took one brief glance at this terrifying prospect, stepped hurriedly back from the edge of the cliff and looked at Mallory in a silently dismayed incredulity.

'I'm afraid so,' Mallory said.

'But this is terrible. Even when I climbed the south cliff in Navarone—'

'You didn't climb the south cliff in Navarone,' Mallory said unkindly. 'Andrea and I pulled you up at the end of a rope.'

'Did you? I forget. But this—this is a climber's nightmare.'

'So we don't have to climb it. Just lower ourselves down. You'll be all right—as long as you don't start rolling.'

'I'll be all right as long as I don't start rolling,' Miller repeated mechanically. He watched Mallory join two ropes together and pass them around the bole of a stunted pine. 'How about Petar and Maria?'

'Petar doesn't have to see to make this descent. All he has to do is to lower himself on this rope—and Petar is as strong as a horse. Somebody will be down there before him to guide his feet on to the ledge. Andrea will look after the young lady here. Now hurry. Neufeld and his men will be up with us any minute here—and if they catch up on this cliff-face, well that's that. Andrea, off you go with Maria.'

Immediately, Andrea and the girl swung over the edge of the gully and began to lower themselves swiftly down the rope. Groves watched them, hesitated, then moved towards Mallory.

'I'll go last, sir, and take the rope with me.'

Miller took his arm and led him some feet away. He said, kindly: 'Generous, son, generous, but it's just not on. Not as long as Dusty Miller's life depends on it. In a situation like this, I must explain, all our lives depend upon the anchor-man. The Captain, I am informed, is the best anchor-man in the world.'

'He's what?'

'It's one of the non-coincidences why he was chosen to lead this mission. Bosnia is known to have rocks and cliffs and mountains all over it. Mallory was climbing the Himalayas, laddie, before you were climbing out of your cot. Even you are not too young to have heard of him.'

'*Keith* Mallory? The New Zealander?'

'Indeed. Used to chase sheep around, I gather. Come on, your turn.'

The first five made it safely. Even the last but one, Miller, made the descent to the ledge without incident, principally by employing his favourite mountain-climbing technique of keeping his eyes closed all the time. Then Mallory came last, coiling the rope with him as he came, moving quickly and surely and hardly ever seeming to look where he put his feet but at the same time not as much as disturbing the slightest pebble or piece of shale. Groves observed the descent with a look of almost awed disbelief in his eyes.

Mallory peered over the edge of the ledge. Because of a slight bend in the gorge above, there was a sharp cut-off in the moonlight just below where they stood so that while the phosphorescent whiteness of the rapids was in clear moonlight, the lower part of the slope beneath their feet was in deep shadow. Even as he watched, the moon was obscured by a shadow, and all the dimly-seen detail in the slope below vanished. Mallory knew that they could never afford to wait until the moon reappeared, for Neufeld and his men could well have arrived by then. Mallory belayed a rope round an outcrop of rock and said to Andrea and Maria: 'This one's really dangerous. Watch for loose boulders.'

Andrea and Maria took well over a minute to make their invisible descent, a double tug on the rope announcing their safe arrival at the bottom. On the way down they had started several small avalanches, but Mallory had no fears that the next man down would trigger off a fall of rock that would injure or even kill Andrea and Maria; Andrea had lived too long and too dangerously to die in so useless and so foolish a fashion—and he would undoubtedly warn the next man down of the same danger. For the tenth time Mallory glanced up towards the top of the slope they had just descended but if Neufeld, Droshny and his men had just arrived they were keeping very quiet about it and being most circumspect indeed: it was not a difficult conclusion to arrive at that, after the events of the past few hours, circumspection would be the last thing in their minds.

The moon broke through again as Mallory finally made his descent. He cursed the exposure it might offer if any of the enemy suddenly appeared on the cliff-top, even although he knew that Andrea would be guarding against precisely that danger; on the other hand it afforded him the opportunity of descending at twice the speed he could have made in the earlier darkness. The watchers below watched tensely as Mallory, without any benefit of rope, made his perilous descent: but he never even looked like making one mistake. He descended safely to the boulder-strewn shore and gazed out over the rapids.

He said to no one in particular: 'You know what's going to happen if they arrive at the top and find us half-way across here and the moon shining down on us?' The ensuing silence left no doubt but they all knew what was going to happen. 'Now is all the time. Reynolds, you think you can make it?' Reynolds nodded. 'Then leave your gun.'

Mallory knotted a bowline round Reynolds's waist, taking the strain, if one were to arise, with Andrea and Groves. Reynolds launched himself bodily into the rapids, heading for the first of the rounded boulders which offered so treacherous a hold in that seething foam. Twice he was knocked off his feet, twice he regained them, reached the rock, but immediately beyond it was washed away off balance and swept down-river. The men on the bank hauled him ashore again, coughing and spluttering and fighting mad. Without a word to or look at anybody Reynolds again hurled himself into the rapids, and this time so determined was the fury of his assault that he succeeded in reaching the far bank without once being knocked off his feet.

He dragged himself on to the stony beach, lay there for some moments recovering from his exhaustion, then rose, crossed to a stunted pine at the base of the cliff rising on the other side, undid the rope round his waist and belayed it securely round the bole of the tree. Mallory, on his side, took two turns round a large rock and gestured to Andrea and the girl.

Mallory glanced upwards again to the top of the gully. There were still no signs of the enemy. Even so, Mallory felt that they could afford to wait no longer, that they had already pushed their luck too far. Andrea and Maria were barely half-way across when he told Groves to give Petar a hand across the rapids. He hoped to God the rope would hold, but hold it did for Andrea and Maria made it safely to the far bank. No sooner had they grounded than Mallory sent Miller on his way, carrying a pile of automatic arms over his left shoulder.

Groves and Petar also made the crossing without incident. Mallory himself had to wait until Miller reached the far bank, for he knew the chances of his being carried away were high and if he were, then Miller too would be precipitated into the water and their guns rendered useless.

Mallory waited until he saw Andrea give Miller a hand into the shallow water on the far bank and waited no longer. He unwound the rope from the rock he had been using as a belay, fastened a bowline round his own waist and plunged into the water. He was swept away at exactly the same point where Reynolds had been on his first attempt and was finally dragged ashore by his friends on the far bank with a fair amount of the waters of the Neretva in his stomach but otherwise unharmed.

'Any injuries, any cracked bones or skulls?' Mallory asked. He himself felt as if he had been over Niagara in a barrel. 'No? Fine.' He looked at Miller. 'You stay here with me. Andrea, take the others up round the first corner there and wait for us.'

'Me?' Andrea objected mildly. He nodded towards the gully. 'We've got friends that might be coming down there at any moment.'

Mallory took him some little way aside. 'We also have friends,' he said quietly, 'who might just possibly be coming down-river from the dam garrison.' He nodded at the two sergeants, Petar and Maria. 'What would happen to them if they ran into an Alpenkorps patrol, do you think?'

'I'll wait for you round the corner.'

Andrea and the four others made their slow way up-river, slipping and stumbling over the wetly slimy rocks and boulders. Mallory and Miller withdrew into the protection and concealment of two large boulders and stared upwards.

Several minutes passed. The moon still shone and the top of the gully was still innocent of any sign of the enemy. Miller said uneasily: 'What do you think has gone wrong? They're taking a damned long time about turning up.'

'No, I think that it's just that they are taking a damned long time in turning back.'

'Turning back?'

'They don't *know* where we've gone.' Mallory pulled out his map, examined it with a carefully hooded pencil-torch. 'About three-quarters of a mile down the railway track, there's a sharp turn to the left. In all probability the locomotive would have left the track there. Last time Neufeld and Droshny saw us we were aboard that locomotive and the logical thing for them to have done would have been to follow the track till they came to where we had abandoned the locomotive, expecting to find us somewhere in the vicinity. When they found the crashed engine, they would know at once what would have happened—but that would have given them another mile and a half to ride—and half of that uphill on tired ponies.'

'That must be it. I wish to God,' Miller went on grumblingly, 'that they'd hurry up.'

'What is this?' Mallory queried. 'Dusty Miller yearning for action?'

'No, I'm not,' Miller said definitely. He glanced at his watch. 'But time is getting very short.'

'Time,' Mallory agreed soberly, 'is getting terribly short.'

And then they came. Miller, glancing upward, saw a faint metallic glint in the moonlight as a head peered cautiously over the edge of the gully. He touched Mallory on the arm.

'I see him,' Mallory murmured. Together both men reached inside their tunics, pulled out their Lugers and removed their waterproof coverings. The helmeted head gradually resolved itself into a figure standing fully silhouetted in the moonlight against the sharply etched skyline. He began what was obviously meant to be a cautious descent, then suddenly flung up both arms and fell backwards and outwards. If he cried out, from where Mallory and Miller were the cry could not have been heard above the rushing of the waters. He struck the ledge half-way down, bounced off and outwards for a quite incredible distance, then landed spread-eagled on the stony river bank below, pulling down a small avalanche behind him.

Miller was grimly philosophical. 'Well, you said it was dangerous.'

Another figure appeared over the lip of the precipice to make the second attempt at a descent, and was followed in short order by several more men. Then, for the space of a few minutes, the moon went behind a cloud, while Mallory and Miller stared across the river until their eyes ached, anxiously and vainly trying to pierce the impenetrable darkness that shrouded the slope on the far side.

The leading climber, when the moon did break through, was just below the ledge, cautiously negotiating the lower slope. Mallory took careful aim with his Luger, the climber stiffened convulsively, toppled backwards and fell to his death. The following figure, clearly oblivious of the fate of his companion, began the descent of the lower slope. Both Mallory and Miller sighted their Lugers but just then the moon was suddenly obscured again and they had to lower their guns. When the moon again reappeared, four men had already reached the safety of the opposite bank, two of whom, linked together by a rope, were just beginning to venture the crossing of the ford.

Mallory and Miller waited until they had safely completed two thirds of the crossing of the ford. They formed a close and easy target and at that range it was impossible that Mallory and Miller should miss, nor did they. There was a momentary reddening of the white waters of the rapids, as much imagined as seen, then, still lashed together they were swept away down the gorge. So furiously were their bodies tumbled over and over by the rushing waters, so often did cartwheeling arms and legs break surface, that they might well have given the appearance of men who, though without hope, were still desperately struggling for their lives. In any event, the two men left standing on the far bank clearly did not regard the accident as being significant of anything amiss in any sinister way. They stood and watched the vanishing bodies of their companions in perplexity, still unaware of what was happening. A matter of two or three seconds later and they would never have been aware of anything else again but once more a wisp of errant dark cloud covered the moon and they still had a little time, a very little time, to live. Mallory and Miller lowered their guns.

Mallory glanced at his watch and said irritably: 'Why the hell don't they start firing? It's five past one.'

'Why don't who start firing?' Miller asked cautiously.

'You heard. You were there. I asked Vis to ask Vukalovic to give us sound cover at one. Up by the Zenica Gap there, less than a mile away. Well, we can't wait any longer. It'll take—' He broke off and listened to the sudden outburst of rifle fire, startlingly loud even at that comparatively close distance, and smiled. 'Well, what's five minutes here or there. Come on. I have the feeling that Andrea must be getting a little anxious about us.'

Andrea was. He emerged silently from the shadows as they rounded the first bend in the river. He said reproachfully: 'Where have you two been? You had me worried stiff.'

'I'll explain in an hour's time—if we're all still around in an hour's time,' Mallory amended grimly. 'Our friends the bandits are two minutes behind. I think they'll be coming in force—although they've lost four already—six including the two Reynolds got from the locomotive. You stop at the next bend up-river and hold them off. You'll have to do it by yourself. Think you can manage?'

'This is no time for joking,' Andrea said with dignity. 'And then?'

'Groves and Reynolds and Petar and his sister come with us up-river, Reynolds and Groves as nearly as possible to the dam, Petar and Maria wherever they can find some suitable shelter, possibly in the vicinity of the swing bridge—as long as they're well clear of that damned great boulder perched above it.'

'Swing bridge, sir?' Reynolds asked. 'A boulder?'

'I saw it when we got off the locomotive to reconnoitre.'

'*You* saw it. Andrea didn't.'

'I mentioned it to him,' Mallory went on impatiently. He ignored the disbelief in the sergeant's face and turned to Andrea. 'Dusty and I can't wait any longer. Use your Schmeisser to stop them.' He pointed north-westwards towards the Zenica Gap, where the rattle of musketry was now almost continuous. 'With all that racket going on, they'll never know the difference.'

Andrea nodded, settled himself comfortably behind a pair of large boulders and slid the barrel of his Schmeisser into the V between them. The remainder of the party moved upstream, scrambling awkwardly around and over the slippery boulders and rocks that covered the right-hand bank of the Neretva, until they came to a rudimentary path that had been cleared among the stones. This they followed for perhaps a hundred yards, till they came to a slight bend in the gorge. By mutual consent and without any order being given, all six stopped and gazed upwards.

The towering breath-taking ramparts of the Neretva dam wall had suddenly come into full view. Above the dam on either side precipitous walls of rock soared up into the night sky, at first quite vertical then both leaning out in an immense overhang which seemed to make them almost touch at the top, although this, Mallory knew from the observation he had made from above, was an optical illusion. On top of the dam wall itself the guard-houses and radio huts were clearly visible, as were the pigmy shapes of several patrolling German soldiers. From the top of the eastern side of the dam, where the huts were situated, an iron ladder—Mallory knew it was painted green, but in the half-shadow cast by the dam wall it looked black—fastened by iron supports to the bare rock face, zig-zagged downwards to the foot of the gorge, close by where foaming white jets of water boiled from the outlet pipes at the base of the dam wall. Mallory tried to estimate how many steps there would be in that ladder. Two hundred, perhaps two hundred and fifty, and once you started to climb or descend you just had to keep on going, for nowhere was there any platform or back-rest to afford even the means for a temporary respite. Nor did the ladder at any point afford the slightest scrap of cover from watchers on the bridge. As an assault route, Mallory mused, it was scarcely the one he would have chosen: he could not conceive of a more hazardous one.

About half-way between where they stood and the foot of

the ladder on the other side, a swing bridge spanned the
boiling waters of the gorge. There was little about its ancient,
rickety and warped appearance to inspire any confidence:
and what little confidence there might have been could
hardly have survived the presence of an enormous boulder,
directly above the eastern edge of the bridge, which seemed
in imminent danger of breaking loose from its obviously
insecure footing in the deep scar in the cliff-side.

Reynolds assimilated all of the scene before him, then
turned to Mallory. He said quietly: 'We've been very
patient, sir.'

'You've been very patient, Sergeant—and I'm grateful. You
know, of course, that there is a Yugoslav division trapped in
the Zenica Cage—that's just behind the mountains to our
left, here. You know, too, that the Germans are going to
launch two armoured divisions across the Neretva bridge at
two a.m. this morning and that if once they do get across
—and normally there would be nothing to stop them—the
Yugoslavs, armed with only their pop-guns and with hardly
any ammunition left, would be cut to pieces. You know
the only way to stop them is to destroy the Neretva bridge?
You know that this counter-espionage and rescue mission was
only a cover for the real thing?'

Reynolds said bitterly: 'I know that—now.' He pointed
down the gorge. 'And I also know that the bridge lies that
way.'

'And so it does. I also know that even if we could
approach it—which would be quite impossible—we couldn't
blow that bridge up with a truckload of explosives; steel
bridges anchored in reinforced concrete take a great deal of
destroying.' He turned and looked at the dam. 'So we do it
another way. See that dam wall there—there's thirty million
tons of water behind it—enough to carry away the Sydney
bridge, far less the one over the Neretva.'

Groves said in a low voice: 'You're crazy,' and then, as
an afterthought, 'sir.'

'Don't we know it? But we're going to blow up that dam
all the same. Dusty and I.'

'But—but all the explosives we have are a few hand-grenades,' Reynolds said, almost desperately. 'And in that dam wall there must be ten- to twenty-feet thicknesses of reinforced concrete. Blow it up? How?'

Mallory shook his head. 'Sorry.'

'Why, you close-mouthed—'

'Be quiet! Dammit, man, will you never, *never* learn. Even up to the very last minute you could be caught and made to tell—and then what would happen to Vukalovic's division trapped in the Zenica Cage? What you don't know, you can't tell.'

'But you know.' Reynolds's voice was thick with resentment. 'You and Dusty and Andrea—Colonel Stavros—*you* know. Groves and I knew all along that you knew, and *you* could be made to talk.'

Mallory said with considerable restraint: 'Get Andrea to talk? Perhaps you might—if you threatened to take away his cigars. Sure, Dusty and I could talk—but *someone* had to know.'

Groves said in the tone of a man reluctantly accepting the inevitable: 'How do you get behind that dam wall—you can't blow it up from the front, can you?'

'Not with the means at present available to us,' Mallory agreed. 'We get behind it. We climb up there.' Mallory pointed to the precipitous gorge wall on the other side.

'We climb up there, eh?' Miller asked conversationally. He looked stunned.

'Up the ladder. But not all the way. Three-quarters of the way up the ladder we leave it and climb vertically up the cliff-face till we're about forty feet above the top of the dam wall, just where the cliff begins to overhang there. From there, there's a ledge—well, more of a crack, really—'

'A crack!' Miller said hoarsely. He was horror-stricken.

'A crack. It stretches about a hundred and fifty feet clear across the top of the dam wall at an ascending angle of maybe twenty degrees. We go that way.'

Reynolds looked at Mallory in an almost dazed incredulity. 'It's madness!'

'Madness!' Miller echoed.

'I wouldn't do it from choice,' Mallory admitted. 'Nevertheless, it's the only way in.'

'But you're bound to be seen,' Reynolds protested.

'Not bound to be.' Mallory dug into his rucksack and produced from it a black rubber frogman's suit, while Miller reluctantly did the same from his. As both men started to pull their suits on, Mallory continued: 'We'll be like black flies against a black wall.'

'He hopes,' Miller muttered.

'Then with any luck we expect them to be looking the other way when the RAF start in with the fireworks. And if we do seem in any danger of discovery—well, that's where you and Groves come in. Captain Jensen was right—as things have turned out, we couldn't have done this without you.'

'Compliments?' Groves said to Reynolds. 'Compliments from the Captain? I've a feeling there's something nasty on the way.'

'There is,' Mallory admitted. He had his suit and hood in position now and was fixing into his belt some pitons and a hammer he had extracted from his rucksack. 'If we're in trouble, you two create a diversion.'

'What kind of diversion?' Reynolds asked suspiciously.

'From somewhere near the foot of the dam you start firing up at the guards atop the dam wall.'

'But—but we'll be completely exposed.' Groves gazed across at the rocky scree which composed the left bank at the base of the dam and at the foot of the ladder. 'There's not an ounce of cover. What kind of chance will we have?'

Mallory secured his rucksack and hitched a long coil of rope over his shoulder. 'A very poor one, I'm afraid.' He looked at his luminous watch. 'But then, for the next forty-five minutes you and Groves are expendable. Dusty and I are not.'

'Just like that?' Reynolds said flatly. 'Expendable.'

'Just like that.'

'Want to change places?' Miller said hopefully. There was no reply for Mallory was already on his way. Miller, with a last apprehensive look at the towering rampart of rock above, gave a last hitch to his rucksack and followed. Reynolds made to move off, but Groves caught him by the arm and signed to Maria to go ahead with Petar. He said to her: 'We'll wait a bit and bring up the rear. Just to be sure.'

'What is it?' Reynolds asked in a low voice.

'This. Our Captain Mallory admitted that he has already made four mistakes tonight. I think he's making a fifth now.'

'I'm not with you.'

'He's putting all our eggs in one basket and he's overlooked certain things. For instance, asking the two of us to stand by at the base of the dam wall. If we have to start a diversion, one burst of machine-gun fire from the top of the dam wall will get us both in seconds. One man can create as successful a diversion as two—and where's the point in the two of us getting killed? Besides, with one of us left alive, there's always the chance that something can be done to protect Maria and her brother. I'll go to the foot of the dam while you—'

'Why should you be the one to go? Why not—'

'Wait, I haven't finished yet. I also think Mallory's very optimistic if he thinks that Andrea can hold off that lot coming up the gorge. There must be at least twenty of them and they're not out for an evening's fun and games. They're out to kill us. So what happens if they do overwhelm Andrea and come up to the swing bridge and find Maria and Petar there while we are busy being sitting targets at the base of the dam wall? They'll knock them both off before you can bat an eyelid.'

'Or maybe not knock them off,' Reynolds muttered. 'What if Neufeld were to be killed before they reached the swing bridge? What if Droshny were the man in charge—Maria and Petar might take some time in dying.'

'So you'll stay near the bridge and keep our backs covered? With Maria and Petar in shelter somewhere near?'

'You're right, I'm sure you're right. But I don't like it,' Reynolds said uneasily. 'He gave us his orders and he's not a man who likes having his orders disobeyed.'

'He'll never know—even if he ever comes back, which I very much doubt, he'll never know. *And* he's started to make mistakes.'

'Not this kind of mistake.' Reynolds was still more than vaguely uneasy.

'Am I right or not?' Groves demanded.

'I don't think it's going to matter a great deal at the end of the day,' Reynolds said wearily. 'Okay, let's do it your way.'

The two sergeants hurried off after Maria and Petar.

Andrea listened to the scraping of heavy boots on stones, the very occasional metallic chink of a gun striking against a rock, and waited, stretched out flat on his stomach, the barrel of his Schmeisser rock-steady in the cleft between the boulders. The sounds heralding the stealthy approach up the river bank were not more than forty yards away when Andrea raised himself slightly, squinted down the barrel and squeezed the trigger.

The reply was immediate. At once three or four guns, all of them, Andrea realized, machine-pistols, opened up. Andrea stopped firing, ignored the bullets whistling above his head and ricocheting from the boulders on either side of him, carefully lined up on one of the flashes issuing from a machine-pistol and fired a one-second burst. The man behind the machine-pistol straightened convulsively, his up-flung right arm sending his gun spinning, then slowly toppled sideways in the Neretva and was carried away in the whitely swirling waters. Andrea fired again and a second man twisted round and fell heavily among the rocks. There came a suddenly barked order and the firing down-river ceased.

There were eight men in the down-river group and now one of them detached himself from the shelter of a boulder and crawled towards the second man who had been hit: as he moved, Droshny's face revealed his usual wolfish grin, but it was clear that he was feeling very far from smiling. He bent over the huddled figure in the stones, and turned him on his back: it was Neufeld, with blood streaming down from a gash in the side of the head. Droshny straightened, his face vicious in anger, and turned round as one of his Cetniks touched his arm.

'Is he dead?'

'Not quite. Concussed and badly. He'll be unconscious for hours, maybe days. I don't know, only a doctor can tell.' Droshny beckoned to two other men. 'You three—get him across the ford and up to safety. Two stay with him, the other come back. And for God's sake tell the others to hurry up and get here.'

His face still contorted with anger and for the moment oblivious of all danger, Droshny leapt to his feet and fired a long continuous burst upstream, a burst which apparently left Andrea completely unmoved, for he remained motionless where he was, resting peacefully with his back to his protective boulder, watching with mild interest but apparent unconcern as ricochets and splintered fragments of rock flew off in all directions.

The sound of the firing carried clearly to the ears of the guards patrolling the top of the dam. Such was the bedlam of small-arms fire all around and such were the tricks played on the ears by the baffling variety of echoes that reverberated up and down the gorge and over the surface of the dam itself, that it was quite impossible precisely to locate the source of the recent bursts of machine-pistol fire: what was significant, however, was that it *had* been machine-gun fire and up to that moment the sounds of musketry had consisted exclusively of rifle fire. And it *had* seemed to emanate from the south, from the gorge below the dam. One of the guards on the dam went worriedly to the captain in charge, spoke briefly, then walked quickly across to one of the small huts on the raised concrete platform at the eastern end of the dam wall. The hut, which had no front, only a rolled-up canvas protection, held a large radio transceiver manned by a corporal.

'Captain's orders,' the sergeant said. 'Get through to the bridge at Neretva. Pass a message to General Zimmermann that we—the captain, that is—is worried. Tell him that there's a great deal of small-arms fire all around us and that some of it seems to be coming from down-river.'

The sergeant waited impatiently while the operator put the call through and even more impatiently as the ear-phones crackled two minutes later and the operator started writing down the message. He took the completed message from the operator and handed it to the captain, who read it out aloud.

'General Zimmermann says, "There is no cause at all for anxiety, the noise is being made by our Yugoslav friends up by the Zenica Gap who are whistling in the dark because they are momentarily expecting an all-out assault by units of the 11th Army Corps. And it will be a great deal noisier later on when the RAF starts dropping bombs in all the wrong places. But they won't be dropping them near you, so don't worry." ' The captain lowered the paper. 'That's good enough for me. If the General says we are not to worry, then that's good enough for me. You know the General's reputation, sergeant?'

'I know his reputation, sir.' Some distance away and from some unidentifiable direction, came several more bursts of machine-pistol fire. The sergeant stirred unhappily.

'You are still troubled by something?' the captain asked.

'Yes, sir. I know the general's reputation, of course, and trust him implicitly.' He paused then went on worriedly: 'I could have sworn that that last burst of machine-pistol fire came from down the gorge there.'

'You're becoming just an old woman, sergeant,' the captain said kindly, 'and you must report to our divisional surgeon soon. Your ears need examining.'

The sergeant, in fact, was not becoming an old woman and his hearing was in considerably better shape than that of the officer who had reproached him. The current burst of machine-pistol firing was, as he'd thought, coming from the gorge, where Droshny and his men, now doubled in numbers, were moving forward, singly or in pairs, but never more than two at a time, in a series of sharp but very short rushes, firing as they went. Their firing, necessarily wildly inaccurate as they stumbled and slipped on the treacherous going under-foot, elicited no response from Andrea, possibly because he felt himself in no great danger, probably because he was conserving his ammunition. The latter supposition seemed the more likely as Andrea had slung his Schmeisser and was now examining with interest a stick-grenade which he had just withdrawn from his belt.

Farther up-river, Sergeant Reynolds, standing at the eastern edge of the rickety wooden bridge which spanned the nar-rowest part of the gorge where the turbulent, racing, foaming waters beneath would have offered no hope of life at all to any person so unfortunate as to fall in there, looked unhappily down the gorge towards the source of the machine-pistol firing and wondered for the tenth time whether he should take a chance, re-cross the bridge and go to Andrea's aid: even in the light of his vastly revised estimate of Andrea, it seemed impossible, as Groves had said, that one man could for long hold off twenty others bent on vengeance. On the other hand, he had promised Groves to remain there to look after Petar and Maria. There came another burst of firing from down-river. Reynolds made his mind up. He would offer his gun to Maria to afford herself and Petar what protection it might, and leave them for as little time as might be necessary to give Andrea what help he required.

He turned to speak to her, but Maria and Petar were no longer there. Reynolds looked wildly around, his first reaction was that they had both fallen into the rapids, a reaction that he at once dismissed as ridiculous. Instinctively he gazed up the bank towards the base of the dam, and, even although the moon was then obscured by a large bank of cloud, he saw them at once, making their way towards the foot of the iron ladder, where Groves was standing. For a brief moment he puzzled why they should have moved upstream without permission, then remembered that neither he nor Groves had, in fact, remembered to give them instructions to remain by the bridge. Not to worry, he thought, Groves will soon send them back down to the bridge again and when they arrived he would tell them of his decision to return to Andrea's aid. He felt vaguely relieved at the prospect, not because he entertained fears of what might possibly happen to him when he rejoined Andrea and faced up to Droshny and his men but because it postponed, if even only briefly, the necessity of implementing a decision which could be only marginally justifiable in the first place.

Groves, who had been gazing up the seemingly endless series of zig-zags of that green iron ladder so precariously, it seemed, attached to that vertical cliff-face, swung round at the soft grate of approaching footsteps on the shale and stared at Maria and Petar, walking, as always, hand in hand. He said angrily: 'What in God's name are you people doing here? You've no right to be here—can't you see, the guards have only to look down and you'll be killed? Go on. Go back and rejoin Sergeant Reynolds at the bridge. Now!'

Maria said softly: 'You are kind to worry, Sergeant Groves. But we don't want to go. We want to stay here.'

'And what in hell's name good can you do by staying here?' Groves asked roughly. He paused, then went on, almost kindly: 'I know who you are now, Maria. I know what you've done, how good you are at your own job. But this is not your job. Please.'

'No.' She shook her head. 'And I *can* fire a gun.'

'You haven't got one to fire. And Petar here, what right have you to speak for him. Does he know where he is?'

Maria spoke rapidly to her brother in incomprehensible Serbo-Croat: he responded by making his customary odd sounds in his throat. When he had finished, Maria turned to Groves.

'He says he knows he is going to die tonight. He has what you people call the second sight and he says there is no future beyond tonight. He says he is tired of running. He says he will wait here till the time comes.'

'Of all the stubborn, thick-headed—'

'Please, Sergeant Groves.' The voice, though still low, was touched by a new note of asperity. 'His mind is made up, and you can never change it.'

Groves nodded in acceptance. He said: 'Perhaps I can change yours.'

'I do not understand.'

'Petar cannot help us anyway, no blind man could. But you can. If you would.'

'Tell me.'

'Andrea is holding off a mixed force of at least twenty Cetniks and German troops.' Groves smiled wryly. 'I have recent reason to believe that Andrea probably has no equal anywhere as a guerilla fighter, but one man cannot hold off twenty for ever. When he goes, then there is only Reynolds left to guard the bridge—and if he goes, then Droshny and his men will be through in time to warn the guards, almost certainly in time to save the dam, certainly in time to send a radio message through to General Zimmermann to pull his tanks back on to high ground. I think, Maria, that Reynolds may require your help. Certainly, you can be of no help here—but if you stand by Reynolds you *could* make all the difference between success and failure. And you did say you can fire a gun.'

'And as *you* pointed out, I haven't got a gun.'

'That was then. You have now.' Groves unslung his Schmeisser and handed it to her along with some spare ammunition.

'But—' Maria accepted gun and ammunition reluctantly. 'But now *you* haven't a gun.'

'Oh yes I have.' Groves produced his silenced Luger from his tunic. 'This is all I want tonight. *I* can't afford to make any noise tonight, not so close to the dam as this.'

'But I *can't* leave my brother.'

'Oh, I think you can. In fact, you're going to. No one on earth can help your brother any more. Not now. Please hurry.'

'Very well.' She moved off a few reluctant paces, stopped, turned and said: 'I suppose you think you're very clever, Sergeant Groves?'

'I don't know what you're talking about,' Groves said woodenly. She looked at him steadily for a few moments, then turned and made her way down-river. Groves smiled to himself in the near-darkness.

The smile vanished in the instant of time that it took for the gorge to be suddenly flooded with bright moonlight as a black, sharply-edged cloud moved away from the face of the moon. Groves called softly, urgently to Maria: 'Face down on the rocks and keep still,' saw her at once do what he ordered, then looked up the green ladder, his face registering the strain and anxiety in his mind.

About three-quarters of the way up the ladder, Mallory and Miller, bathed in the brilliant moonlight, clung to the top of one of the angled sections as immoblie as if they had been carved from the rock itself. Their unmoving eyes, set in equally unmoving faces, were obviously fixed on—or transfixed by—the same point in space.

That point was a scant fifty feet away, above and to their left, where two obviously very jumpy guards were leaning anxiously over the parapet at the top of the dam: they were gazing into the middle distance, down the gorge, towards the location of what seemed to be the sound of firing. They had only to move their eyes downwards and discovery for Groves and Maria was certain: they had only to shift their gaze to the left and discovery for Mallory and Miller would have been equally certain. And death for all inevitable.

XI

SATURDAY 0120-0135

Like Mallory and Miller, Groves, too, had caught sight of the two German sentries leaning out over the parapet at the top of the dam and staring anxiously down the gorge. As a situation for conveying a feeling of complete nakedness, exposure and vulnerability, it would, Groves felt, take a lot of beating. And if he felt like that, how must Mallory and Miller, clinging to the ladder and less than a stone's throw from the guards, be feeling? Both men, Groves knew, carried silenced Lugers, but their Lugers were inside their tunics and their tunics encased in their zipped-up frogmen's suits, making them quite inaccessible. At least, making them quite inaccessible without, clinging as they were to the ladder, performing a variety of contortionist movements to get at

them—and it was certain that the least untoward movement
would have been immediately spotted by the two guards. How
it was that they hadn't already been seen, even without
movement, was incomprehensible to Groves: in that bright
moonlight, which cast as much light on the dam and in the
gorge as one would have expected on any reasonably dull
afternoon, any normal peripheral vision should have picked
them all up immediately. And it was unlikely that any
front-line troops of the Wehrmacht had less than standard
peripheral vision. Groves could only conclude that the in-
tentness of the guards' gaze did not necessarily mean that
they were looking intently; it could have been that all their
being was at that moment concentrated on their hearing,
straining to locate the source of the desultory machine-pistol
fire down the gorge. With infinite caution Groves eased his
Luger from his tunic and lined it up. At that distance, even
allowing for the high muzzle-velocity of the gun, he reckoned
his chances of getting either of the guards to be so remote
as to be hardly worth considering: but at least, as a gesture,
it was better than nothing.

Groves was right on two counts. The two sentries on the
parapet, far from being reassured by General Zimmermann's
encouraging reassurance, were in fact concentrating all their
being on listening to the down-river bursts of machine-pistol
fire, which were becoming all the more noticeable, not only
because they seemed—as they were—to be coming closer, but
also because the ammunition of the Partisan defenders of the
Zenica Gap was running low and their fire was becoming more
sporadic. Groves had been right, too, about the fact that
neither Mallory nor Miller had made any attempt to get
at their Lugers. For the first few seconds, Mallory, like
Groves, had felt sure that any such move would be bound
to attract immediate attention, but, almost at once and long
before the idea had occurred to Groves, Mallory had realized
that the men were in such a trance-like state of listening that
a hand could almost have passed before their faces without
their being aware of it. And now, Mallory was certain, there
would be no need to do anything at all because, from his
elevation, he could see something that was quite invisible to

Groves from his position at the foot of the dam: another dark band of cloud was almost about to pass across the face of the moon.

Within seconds, a black shadow flitting across the waters of the Neretva dam turned the colour from dark green to the deepest indigo, moved rapidly across the top of the dam wall, blotted out the ladder and the two men clinging to it, then engulfed the gorge in darkness. Groves sighed in soundless relief and lowered his Luger. Maria rose and made her way down-river towards the bridge. Petar moved his unseeing gaze around in the sightless manner of the blind. And, up above, Mallory and Miller at once began to climb again.

Mallory now abandoned the ladder at the top of one of its zigs and struck vertically up the cliff-face. The rock-face, providentially, was not completely smooth, but such hand- and foot-holds as it afforded were few and small and awkwardly situated, making for a climb that was as arduous as it was technically difficult: normally, had he been using the hammer and pitons that were stuck in his belt, Mallory would have regarded it as a climb of no more than moderate difficulty: but the use of pitons was quite out of the question. Mallory was directly opposite the top of the dam wall and no more than 35 feet from the nearest guard: one tiny chink of hammer on metal could not fail to register on the hearing of the most inattentive listener: and, as Mallory had just observed, inattentive listening was the last accusation that could have been levelled against the sentries on the dam. So Mallory had to content himself with the use of his natural talents and the vast experience gathered over many years of rock-climbing and continue the climb as he was doing, sweating profusely inside the hermetic rubber suit, while Miller, now some forty feet below, peered upwards with such tense anxiety on his face that he was momentarily oblivious of his own precarious perch on top of one of the slanted ladders, a predicament which would normally have sent him into a case of mild hysterics.

Andrea, too, was at that moment peering at something about fifty feet away, but it would have required a hyper-active imagination to detect any signs of anxiety in that dark and rugged face. Andrea, as the guards on the dam had so recently been doing, was listening rather than looking. From his point of view all he could see was a dark and shapeless jumble of wetly glistening boulders with the Neretva rushing whitely alongside. There was no sign of life down there, but that only meant that Droshny, Neufeld and his men, having learnt their lessons the hard way—for Andrea could not know at this time that Neufeld had been wounded —were inching their way forward on elbows and knees, not once moving out from one safe cover until they had located another.

A minute passed, then Andrea heard the inevitable: a barely discernible 'click,' as two pieces of stone knocked together. It came, Andrea estimated, from about thirty feet away. He nodded as if in satisfaction, armed the grenade, waited two seconds, then gently lobbed it downstream, dropping flat behind his protective boulder as he did so. There was the typically flat crack of a grenade explosion, accompanied by a briefly white flash of light in which two soldiers could be seen being flung bodily sideways.

The sound of the explosion came clearly to Mallory's ear. He remained still, allowing only his head to turn slowly till he was looking down on top of the dam wall, now almost twenty feet beneath him. The same two guards who had been previously listening so intently stopped their patrol a second time, gazed down the gorge again, looked at each other uneasily, shrugged uncertainly, then resumed their patrol. Mallory resumed his climb.

He was making better time now. The former negligible finger and toe holds had given way, occasionally, to small fissures in the rock into which he was able to insert the odd piton to give him a great deal more leverage than would have otherwise been possible. When next he stopped climbing and looked upwards he was no more than six feet below the longitudinal crack he had been looking for—and, as he had said to Miller earlier, it *was* no more than a crack. Mallory made to begin again, then paused, his head cocked towards the sky.

Just barely audible at first above the roaring of the waters

of the Neretva and the sporadic small-arms fire from the
direction of the Zenica Gap, but swelling in power with
the passing of every second, could be heard a low and distant
thunder, a sound unmistakable to all who had ever heard it
during the war, a sound that heralded the approach of
squadrons, of a fleet of heavy bombers. Mallory listened to the
rapidly approaching clamour of scores of aero engines and
smiled to himself.

Many men smiled to themselves that night when they
heard the approach from the west of those squadrons of
Lancasters. Miller, still perched on his ladder and still exercising all his available will-power not to look down, managed to
smile to himself, as did Groves at the foot of the ladder and
Reynolds by the bridge. On the right bank of the Neretva,
Andrea smiled to himself, reckoned that the roar of those
fast-approaching engines would make an excellent cover for
any untoward sound and picked another grenade from his
belt. Outside a soup tent high up in the biting cold of the
Ivenici plateau, Colonel Vis and Captain Vlanovich smiled
their delight at each other and solemnly shook hands. Behind
the southern redoubts of the Zenica Cage, General Vukalovic
and his three senior officers, Colonel Janzy, Colonel Lazlo and
Major Stephan, for once removed the glasses through which
they had been so long peering at the Neretva bridge and the
menacing woods beyond and smiled their incredulous relief at
one another. And, most strangely of all, already seated in his
command truck just inside the woods to the south of the
Neretva bridge, General Zimmermann smiled perhaps the most
broadly of all.

Mallory resumed his climb, moving even more quickly
now, reached the longitudinal crack, worked his way up
above it, pressed a piton into a convenient crack in the
rock, withdrew his hammer from his belt and prepared to
wait. Even now, he was not much more than forty feet above
the dam wall, and the piton that Mallory now wanted to
anchor would require not one blow but a dozen of them, and
powerful ones at that: the idea that, even above the approaching thunder of the Lancasters' engines, the metallic
hammering would go unremarked was preposterous. The

sound of the heavy aero engines was now deepening by the moment.

Mallory glanced down directly beneath him. Miller was gazing upward, tapping his wristwatch as best a man can when he has both arms wrapped round the same rung of a ladder, and making urgent gestures. Mallory, in turn, shook his head and made a downward restraining motion with his free hand. Miller shook his own head in resignation.

The Lancasters were on top of them now. The leader arrowed in diagonally across the dam, lifted slightly as it came to the high mountains on the other side and then the earth shook and ripples of dark waters shivered their erratic way across the surface of the Neretva dam before the first explosion reached their ears, as the first stick of 1,000-pound bombs crashed squarely into the Zenica Gap. From then on the sound of the explosions of the bombs raining down on the Gap were so close together as to be almost continuous: what little time-lapse there was between some of the explosions was bridged by the constantly rumbling echoes that rumbled through the mountains and valleys of central Bosnia.

Mallory had no longer any need to worry about sound any more, he doubted he could even have heard himself speak, for most of those bombs were landing in a concentrated area less than a mile from where he clung to the side of the cliff, their explosions making an almost constant white glare that showed clearly above the mountains to the west. He hammered home his piton, belayed a rope around it, and dropped the rope to Miller, who immediately seized it and began to climb: he looked, Mallory thought, uncommonly like one of the early Christian martyrs. Miller was no mountaineer, but, no mistake, he knew how to climb a rope: in a remarkably short time he was up beside Mallory, feet firmly wedged into the longitudinal crack, both hands gripping tightly to the piton.

'Think you can hang on that piton?' Mallory asked. He almost had to shout to make himself heard above the still undiminished thunder of the falling bombs.

'Just try to prise me away.'

'I won't,' Mallory grinned.

He coiled up the rope which Miller had used for his ascent, hitched it over his shoulder and started to move quickly along the longitudinal crack. 'I'll take this across the top of the dam, belay it to another piton. Then you can join me. Right?'

Miller looked down into the depths and shuddered. 'If you think I'm going to stay here, you must be mad.'

Mallory grinned again and moved away.

To the south of the Neretva bridge, General Zimmermann, with an aide by his side, was still listening to the sounds of the aerial assault on the Zenica Gap. He glanced at his watch.

'Now,' he said. 'First-line assault troops into position.'

At once heavily armed infantry, bent almost double to keep themselves below parapet level, began to move quickly across the Neretva bridge: once on the other side, they spread out east and west along the northern bank of the river, concealed from the Partisans by the ridge of high ground abutting on the river bank. Or they thought they were concealed: in point of fact a Partisan scout, equipped with night-glasses and field telephone, lay prone in a suicidally positioned slit-trench less than a hundred yards from the bridge itself, sending back a constant series of reports to Vukalovic.

Zimmermann glanced up at the sky and said to his aide: 'Hold them. The moon's coming through again.' Again he looked at his watch. 'Start the tank engines in twenty minutes.'

'They've stopped coming across the bridge, then?' Vukalovic said.

'Yes, sir.' It was the voice of his advance scout. 'I think it's because the moon is about to break through in a minute or two.'

'I think so too,' Vukalovic said. He added grimly: 'And I suggest you start working your way back before it does break through or it will be the last chance you'll ever have.'

Andrea, too, was regarding the night sky with interest. His gradual retreat had now taken him into a particularly

unsatisfactory defensive position, practically bereft of all
cover: a very unhealthy situation to be caught in, he
reflected, when the moon came out from behind the clouds.
He paused for a thoughtful moment, then armed another
grenade and lobbed it in the direction of a cluster of dimly
seen boulders about fifty feet away. He did not wait to see
what effect it had, he was already scrambling his way up-river
before the grenade exploded. The one certain effect it did have
was to galvanize Droshny and his men into immediate and
furious retaliation, at least half a dozen machine-pistols
loosing off almost simultaneous bursts at the position Andrea
had so recently and prudently vacated. One bullet plucked
at the sleeve of his tunic, but that was as near as anything
came. He reached another cluster of boulders without
incident and took up a fresh defensive position behind them:
when the moon did break through it would be Droshny and
his men who would be faced with the unpalatable prospect of
crossing that open stretch of ground.

Reynolds, crouched by the swing bridge with Maria now
by his side, heard the flat crack of the exploding grenade and
guessed that Andrea was now no more than a hundred
yards downstream on the far bank. And like so many people
at that precise instant, Reynolds, too, was gazing up at what
could be seen of the sky through the narrow north-west gap
between the precipitous walls of the gorge.

Reynolds had intended going to Andrea's aid as soon as
Groves had sent Petar and Maria back to him, but three factors
had inhibited him from taking immediate action. In the
first place, Groves had been unsuccessful in sending back
Petar: secondly, the frequent bursts of machine-pistol firing
down the gorge, coming steadily closer, were indication
enough that Andrea was making a very orderly retreat and
was still in fine fighting fettle: and thirdly, even if Droshny
and his men did get Andrea, Reynolds knew that by taking up
position behind the boulder directly above the bridge, he
could deny Droshny and his men the crossing of the bridge for
an indefinite period.

But the sight of the large expanse of starlit sky coming
up behind the dark clouds over the moon made Reynolds

forget the tactically sound and cold-blooded reasons for remaining where he was. It was not in Reynolds's nature to regard any other man as an expendable pawn and he suspected strongly that when he was presented with a sufficiently long period of moonlight Droshny would use it to make the final rush that would overwhelm Andrea. He touched Maria on the shoulder.

'Even the Colonel Stavroses of this world need a hand at times. Stay here. We shouldn't be long.' He turned and ran across the swaying swing bridge.

Damn it, Mallory thought bitterly, damn it, damn it and damn it all. Why couldn't there have been heavy dark cloud covering the entire sky? Why couldn't it have been raining? Or snowing? Why hadn't they chosen a moonless night for this operation? But he was, he knew, only kicking against the pricks. No one had had any choice, for tonight was the only time there was. But still, that damnable moon.

Mallory looked to the north, where the northern wind, driving banded cloud across the moon, was leaving behind it a large expanse of starlit sky. Soon the entire dam and gorge would be bathed in moonlight for a considerable period: Mallory thought wryly that he could have wished himself to be in a happier position for that period.

By this time, he had traversed about half the length of the longitudinal crack. He glanced to his left and reckoned he had still between thirty and forty feet to go before he was well clear of the dam wall and above the waters of the dam itself. He glanced to his right and saw, not to his surprise, that Miller was still where he had left him, clinging to the piton with both hands as if it were his dearest friend on earth, which at that moment it probably was. He glanced downwards: he was directly above the dam wall now, some fifty feet above it, forty feet above the roof of the guardhouse. He looked at the sky again: a minute, no more, and the moon would be clear. What was it that he had said to Reynolds that afternoon? Yes, that was it. For now is all the time there may be. He was beginning to wish he hadn't said that. He was a New Zealander, but only a second-generation New

Zealander: all his forebears were Scots and everyone knew how the Scots indulged in those heathenish practices of second sight and peering into the future. Mallory briefly indulged in the mental equivalent of a shoulder shrug and continued on his traverse.

At the foot of the iron ladder, Groves, to whom Mallory was now no more than a half-seen, half-imagined dark shape against a black cliff-face, realized that Mallory was soon going to move out of his line of sight altogether, and when that happened he would be in no position to give Mallory any covering fire at all. He touched Petar on the shoulder and with the pressure of his hand indicated that he should sit down at the foot of the ladder. Petar looked at him sightlessly, uncomprehendingly, then suddenly appeared to gather what was expected of him, for he nodded obediently and sat down. Groves thrust his silenced Luger deep inside his tunic and began to climb.

A mile to the west, the Lancasters were still pounding the Zenica Gap. Bomb after bomb crashed down with surprising accuracy into that tiny target area, blasting down trees, throwing great eruptions of earth and stones into the air, starting all over the area scores of small fires which had already incinerated nearly all the German plywood tanks. Seven miles to the south, Zimmermann still listened with interest and still with satisfaction to the continuing bombardment to the north. He turned to the aide seated beside him in the command car.

'You will have to admit that we must give the Royal Air Force full marks for industry, if for nothing else. I hope our troops are well clear of the area?'

'There's not a German soldier within two miles of the Zenica Gap, Herr General.'

'Excellent, excellent.' Zimmermann appeared to have forgotten about his earlier forebodings. 'Well, fifteen minutes. The moon will soon be through, so we'll hold our infantry. The next wave of troops can go across with the tanks.'

Reynolds, making his way down the right bank of the

Neretva towards the sound of firing, now very close indeed, suddenly became very still indeed. Most men react the same way when they feel the barrel of a gun grinding into the side of their necks. Very cautiously, so as not to excite any nervous trigger-fingers, Reynolds turned both eyes and head slightly to the right and realized with a profound sense of relief that this was one instance where he need have no concern about jittery nerves.

'You had your orders,' Andrea said mildly. 'What are you doing here?'

'I—I thought you might need some help.' Reynolds rubbed the side of his neck. 'Mind you, I could have been wrong.'

'Come on. It's time we got back and crossed the bridge.' For good measure and in very quick succession, Andrea spun another couple of grenades down-river, then made off quickly up the river bank, closely followed by Reynolds.

The moon broke through. For the second time that night, Mallory became absolutely still, his toes jammed into the longitudinal crack, his hands round the piton which he had thirty seconds earlier driven into the rock and to which he had secured the rope. Less than ten feet from him Miller, who with the aid of the rope had already safely made the first part of the traverse, froze into similar immobility. Both men stared down on to the top of the dam wall.

There were six guards visible, two at the farther or western end, two at the middle and the remaining two almost directly below Mallory and Miller. How many more there might have been inside the guard-house neither Mallory nor Miller had any means of knowing. All they could know for certain was that their exposed vulnerability was complete, their position desperate.

Three-quarters of the way up the iron ladder, Groves, too, became very still. From where he was, he could see Mallory, Miller and the two guards very clearly indeed. He knew with a sudden conviction that this time there would be no escape, they could never be so lucky again. Mallory, Miller, Petar or himself—who would be the first to be spotted? On balance, he thought he himself was the most likely candidate. Slowly, he wrapped his left arm round the ladder, pushed his right hand inside his tunic, withdrew his Luger and laid the barrel along his left forearm.

The two guards on the eastern end of the dam wall were restless, apprehensive, full of nameless fears. As before, they both leaned out over the parapet and stared down the valley. They can't help but see me, Groves thought, they're *bound* to see me, good God, I'm almost directly in their line of sight. Discovery must be immediate.

It was, but not for Groves. Some strange instinct made one of the guards glance upwards and to his left and his mouth fell open at the astonishing spectacle of two men in rubber suits clinging like limpets to the sheer face of the cliff. It took him several interminable seconds before he could recover himself sufficiently to reach out blindly and grab his companion by the arm. His companion followed the other guard's line of sight, then his jaw, too, dropped in an almost comical fashion. Then, at precisely the same moment, both men broke free from their thrall-like spell and swung their guns, one a Schmeisser, the other a pistol, upwards to line up on the two men pinned helplessly to the cliff-face.

Groves steadied his Luger against both his left arm and the side of the ladder, sighted unhurriedly along the barrel and squeezed the trigger. The guard with the Schmeisser dropped the weapon, swayed briefly on his feet and started to fall outwards. Almost three seconds passed before the other guard, startled and momentarily quite uncomprehending, reached out to grab his companion, but he was far too late, he never even succeeded in touching him. The dead man, moving in an almost grotesquely slow-motion fashion, toppled wearily over the edge of the parapet and tumbled head over heels into the depths of the gorge beneath.

The guard with the pistol leaned far out over the parapet, staring in horror after his falling comrade. It was quite obvious that he was momentarily at a total loss to understand what had happened, for he had heard no sound of a shot. But realization came within the second as a piece of concrete chipped away inches from his left elbow and a spent bullet ricocheted its whistling way into the night sky. The guard's eyes lifted and widened in shock, but this time the shock had no inhibiting effect on the speed of his reactions. More in blind hope than in any real expectation of success, he loosed off two quick snap-shots and bared his teeth in satisfaction as he heard Groves cry out and saw the right hand, the forefinger still holding the Luger by the trigger-guard, reach up to clutch the shattered left shoulder.

Groves's face was dazed and twisted with pain, the eyes already clouded by the agony of the wound, but those responsible for making Groves a commando sergeant had not picked him out with a pin, and Groves was not quite finished yet. He brought his Luger down again. There was something terribly wrong with his vision now, he dimly realized, he thought he had a vague impression that the guard on the parapet was leaning far out, pistol held in both hands to make sure of his killing shot, but he couldn't be sure. Twice Groves squeezed the trigger of his Luger and then he closed his eyes, for the pain was gone and he suddenly felt very sleepy.

The guard by the parapet pitched forward. He reached out desperately to grab the coaming of the parapet, but to pull himself back to safety he had to swing his legs up to retain his balance and he found he could no longer control his legs, which slid helplessly over the edge of the parapet. His body followed his legs almost of its own volition, for the last vestiges of strength remain for only a few seconds with a man through whose lungs two Luger bullets have just passed. For a moment of time his clawed hands hooked despairingly on to the edge of the parapet and then his fingers opened.

Groves seemed unconscious now, his head lolling on his chest, the left-hand sleeve and left-hand side of his uniform already saturated with blood from the terrible wound in his shoulder. Were it not for the fact that his right arm was jammed between a rung of the ladder and the cliff-face behind it, he must certainly have fallen. Slowly, the fingers of his right hand opened and the Luger fell from his hand.

Seated at the foot of the ladder, Petar started as the Luger struck the shale less than a foot from where he was sitting.

He looked up instinctively, then rose, made sure that the inevitable guitar was firmly secured across his back, reached out for the ladder and started climbing.

Mallory and Miller stared down, watching the blind singer climb up towards the wounded and obviously unconscious Groves. After a few moments, as if by telepathic signal, Mallory glanced across at Miller who caught his eyes almost at once. Miller's face was strained, almost haggard. He freed one hand momentarily from the rope and made an almost desperate gesture in the direction of the wounded sergeant. Mallory shook his head.

Miller said hoarsely: 'Expendable, huh?'

'Expendable.'

Both men looked down again. Petar was now not more than ten feet below Groves, and Groves, though Mallory and Miller could not see this, had his eyes closed and his right arm was beginning to slip through the gap between the rung and the rock. Gradually, his right arm began to slip more quickly, until his elbow was free, and then his arm came free altogether and slowly, so very slowly, he began to topple outwards from the wall. But Petar got to him first, standing on the step beneath Groves and reaching out an arm to encircle him and press him back against the ladder. Petar had him and for the moment Petar could hold him. But that was all he could do.

The moon passed behind a cloud.

Miller covered the last ten feet separating him from Mallory. He looked at Mallory and said: 'They're both going to go, you know that?'

'I know that.' Mallory sounded even more tired than he looked. 'Come on. Another thirty feet and we should be in position.' Mallory, leaving Miller where he was, continued his traverse along the crack. He was moving very quickly now, taking risks that no sane cragsman would ever have contemplated, but he had no option now, for time was running out. Within a minute he had reached a spot where he judged that he had gone far enough, hammered home a piton and securely belayed the rope to it.

He signalled to Miller to come and join him. Miller began

the last stage of the traverse, and as he was on his way across, Mallory unhitched another rope from his shoulders, a sixty-foot length of climbers' rope, knotted at fifteen-inch intervals. One end of this he fastened to the same piton as held the rope that Miller was using for making his traverse: the other end he let fall down the cliff-side. Miller came up and Mallory touched him on the shoulder and pointed downwards.

The dark waters of the Neretva dam were directly beneath them.

XII

SATURDAY 0135-0200

Andrea and Reynolds lay crouched among the boulders at the western end of the elderly swing bridge over the gorge. Andrea looked across the length of the bridge, his gaze travelling up the steep gully behind it till it came to rest on the huge boulder perched precariously at the angle where the steep slope met the vertical cliff-face behind it. Andrea rubbed a bristly chin, nodded thoughtfully and turned to Reynolds.

'You cross first. I'll give you covering fire. You do the same for me when you get to the other side. Don't stop, don't look round. Now.'

Reynolds made for the bridge in a crouching run, his footsteps seeming to him abnormally loud as he reached the rotting planking of the bridge itself. The palms of his hands gliding lightly over the hand ropes on either side he continued without check or diminution of speed, obeying Andrea's instructions not to risk a quick backward glance, and feeling a very strange sensation between his shoulder-blades. To his mild astonishment he reached the far bank without a shot being fired, headed for the concealment and shelter offered by a large boulder a little way up the bank, was startled momentarily to see Maria hiding behind the same boulder, then whirled round and unslung his Schmeisser.

On the far bank there was no sign of Andrea. For a brief moment Reynolds experienced a quick stab of anger, thinking Andrea had used this ruse merely to get rid of him, then smiled to himself as he heard two flat explosive sounds some little way down the river on the far bank. Andrea, Reynolds remembered, had still had two grenades left and Andrea was not the man to let such handy things rust from disuse. Besides, Reynolds realized, it would provide Andrea with extra valuable seconds to make good his escape, which indeed it did for Andrea appeared on the far bank almost immediately and, like Reynolds, effected the crossing of the bridge entirely without incident. Reynolds called softly and Andrea joined them in the shelter of the boulder.

Reynolds said in a low voice: 'What's next?'

'First things first.' Andrea produced a cigar from a waterproof box, a match from another waterproof box, struck the match in his huge cupped hands and puffed in immense satisfaction. When he removed the cigar, Reynolds noticed that he held it with the glowing end safely concealed in the curved palm of his hand. 'What's next? I tell you what's next. Company coming to join us across the bridge, and coming very soon, too. They've taken crazy risks to try to get me—and paid for them—which shows they are pretty desperate. Crazy men don't hang about for long. You and Maria here move fifty or sixty yards nearer the dam and take cover there—and keep your guns on the far side of the bridge.'

'You staying here?' Reynolds asked.

Andrea blew out a noxious cloud of cigar smoke. 'For the moment, yes.'

'Then I'm staying, too.'

'If you want to get killed, it's all right by me,' Andrea said mildly. 'But this beautiful young lady here wouldn't look that way any more with the top of her head blown off.'

Reynolds was startled by the crudeness of the words. He said angrily: 'What the devil do you mean?'

'I mean this.' Andrea's voice was no longer mild. 'This boulder gives you perfect concealment from the bridge. But

Droshny and his men can move another thirty or forty yards farther up the bank on their side. What concealment will you have then?'

'I never thought of that,' Reynolds said.

'There'll come a day when you say that once too often,' Andrea said sombrely, 'and then it will be too late to think of anything again.'

A minute later they were in position. Reynolds was hidden behind a huge boulder which afforded perfect concealment both from the far side of the bridge and from the bank on the far side up to the point where it petered out: it did not offer concealment from the dam. Reynolds looked to his left where Maria was crouched farther in behind the rock. She smiled at him, and Reynolds knew he had never seen a braver girl, for the hands that held the Schmeisser were trembling. He moved out a little and peered down-river, but there appeared to be no signs of life whatsoever at the western edge of the bridge. The only signs of life at all, indeed, were to be seen behind the huge boulder up in the gully, where Andrea, completely screened from anyone at or near the far side of the bridge, was industriously loosening the foundations of rubble and earth round the base of the boulder.

Appearances, as always, were deceptive. Reynolds had judged there to be no life at the western end of the bridge but there was, in fact, life and quite a lot of it, although admittedly there was no action. Concealed in the massive boulders about twenty feet back from the bridge, Droshny, a Cetnik sergeant and perhaps a dozen German soldiers and Cetniks lay in deep concealment among the rocks.

Droshny had binoculars to his eyes. He examined the ground in the neighbourhood of the far side of the swing bridge, then traversed to his left up beyond the boulder where Reynolds and Maria lay hidden until he reached the dam wall. He lifted the glasses, following the dimly-seen zig-zag outline of the iron ladder, checked, adjusted the focus as finely as possible, then stared again. There could be no doubt: there were two men clinging to the ladder, about three-quarters of the way up towards the top of the dam.

'Good God in heaven!' Droshny lowered the binoculars, the gaunt craggy features registering an almost incredulous horror, and turned to the Cetnik sergeant by his side. 'Do you know what they mean to do?'

'The dam!' The thought had not occurred to the sergeant until that instant but the stricken expression on Droshny's face made the realization as immediate as it was inevitable. 'They're going to blow up the dam!' It did not occur to either man to wonder *how* Mallory could possibly blow up the dam: as other men had done before them, both Droshny and the sergeant were beginning to discover in Mallory and his *modus operandi* an extraordinary quality of inevitability that transformed remote possibilities into very likely probabilities.

'General Zimmermann!' Droshny's gravelly voice had become positively hoarse. 'He must be warned! If that dam bursts while his tanks and troops are crossing—'

'Warn him? Warn him? How in God's name can we warn him?'

'There's a radio up on the dam.'

The sergeant stared at him. He said: 'It might as well be on the moon. There'll be a rear-guard, they're bound to have left a rear-guard. Some of us are going to get killed crossing that bridge, Captain.'

'You think so?' Droshny glanced up sombrely at the dam. 'And just what do you think is going to happen to us all down here if *that* goes?'

Slowly, soundlessly and almost invisibly, Mallory and Miller swam northwards through the dark waters of the Neretva dam, away from the direction of the dam wall. Suddenly Miller, who was slightly in the lead, gave a low exclamation and stopped swimming.

'What's up?' Mallory asked.

'This is up.' With an effort Miller lifted a section of what appeared to be a heavy wire cable just clear of the water. 'Nobody mentioned this little lot.'

'Nobody did,' Mallory agreed. He reached under the water. 'And there's a steel mesh below.'

'An anti-torpedo net?'

'Just that.'

'Why?' Miller gestured to the north where, at a distance of less than two hundred yards, the dam made an abrupt right-angled turn between the towering cliff-faces. 'It's impossible for any torpedo bomber—any bomber—to get a run-in on the dam wall.'

'Someone should have told the Germans. They take no chances—and it makes things a damned sight more difficult for us.' He peered at his watch. 'We'd better start hurrying. We're late.'

They eased themselves over the wire and started swimming again, more quickly this time. Several minutes later, just after they had rounded the corner of the dam and lost sight of the dam wall, Mallory touched Miller on the shoulder. Both men trod water, turned and looked back in the direction from which they had come. To the south, not much more than two miles away, the night sky had suddenly blossomed into an incandescent and multi-coloured beauty as scores of parachute flares, red and green and white and orange, drifted slowly down towards the Neretva river.

'Very pretty, indeed,' Miller conceded. 'And what's all this in aid of?'

'It's in aid of us. Two reasons. First of all, it will take any person who looks at that—and *everyone* will look at it—at least ten minutes to recover his night-sight, which means that any odd goings-on in this part of the dam are all that less likely to be observed: and if everyone is going to be busy looking that way, then they can't be busy looking this way at the same time.'

'Very logical,' Miller approved. 'Our friend Captain Jensen doesn't miss out on very much, does he?'

'He has, as the saying goes, all his marbles about him.' Mallory turned again and gazed to the east, his head cocked the better to listen. He said: 'You have to hand it to them. Dead on target, dead on schedule. I hear him coming now.'

The Lancaster, no more than five hundred feet above the surface of the dam, came in from the east, its engine throttled back almost to stalling speed. It was still two hundred yards short of where Mallory and Miller were treading water when suddenly huge black silk parachutes bloomed beneath it: almost simultaneously, engine-power was increased to maximum revolutions and the big bomber went into a steeply banking climbing turn to avoid smashing into the mountains on the far side of the dam.

Miller gazed at the slowly descending black parachutes, turned, and looked at the brilliantly burning flares to the south. 'The skies,' he announced, 'are full of things tonight.'

He and Mallory began to swim in the direction of the falling parachutes.

Petar was near to exhaustion. For long minutes now he had been holding Groves's dead weight pinned against the iron ladder and his aching arms were beginning to quiver with the strain. His teeth were clenched hard, his face, down which rivulets of sweat poured, was twisted with the effort and the agony of it all. Plainly, Petar could not hold out much longer.

It was by the light of those flares that Reynolds, still crouched with Maria in hiding behind the big boulder, first saw the predicament of Petar and Groves. He turned to glance at Maria: one look at the stricken face was enough to tell Reynolds that she had seen it, too.

Reynolds said hoarsely: 'Stay here. I must go and help them.'

'No!' She caught his arm, clearly exerting all her will to keep herself under control: her eyes, as they had been when Reynolds had first seen her, had the look of a hunted animal about them. 'Please, Sergeant, no. You must stay here.'

Reynolds said desperately: 'Your brother—'

'There are more important things—'

'Not for you there aren't.' Reynolds made to rise, but she clung to his arm with surprising strength, so that he couldn't release himself without hurting her. He said, almost gently: 'Come on, lass, let me go.'

'No! If Droshny and his men get across—' She broke off as the last of the flares finally fizzled to extinction, casting the entire gorge into what was, by momentary contrast, an almost total darkness. Maria went on simply: 'You'll have to stay now, won't you?'

'I'll have to stay now.' Reynolds moved out from the shelter of the boulder and put his night-glasses to his eyes. The swing bridge, and as far as he could tell, the far bank seemed innocent of any sign of life. He traversed up the gully and could just make out the form of Andrea, his excavations finished, resting peacefully behind the big boulder. Again with a feeling of deep unease, Reynolds trained his glasses on the bridge. He suddenly became very still. He removed the glasses, wiped the lenses very carefully, rubbed his eyes and lifted the glasses again.

His night-sight, momentarily destroyed by the flares, was now almost back to normal and there could be no doubt or any imagination about what he was seeing—seven or eight men, Droshny in the lead, flat on their stomachs, were inching their way on elbows, hands and knees across the wooden slats of the swing bridge.

Reynolds lowered the glasses, stood upright, armed a grenade and threw it as far as he could towards the bridge. It exploded just as it landed, at least forty yards short of the bridge. That it achieved nothing but a flat explosive bang and the harmless scattering of some shale was of no account, for it had never been intended to reach the bridge: it had been intended as a signal for Andrea, and Andrea wasted no time.

He placed the soles of both feet against the boulder, braced his back against the cliff-face and heaved. The boulder moved the merest fraction of an inch. Andrea momentarily relaxed, allowing the boulder to roll back, then repeated the process: this time the forward motion of the boulder was quite perceptible. Andrea relaxed again, then pushed for the third time.

Down below on the bridge, Droshny and his men, uncertain as to the exact significance of the exploding grenade, had frozen into complete immobility. Only their eyes moved, darting almost desperately from side to side to locate the source of a danger that lay so heavily in the air as to be almost palpable.

The boulder was distinctly rocking now. With every additional heave it received from Andrea, it was rocking an additional inch farther forward, an additional inch farther backwards. Andrea had slipped farther and farther down until now he was almost horizontal on his back. He was gasping for breath and sweat was streaming down his face. The boulder rolled back almost as if it were going to fall upon him and crush him. Andrea took a deep breath, then convulsively straightened back and legs in one last titanic heave. For a moment the boulder teetered on the point of imbalance, reached the point of no return and fell away.

Droshny could most certainly have heard nothing and, in that near darkness, it was certain as could be that he had seen nothing. It could only have been an instinctive awareness of impending death that made him glance upwards in sudden conviction that this was where the danger lay. The huge boulder, just rolling gently when Droshny's horror-stricken eyes first caught sight of it, almost at once began to bound in ever-increasing leaps, hurtling down the slope directly towards them, trailing a small avalanche behind it. Droshny screamed a warning. He and his men scrambled desperately to their feet, an instinctive reaction that was no more than a useless and token gesture in the face of death, because, for most of them, it was already far too late and they had no place to go.

With one last great leap the hurtling boulder smashed straight into the centre of the bridge, shattering the flimsy woodwork and slicing the bridge in half. Two men who had been directly in the path of the boulder died instantaneously: five others were catapulted into the torrent below and swept away to almost equally immediate death. The two broken sections of the bridge, still secured to either bank by the suspension ropes, hung down into the rushing waters, their lowermost parts banging furiously against the boulder-strewn banks.

There must have been at least a dozen parachutes attached to the three dark cylindrical objects that now lay floating, though more than half submerged, in the equally dark waters of the

Neretva dam. Mallory and Miller sliced those away with their knives, then joined the three cylinders in line astern, using short wire strops that had been provided for that precise purpose. Mallory examined the leading cylinder and gently eased back a lever set in the top. There was a subdued roar as compressed air violently aerated the water astern of the leading cylinder and sent it surging forward, tugging the other two cylinders behind it. Mallory closed the lever and nodded to the other two cylinders.

'These levers on the right-hand side control the flooding valves. Open that one till you just have negative buoyancy and no more. I'll do the same on this one.'

Miller cautiously turned a valve and nodded at the leading cylinder. 'What's that for?'

'Do *you* fancy towing a ton and a half of amatol as far as the dam wall? Propulsion unit of some kind. Looks like a sawn-off section of a twenty-one-inch torpedo tube to me. Compressed air, maybe at a pressure of five thousand pounds a square inch, passing through reduction gear. Should do the job all right.'

'Just so long as Miller doesn't have to do it.' Miller closed the valve on the cylinder. 'About that?'

'About that.' All three cylinders were now just barely submerged. Again Mallory eased back the compressed air lever on the leading cylinder. There was a throaty burble of sound, a sudden flurry of bubbles streaming out astern and then all three cylinders were under way, heading down towards the angled neck of the dam, both men clinging to and guiding the leading cylinder.

When the swing bridge had disintegrated under the impact of the boulder, seven men had died: but two still lived.

Droshny and his sergeant, furiously buffeted and badly bruised by the torrent of water, clung desperately to the broken end of the bridge. At first, they could do no more than hold on, but gradually, and after a most exhausting struggle, they managed to haul themselves clear of the rapids and hang there, arms and legs hooked round broken sections of what remained of the bridge, fighting for breath. Droshny made a signal to some unseen person or persons across the rapids, then pointed upwards in the direction from which the boulder had come.

Crouched among the boulders on the far side of the river, three Cetniks—the fortunate three who had not yet moved on to the bridge when the boulder had fallen—saw the signal and understood. About seventy feet above where Droshny—completely concealed from sight on that side by the high bank of the river—was still clinging grimly to what was left of the bridge, Andrea, now bereft of cover, had begun to make a precarious descent from his previous hiding-place. On the other side of the river, one of the three Cetniks took aim and fired.

Fortunately for Andrea, firing uphill in semi-darkness is a tricky business at the best of times. Bullets smashed into the cliff-face inches from Andrea's left shoulder, the whining ricochets leaving him almost miraculously unscathed. There would be a correction factor for the next burst, Andrea knew: he flung himself to one side, lost his balance and what little precarious purchase he had and slid and tumbled helplessly down the boulder-strewn slope. Bullets, many bullets, struck close by him on his way down, for the three Cetniks on the right bank, convinced now that Andrea was the only person left for them to deal with, had risen, advanced to the edge of the river and were concentrating all their fire on Andrea.

Again fortunately for Andrea, this period of concentration lasted for only a matter of a few seconds. Reynolds and Maria emerged from cover and ran down the bank, stopping momentarily to fire at the Cetniks across the river, who at once forgot all about Andrea to meet this new and unexpected threat. Just as they did so, Andrea, in the midst of a small avalanche, still fighting furiously but hopelessly to arrest his fall, struck the bank of the river with appalling force, struck the side of his head against a large stone and collapsed, his head and shoulders hanging out over the wild torrent below.

Reynolds flung himself flat on the shale of the river bank,

forced himself to ignore the bullets striking to left and right of him and whining above him and took a slow and careful aim. He fired a long burst, a very long one, until the magazine of his Schmeisser was empty. All three Cetniks crumpled and died.

Reynolds rose. He was vaguely surprised to notice that his hands were shaking. He looked at Andrea, lying unconscious and dangerously near the side of the bank, took a couple of paces in his direction, then checked and turned as he heard a low moan behind him. Reynolds broke into a run.

Maria was half-sitting, half-lying on the stony bank. Both hands cradled her leg just above the right knee and the blood was welling between her fingers. Her face, normally pale enough, was ashen and drawn with shock and pain. Reynolds cursed bitterly but soundlessly, produced his knife and began to cut away the cloth around the wound. Gently, he pulled away the material covering the wound and smiled reassuringly at the girl: her lower lip was caught tightly between her teeth and she watched him steadily with eyes dimmed by pain and tears.

It was a nasty enough looking flesh wound, but, Reynolds knew, not dangerous. He reached for his medical pack, gave her a reassuring smile and then forgot all about his medical pack. The expression in Maria's eyes had given way to one of shock and fear and she was no longer looking at him.

Reynolds twisted round. Droshny had just hauled himself over the edge of the river bank, had risen to his feet and was now heading purposefully towards Andrea's prostrate body, with the obvious intention of heaving the unconscious man into the gorge.

Reynolds picked up his Schmeisser and pulled the trigger. There was an empty click—he'd forgotten the magazine had been emptied. He glanced around almost wildly in an attempt to locate Maria's gun, but there was no sign of it. He could wait no longer. Droshny was only a matter of feet from where Andrea lay. Reynolds picked up his knife and rushed along the bank. Droshny saw him coming and he saw too that

Reynolds was armed with only a knife. He smiled as a wolf would smile, took one of his wickedly-curved knives from his belt and waited.

The two men approached closely and circled warily. Reynolds had never wielded a knife in anger in his life and so had no illusions at all as to his chances: hadn't Neufeld said that Droshny was the best man in the Balkans with a knife? He certainly looked it, Reynolds thought. His mouth felt very dry.

Thirty yards away Maria, dizzy and weak with pain and dragging her wounded leg, crawled towards the spot where she thought her gun had fallen when she had been hit. After what seemed a very long time, but what was probably no more than ten seconds, she found it half-hidden among rocks. Nauseated and faint from the pain of her wounded leg, she forced herself to sit up and brought the gun to her shoulder. Then she lowered it again.

In her present condition, she realized vaguely, it would have been impossible for her to hit Droshny without almost certainly hitting Reynolds at the same time: in fact, she might well have killed Reynolds while missing Droshny entirely. For both men were now locked chest to chest, each man's knife-hand—the right—clamped in the grip of the other's left.

The girl's dark eyes, which had so recently reflected pain and shock and fear, now held only one expression—despair. Like Reynolds, Maria knew of Droshny's reputation—but, unlike Reynolds, she had seen Droshny kill with that knife and knew too well how lethal a combination that man and that knife were. A wolf and a lamb, she thought, a wolf and a lamb. After he kills Reynolds—her mind was dulled now, her thoughts almost incoherent—after he kills Reynolds I shall kill him. But first, Reynolds would have to die, for there could be no help for it. And then the despair left the dark eyes to be replaced by an almost unthinkable hope for she knew with an intuitive certainty that with Andrea by one's side hope need never be abandoned.

Not that Andrea was as yet by anyone's side. He had forced himself up to his hands and knees and was gazing down uncomprehendingly at the rushing white waters below, shaking his leonine head from side to side in an attempt to clear it. And then, still shaking his head, he levered himself painfully to his feet and he wasn't shaking his head any more. In spite of her pain, Maria smiled.

Slowly, inexorably, the Cetnik giant twisted Reynolds's knife-hand away from himself while at the same time bringing the lancet point of his own knife nearer to Reynolds's throat. Reynolds's sweat-sheened face deflected his desperation, his total awareness of impending defeat and death. He cried out with pain as Droshny twisted his right wrist almost to breaking-point, forcing him to open his fingers and drop his knife. Droshny kneed him viciously at the same time, freeing his left hand to give Reynolds a violent shove that sent him staggering to crash on his back against the stones and lie there winded and gasping in agony.

Droshny smiled his smile of wolfish satisfaction. Even although he must have known that the need for haste was paramount he yet had to take time off to carry out the execution in a properly leisurely fashion, to savour to the full every moment of it, to prolong the exquisite joy he always felt at moments like these. Reluctantly, almost, he changed to a throwing grip on his knife and slowly raised it high. The smile was broader than ever, a smile that vanished in an instant of time as he felt a knife being plucked from his own belt. He whirled round. Andrea's face was a mask of stone.

Droshny smiled again. 'The gods have been kind to me.' His voice was low, almost reverent, his tone a caressing whisper. 'I have dreamed of this. It is better that you should die this way. This will teach you, my friend—'

Droshny, hoping to catch Andrea unprepared, broke off in mid-sentence and lunged forward with cat-like speed. The smile vanished again as he looked in almost comical disbelief at his right wrist locked in the vice-like grip of Andrea's left hand.

Within seconds, the tableau was as it had been in the beginning of the earlier struggle, both knife-wrists locked in the opponents' left hands. The two men appeared to be absolutely immobile, Andrea with his face totally impassive, Droshny with his white teeth bared, but no longer in a smile. It was, instead, a vicious snarl compounded of hate and fury and baffled anger—for this time Droshny, to his evident consternation and disbelief, could make no impression whatsoever on his opponent. The impression, this time, was being made on him.

Maria, the pain in her leg in temporary abeyance, and a slowly recovering Reynolds stared in fascination as Andrea's left hand, in almost millimetric slow-motion, gradually twisted Droshny's right wrist so that the blade moved slowly away and the Cetnik's fingers began, almost imperceptibly at first, to open. Droshny, his face darkening in colour and the veins standing out on forehead and neck, summoned every last reserve of strength to his right hand: Andrea, rightly sensing that all of Droshny's power and will and concentration were centred exclusively upon breaking his crushing grip suddenly tore his own right hand free and brought his knife scything round and under and upwards with tremendous power: the knife went in under the breast-bone, burying itself to the hilt. For a moment or two the giant stood there, lips drawn far back over bared teeth smiling mindlessly in the rictus of death, then, as Andrea stepped away, leaving the knife still embedded, Droshny toppled slowly over the edge of the ravine. The Cetnik sergeant, still clinging to the shattered remains of the bridge, stared in uncomprehending horror as Droshny, the hilt of the knife easily distinguishable, fell head-first into the boiling rapids and was immediately lost to sight.

Reynolds rose painfully and shakily to his feet and smiled at Andrea. He said: 'Maybe I've been wrong about you all along. Thank you, Colonel Stavros.'

Andrea shrugged. 'Just returning a favour, my boy. Maybe I've been wrong about you, too.' He glanced at his watch. 'Two o'clock! *Two* o'clock! Where are the others?'

'God, I'd almost forgotten. Maria there is hurt. Groves and Petar are on the ladder. I'm not sure, but I think Groves is in a pretty bad way.'

'They may need help. Get to them quickly. I'll look after the girl.'

At the southern end of the Neretva bridge, General Zimmermann stood in his command car and watched the sweep-second hand of his watch come up to the top.

'Two o'clock,' Zimmermann said, his tone almost conversational. He brought his right hand down in a cutting gesture. A whistle shrilled and at once tank engines roared and treads clattered as the spearhead of Zimmermann's first armoured division began to cross the bridge at Neretva.

XIII

SATURDAY 0200-0215

'Maurer and Schmidt! Maurer and Schmidt!' The captain in charge of the guard on top of the Neretva dam wall came running from the guard-house, looked around almost wildly and grabbed his sergeant by the arm. 'For God's sake, where are Maurer and Schmidt? No one seen them? No one? Get the searchlight.'

Petar, still holding the unconscious Groves pinned against the ladder, heard the sound of the words but did not understand them. Petar, with both arms round Groves, now had his forearms locked at an almost impossible angle between the stanchions and the rock-face behind. In this position, as long as his wrists or forearms didn't break, he could hold Groves almost indefinitely. But Petar's grey and sweat-covered face, the racked and twisted face, were mute testimony enough to the almost unendurable agony he was suffering.

Mallory and Miller also heard the urgently shouted commands, but, like Petar, were unable to understand what it was that was being shouted. It would be something, Mallory thought vaguely, that would bode no good for them, then put the thought from his mind: he had other and more urgently immediate matters to occupy his attention. They had reached the barrier of the torpedo net and he had the supporting cable in one hand, a knife in the other when Miller exclaimed and caught his arm.

'For God's sake, no!' The urgency in Miller's voice had Mallory looking at him in astonishment. 'Jesus, what do I use for brains. That's not a wire.'

'It's not—'

'It's an insulated power cable. Can't you see?'

Mallory peered closely. 'Now I can.'

'Two thousand volts, I'll bet.' Miller still sounded shaken. 'Electric chair power. We'd have been frizzled alive. *And* it would have triggered off an alarm bell.'

'Over the top with them,' Mallory said.

Struggling and pushing, heaving and pulling, for there was only a foot of clear water between the wire and the surface of the water, they managed to ease the compressed air cylinder over and had just succeeded in lifting the nose of the first of the amatol cylinders on to the wire when, less than a hundred yards away, a six-inch searchlight came to life on the top of the dam wall, its beam momentarily horizontal, then dipping sharply to begin a traverse of the water close in to the side of the dam wall.

'That's all we bloody well need,' Mallory said bitterly. He pushed the nose of the amatol block back off the wire, but the wire strop securing it to the compressed air cylinder held it in such a position that it remained with its nose nine inches clear of the water. 'Leave it. Get under. Hang on to the net.'

Both men sank under the water as the sergeant atop the dam wall continued his traverse with the searchlight. The beam passed over the nose of the first of the amatol cylinders, but a black-painted cylinder in dark waters makes a poor subject for identification and the sergeant failed to see it. The light moved on, finished its traverse of the water alongside the dam, then went out.

Mallory and Miller surfaced cautiously and looked swiftly around. For the moment, there was no other sign of immediate danger. Mallory studied the luminous hands of his watch. He said: 'Hurry! For God's sake, hurry! We're almost three minutes behind schedule.'

They hurried. Desperate now, they had the two amatol cylinders over the wire inside twenty seconds, opened the compressed air valve on the leading cylinder and were alongside the massive wall of the dam inside another twenty. At that moment, the clouds parted and the moon broke through again, silvering the dark waters of the dam. Mallory and Miller were now in a helplessly exposed position but there was nothing they could do about it and they knew it. Their time had run out and they had no option other than to secure and arm the amatol cylinders as quickly as ever possible. Whether they were discovered or not could still be all-important: but there was nothing they could do to prevent that discovery.

Miller said softly: 'Forty feet apart and forty feet down, the experts say. We'll be too late.'

'No. Not yet too late. The idea is to let the tanks across first then destroy the bridge before the petrol bowsers and the main infantry battalions cross.'

Atop the dam wall, the sergeant with the searchlight returned from the western end of the dam and reported to the captain.

'Nothing, sir. No sign of anyone.'

'Very good.' The captain nodded towards the gorge. 'Try that side. You may find something there.'

So the sergeant tried the other side and he did find something there, and almost immediately. Ten seconds after he had begun his traverse with the searchlight he picked up the figures of the unconscious Groves and the exhausted Petar and, only feet below them and climbing steadily, Sergeant Reynolds. All three were hopelessly trapped, quite powerless to do anything to defend themselves: Reynolds had no longer even his gun.

On the dam wall, a Wehrmacht soldier, levelling his machine-pistol along the beam of the searchlight, glanced up in astonishment as the captain struck down the barrel of his gun.

'Fool!' The captain sounded savage. 'I want them alive. You two, fetch ropes, get them up here for questioning. We *must* find out what they have been up to.'

His words carried clearly to the two men in the water for, just then, the last of the bombing ceased and the sound of the small-arms fire died away. The contrast was almost too much to be borne, the suddenly hushed silence strangely ominous, deathly, almost, in its sinister foreboding.

'You heard?' Miller whispered.

'I heard.' More cloud, Mallory could see, thinner cloud but still cloud, was about to pass across the face of the moon. 'Fix these float suckers to the wall. I'll do the other charge.' He turned and swam slowly away, towing the second amatol cylinder behind him.

When the beam of the searchlight had reached down from the top of the dam wall Andrea had been prepared for almost instant discovery, but the prior discovery of Groves, Reynolds and Petar had saved Maria and himself, for the Germans seemed to think that they had caught all there were to be caught and, instead of traversing the rest of the gorge with the searchlights, had concentrated, instead, on bringing up to the top of the wall the three men they had found trapped on the ladder. One man, obviously unconscious—that would be Groves, Andrea thought—was hauled up at the end of a rope: the other two, with one man lending assistance to the other, had completed the journey up the ladder by themselves. All this Andrea had seen while he was bandaging Maria's injured leg, but he had said nothing of it to her.

Andrea secured the bandage and smiled at her. 'Better?'

'Better.' She tried to smile her thanks but the smile wouldn't come.

'Fine. Time we were gone.' Andrea consulted his watch. 'If we stay here any longer I have the feeling that we're going to get very, very wet.'

He straightened to his feet and it was this sudden movement that saved his life. The knife that had been intended for his back passed cleanly through his upper left arm. For a moment, almost as if uncomprehending, Andrea stared down at the tip of the narrow blade emerging from his arm then, apparently oblivious of the agony it must have cost him, turned slowly round, the movement wrenching the hilt of the knife from the hand of the man who held it.

The Cetnik sergeant, the only other man to have survived with Droshny the destruction of the swing bridge, stared at Andrea as if he were petrified, possibly because he couldn't understand why he had failed to kill Andrea, more probably because he couldn't understand how a man could suffer such a wound in silence and, in silence, still be able to tear the knife from his grasp. Andrea had now no weapon left him nor did he require one. In what seemed an almost grotesque slow motion, Andrea lifted his right hand: but there was nothing slow-motion about the dreadful edge-handed chopping blow which caught the Cetnik sergeant on the base of the neck. The man was probably dead before he struck the ground.

Reynolds and Petar sat with their backs to the guard-hut at the eastern end of the dam. Beside them lay the still unconscious Groves, his breathing now stertorous, his face ashen and of a peculiar waxed texture. From overhead, fixed to the roof of the guard-house, a bright light shone down on them, while near by was a watchful guard with his carbine trained on them. The Wehrmacht captain of the guard stood above them, an almost awestruck expression on his face.

He said incredulously but in immaculate English: 'You hoped to blow up a dam this size with a few sticks of dynamite? You must be mad!'

'No one told us the dam was as big as this,' Reynolds said sullenly.

'No one told you—God in heaven, talk of mad dogs and Englishmen! And where is this dynamite?'

'The wooden bridge broke.' Reynolds's shoulders were slumped in abject defeat. 'We lost all the dynamite—and all our other friends.'

'I wouldn't have believed it, I just wouldn't have believed it.' The captain shook his head and turned away, then checked as Reynolds called him. 'What is it?'

'My friend here.' Reynolds indicated Groves. 'He is very ill, you can see that. He needs medical attention.'

'Later.' The captain turned to the soldier in the open transceiver cabin. 'What news from the south.'

'They have just started to cross the Neretva bridge, sir.'

The words carried clearly to Mallory, at that moment some distance apart from Miller. He had just finished securing his float to the wall and was on the point of rejoining Miller when he caught a flash of light out of the corner of his eye. Mallory remained still and glanced upward and to his right.

There was a guard on the dam wall above, leaning over the parapet as he moved along, flashing a torch downwards. Discovery, Mallory at once realized, was certain. One or both of the supporting floats were bound to be seen. Unhurriedly, and steadying himself against his float, Mallory unzipped the top of his rubber suit, reached under his tunic, brought out his Luger, unwrapped it from its water-proof cover and eased off the safety-catch.

The pool of light from the torch passed over the water, close in to the side of the dam wall. Suddenly, the beam of the torch remained still. Clearly to be seen in the centre of the light was a small, torpedo-shaped object fastened to the dam wall by suckers and, just beside it, a rubber-suited man with a gun in his hand. And the gun—it had, the sentry automatically noticed, a silencer screwed to the end of the barrel—was pointed directly at him. The sentry opened his mouth to shout a warning but the warning never came for a red flower bloomed in the centre of his forehead, and he leaned forward tiredly, the upper half of his body over the edge of the parapet, his arms dangling downwards. The torch slipped from his lifeless hand and tumbled down into the water.

The impact of the torch on the water made a flat, almost cracking sound. In the now deep silence it was bound to be heard by those above, Mallory thought. He waited tensely, the Luger ready in his hand, but after twenty seconds had passed and nothing happened Mallory decided he could wait no longer. He glanced at Miller, who had clearly heard the sound, for he was staring at Mallory, and at the gun in Mallory's hand with a puzzled frown on his face. Mallory pointed up towards the dead guard hanging over the

parapet. Miller's face cleared and he nodded his understanding. The moon went behind a cloud.

Andrea, the sleeve of his left arm soaked in blood, more than
half carried the hobbling Maria across the shale and through
the rocks: she could hardly put her right foot beneath
her. Arrived at the foot of the ladder, both of them stared
upwards at the forbidding climb, at the seemingly endless zig-
zags of the iron ladder reaching up into the night. With a
crippled girl and his own damaged arm, Andrea thought, the
prospects were poor indeed. And God only knew when
the wall of the dam was due to go up. He looked at his
watch. If everything was on schedule, it was due to go now:
Andrea hoped to God that Mallory, with his passion for
punctuality, had for once fallen behind schedule. The girl
looked at him and understood.

'Leave me,' she said. 'Please leave me.'

'Out of the question,' Andrea said firmly. 'Maria would
never forgive me.'

'Maria?'

'Not you.' Andrea lifted her on to his back and wound
her arms round his neck. 'My wife. I think I'm going to
be terrified of her.' He reached out for the ladder and
started to climb.

The better to see how the final preparations for the attack
were developing, General Zimmermann had ordered his
command car out on to the Neretva bridge itself and now had
it parked exactly in the middle, pulled close in to the right-
hand side. Within feet of him clanked and clattered and
roared a seemingly endless column of tanks and self-propelled
guns and trucks laden with assault troops: as soon as they
reached the northern end of the bridge, tanks and guns
and trucks fanned out east and west along the banks of
the river, to take temporary cover behind the steep escarpment
ahead before launching the final concerted attack.

From time to time, Zimmermann raised his binoculars and
scanned the skies to the west. A dozen times he imagined he

heard the distant thunder of approaching air armadas, a dozen times he deceived himself. Time and again he told himself he was a fool, a prey to useless and fearful imaginings wholly unbecoming to a general in the Wehrmacht: but still this deep feeling of unease persisted, still he kept examining the skies to the west. It never once occurred to him, for there was no reason why it should, that he was looking in the wrong direction.

Less than half a mile to the north, General Vukalovic lowered his binoculars and turned to Colonel Janzy.

'That's it, then.' Vukalovic sounded weary and inexpressibly sad. 'They're across—or almost all across. Five more minutes. Then we counter-attack.'

'Then we counter-attack,' Janzy said tonelessly. 'We'll lose a thousand men in fifteen minutes.'

'We asked for the impossible,' Vukalovic said. 'We pay for our mistakes.'

Mallory, a long trailing lanyard in his hand, rejoined Miller. He said: 'Fixed?'

'Fixed.' Miller had a lanyard in his own hand. 'We pull those leads to the hydrostatic chemical fuses and take off?'

'Three minutes. You know what happens to us if we're still in this water after three minutes?'

'Don't even talk about it,' Miller begged. He suddenly cocked his head and glanced quickly at Mallory. Mallory, too, had heard it, the sound of running footsteps up above. He nodded at Miller. Both men sank beneath the surface of the water.

The captain of the guard, because of inclination, a certain rotundity of figure and very proper ideas as to how an officer of the Wehrmacht should conduct himself, was not normally given to running. He had, in fact, been walking, quickly and nervously, along the top of the dam wall when he caught sight of one of his guards leaning over the parapet in what he could only consider an unsoldierly and slovenly fashion. It then occurred to him that a man leaning over a parapet would normally use his hands and arms to brace himself and he could not see the guard's hands and arms. He remembered the missing Maurer and Schmidt and broke into a run.

The guard did not seem to hear him coming. The captain caught him roughly by the shoulder, then stood back aghast as the dead man slid back off the parapet and collapsed at his feet, face upwards: the place where his forehead had been was not a pretty sight. Seized by a momentary paralysis, the captain stared for long seconds at the dead man, then, by a conscious effort of will, drew out both his torch and pistol, snapped on the beam of the one and released the safety-catch of the other and risked a very quick glance over the dam parapet.

There was nothing to be seen. Rather, there was nobody to be seen, no sign of the enemy who must have killed his guard within the past minute or so. But there *was* something to be seen, additional evidence, as if he ever needed such evidence, that the enemy had been there: a torpedo-shaped object—no, *two* torpedo-shaped objects—clamped to the wall of the dam just at water level. Uncomprehendingly at first, the captain stared at those, then the significance of their presence there struck him with the violence, almost, of a physical blow. He straightened and started running towards the eastern end of the dam, shouting 'Radio! Radio!' at the top of his voice.

Mallory and Miller surfaced. The shouts—they were almost screams—of the running captain of the guard—carried clear over the now silent waters of the dam. Mallory swore.

'Damn and damn and damn again!' His voice was almost vicious in his chagrin and frustration. 'He can give Zimmermann seven, maybe eight minutes warning. Time to pull the bulk of his tanks on to the high ground.'

'So now?'

'So now we pull those lanyards and get the hell out of here.'

The captain, racing along the wall, was now less than thirty yards from the radio hut and where Petar and Reynolds sat with their backs to the guard-house.

'General Zimmermann!' he shouted. 'Get through. Tell him

to pull his tanks to the high ground. Those damned English have mined the dam!'

'Ah, well.' Petar's voice was almost a sigh. 'All good things come to an end.'

Reynolds stared at him, his face masked in astonishment. Automatically, involuntarily, his hand reached out to take the dark glasses Petar was passing him, automatically his eyes followed Petar's hand moving away again and then, in a state of almost hypnotic trance, he watched the thumb of that hand press a catch in the side of the guitar. The back of the instrument fell open to reveal inside the trigger, magazine and gleamingly-oiled mechanism of a sub-machine-gun.

Petar's forefinger closed over the trigger. The sub-machine-gun, its first shell shattering the end of the guitar, stuttered and leapt in Petar's hands. The dark eyes were narrowed, watchful and cool. And Petar had his priorities right.

The soldier guarding the three prisoners doubled over and died, almost cut in half by the first blast of shells. Two seconds later the corporal guard by the radio hut, while still desperately trying to unsling his Schmeisser, went the same way. The captain of the guard, still running, fired his pistol repeatedly at Petar, but Petar still had his priorities right. He ignored the captain, ignored a bullet which struck his right shoulder, and emptied the remainder of the magazine into the radio transceiver, then toppled sideways to the ground, the smashed guitar falling from his nerveless hands, blood pouring from his shoulder and a wound on his head.

The captain replaced his still smoking revolver in his pocket and stared down at the unconscious Petar. There was no anger in the captain's face now, just a peculiar sadness, the dull acceptance of ultimate defeat. His eyes moved and caught Reynolds's: in a moment of rare understanding both men shook their heads in a strange and mutual wonder.

Mallory and Miller, climbing the knotted rope, were almost opposite the top of the dam wall when the last echoes of the firing drifted away across the waters of the dam. Mallory glanced down at Miller, who shrugged as best a man can shrug when hanging on to a rope and shook his head wordlessly. Both men resumed their climb, moving even more quickly than before.

Andrea, too, had heard the shots, but had no idea what their significance might be. At that moment, he did not particularly care. His left upper arm felt as if it were burning in a fierce bright flame, his sweat-covered face reflected his pain and near-exhaustion. He was not yet, he knew, half-way up the ladder. He paused briefly, aware that the girl's grip around his neck was slipping, eased her carefully in towards the ladder, wrapped his left arm round her waist and continued his painfully slow and dogged climb. He wasn't seeing very well now and he thought vaguely that it must be because of the loss of blood. Oddly enough, his left arm was beginning to become numb and the pain was centring more and more on his right shoulder which all the time took the strain of their combined weights.

'Leave me!' Maria said again. 'For God's sake, leave me. You can save yourself.'

Andrea gave her a smile or what he thought was a smile and said kindly: 'You don't know what you're saying. Besides, Maria would murder me.'

'Leave me! Leave me!' She struggled and exclaimed in pain as Andrea tightened his grip. 'You're hurting me.'

'Then stop struggling,' Andrea said equably. He continued his pain-racked, slow-motion climb.

Mallory and Miller reached the longitudinal crack running across the top of the dam wall and edged swiftly along crack and rope until they were directly above the arc lights on the eaves of the guard-house some fifty feet below: the brilliant illumination from those lights made it very clear indeed just what had happened. The unconscious Groves and Petar, the two dead German guards, the smashed radio transceiver and, above all, the sub-machine-gun still lying in the shattered casing of the guitar told a tale that could not be misread. Mallory moved another ten feet along the crack and peered down again: Andrea, with the girl doing her best to help by pulling on the rungs of the ladder, was now almost two-thirds of the way up, but making dreadfully slow progress of it: they'll never make it in time, Mallory thought, it is impossible that they will ever make it in time. It comes to us all, he thought tiredly, some day it's bound to come to us all: but that it should come to the indestructible Andrea pushed fatalistic acceptance beyond its limits. Such a thing was inconceivable: and the inconceivable was about to happen now.

Mallory rejoined Miller. Quickly he unhitched a rope—the knotted rope he and Miller had used to descend to the Neretva dam—secured it to the rope running above the longitudinal crack and lowered it until it touched softly on the roof of the guard-house. He took the Luger in his hand and was about to start sliding down when the dam blew up.

The twin explosions occurred within two seconds of each other: the detonation of 3,000 pounds of high explosive should normally have produced a titanic outburst of sound, but because of the depth at which they took place, the explosions were curiously muffled, felt, almost, rather than heard. Two great columns of water soared up high above the top of the dam wall, but for what seemed an eternity of time but certainly was not more than four or five seconds, nothing appeared to happen. Then, very, very slowly, reluctantly, almost, the entire central section of the dam wall, at least eighty feet in width and right down to its base, toppled outwards into the gorge: the entire section seemed to be all still in one piece.

Andrea stopped climbing. He had heard no sound, but he felt the shuddering vibration of the ladder and he knew what had happened, what was coming. He wrapped both arms around Maria and the stanchions, pressed her close to the ladder and looked over her head. Two vertical cracks made their slow appearance on the outside of the dam wall, then the entire wall fell slowly towards them, almost as if it were hinged on its base, and then was abruptly lost to sight as countless millions of gallons of greenish-dark water came boiling through the shattered dam wall. The sound of the crash of a thousand tons of masonry falling into the gorge below should have been heard miles away: but Andrea could hear nothing above the roaring of the escaping waters. He had time only to notice that the dam wall had vanished and now there was only this mighty green torrent, curiously smooth and calm in its initial stages, then pouring down to strike the gorge beneath in a seething white maelstrom of foam before the awesome torrent was upon them. In a second of time Andrea released one hand, turned the girl's terrified face and buried it against his chest for he knew that if she should impossibly live, then that battering-ram of water, carrying with it sand and pebbles and God only knew what else, would tear the delicate skin from her face and leave her forever scarred. He ducked his own head against the fury of the coming onslaught and locked his hands together behind the ladder.

The impact of the waters drove the breath from his gasping body. Buried in this great falling crushing wall of green, Andrea fought for his life and that of the girl. The strain upon him, battered and already bruising badly from the hammer-blows of this hurtling cascade of water which seemed so venomously bent upon his instant destruction, was, even without the cruel handicap of his badly injured arm, quite fantastic. His arms, it felt, were momentarily about to be torn from their sockets, it would have been the easiest thing in the world to unclasp his hands and let kindly oblivion take the place of the agony that seemed to be tearing limbs and muscles asunder. But Andrea did not let go and Andrea did not break. Other things broke. Several of the ladder supports were torn away from the wall and it seemed that both ladder and climbers must be inevitably swept away. The ladder twisted, buckled and leaned far out from the wall so that Andrea was now as much lying beneath the ladder as hanging on to it: but still Andrea did not let go, still some remaining supports held. Then very gradually, after what seemed to the dazed Andrea an interminable period of time, the dam level dropped, the force of the water weakened, not much but just perceptibly, and Andrea started to climb again. Half a dozen times, as he changed hands on the rungs, his grip loosened and he was almost torn away: half a dozen times his teeth bared in the agony of effort, the great hands clamped tight and he impossibly retained his grip. After almost a minute of this titanic struggle he finally won clear of the worst of the waters and could breathe again. He looked at the girl in his arms. The blonde hair was plastered over her ashen cheeks, the incongruously dark eyelashes closed. The ravine seemed almost full to the top of its precipitously-sided walls with this whitely boiling torrent of water sweeping everything before it, its roar, as it thundered down the gorge with a speed faster than that of an express train, a continuous series of explosions, an insane and banshee shrieking of sound.

Almost thirty seconds elapsed from the time of the blowing up of the dam until Mallory could bring himself to move again. He did not know why he should have been held in thrall for so long. He told himself, rationalizing, that it was because of the hypnotic spectacle of the dramatic fall in the level of the dam coupled with the sight of that great gorge filled almost to the top with those whitely seething waters: but, without admitting it to himself, he knew it was more than that, he knew he could not accept the realization that Andrea and Maria had been swept to their deaths, for Mallory did not know that at that instant Andrea, completely spent and no longer knowing what he was doing, was vainly trying to negotiate the last few steps of the ladder to the top of the dam. Mallory seized the rope and slid down down recklessly, ignoring or not feeling the burning of the skin on the palms of his hands, his mind irrationally filled with murder—irrationally, because it was he who had triggered the explosion that had taken Andrea to his death.

And then, as his feet touched the roof of the guard-house, he saw the ghost—the ghosts, rather—as the heads of Andrea and a clearly unconscious Maria appeared at the top of the ladder. Andrea, Mallory noticed, did not seem to be able to go any farther. He had a hand on the top rung, and was making convulsive, jerking movements, but making no progress at all. Andrea, Mallory knew, was finished.

Mallory was not the only one who had seen Andrea and

the girl. The captain of the guard and one of his men were staring in stupefaction over the awesome scene of destruction, but a second guard had whirled round, caught sight of Andrea's head and brought up his machine-pistol. Mallory, still clinging to the rope, had no time to bring his Luger to bear and release the safety-catch and Andrea should have assuredly died then: but Reynolds had already catapulted himself forward in a desperate dive and brought down the gun in the precise instant that the guard opened fire. Reynolds died instantaneously. The guard died two seconds later. Mallory lined up the still smoking barrel of his Luger on the captain and the guard.

'Drop those guns,' he said.

They dropped their guns. Mallory and Miller swung down from the guard-house roof, and while Miller covered the Germans with his guns, Mallory ran quickly across to the ladder, reached down a hand and helped the unconscious girl and the swaying Andrea to safety. He looked at Andrea's exhausted, blood-flecked face, at the flayed skin on his hands, at the left sleeve saturated in blood and said severely: 'And where the hell have you been?'

'Where have I been?' Andrea asked vaguely. 'I don't know.' He stood rocking on his feet, barely conscious, rubbed a hand across his eyes and tried to smile. 'I think I must have stopped to admire the view.'

General Zimmermann was still in his command car and his car was still parked in the right centre of the bridge at Neretva. Zimmermann had again his binoculars to his eyes, but for the first time he was gazing neither to the west nor to the north. He was gazing instead to the east, up-river towards the mouth of the Neretva gorge. After a little time he turned to his aide, his face at first uneasy, then the uneasiness giving way to apprehension, then the apprehension to something very like fear.

'You hear it?' he asked.

'I hear it, Herr General.'

'And feel it?'

'And I feel it.'

'What in the name of God almighty can it be?' Zimmermann demanded. He listened as a great and steadily increasing roar filled all the air around them. 'That's not thunder. It's far too loud for thunder. And too continuous. And that wind —that wind coming out of the gorge there.' He could now hardly hear himself speak above the almost deafening roar of sound coming from the east. 'It's the dam! The dam at Neretva! They've blown the dam! Get out of here!' he screamed at the driver. 'For God's sake get out of here!'

The command car jerked and moved forward, but it was too late for General Zimmermann, just as it was too late for his massed echelons of tanks and thousands of assault troops concealed on the banks of the Neretva by the low escarpment to the north of them and waiting to launch the devastating attack that was to annihilate the seven thousand fanatically stubborn defenders of the Zenica Gap. A mighty wall of white water, eighty feet high, carrying with it the irresistible pressure of millions of tons of water and sweeping before it a gigantic battering ram of boulders and trees, burst out of the mouth of the gorge.

Mercifully for most of the men in Zimmermann's armoured corps, the realization of impending death and death itself were only moments apart. The Neretva bridge, and all the vehicles on it, including Zimmerman's command car, were swept away to instant destruction. The giant torrent overspread both banks of the river to a depth of almost twenty feet, sweeping before its all-consuming path tanks, guns, armoured vehicles, thousands of troops and all that stood in its way: when the great flood finally subsided, there was not one blade of grass left growing along the banks of the Neretva. Perhaps a hundred or two of combat troops on both sides of the river succeeded in climbing in terror to higher ground and the most temporary of safety for they too would not have long to live, but for ninety-five per cent of Zimmermann's two armoured divisions destruction was as appallingly sudden as it was terrifyingly complete. In sixty seconds, no more, it was all over. The German armoured corps was totally destroyed. But still that mighty wall of water continued to boil forth from the mouth of the gorge.

'I pray God that I shall never see the like again.' General Vukalovic lowered his glasses and turned to Colonel Janzy, his face registering neither jubilation nor satisfaction, only an awestruck wonder mingled with a deep compassion. 'Men should not die like that, even our enemies should not die like that.' He was silent for a few moments, then stirred. 'I think a hundred or two of their infantry escaped to safety on this side, Colonel. You will take care of them?'

'I'll take care of them,' Janzy said sombrely. 'This is a night for prisoners, not killing, for there won't be any fight. It's as well, General. For the first time in my life I'm not looking forward to a fight.'

'I'll leave you then.' Vukalovic clapped Janzy's shoulder and smiled, a very tired smile. 'I have an appointment. At the Neretva dam—or what's left of it.'

'With a certain Captain Mallory?'

'With Captain Mallory. We leave for Italy tonight. You know, Colonel, we could have been wrong about that man.'

'I never doubted him,' Janzy said firmly.

Vukalovic smiled and turned away.

Captain Neufeld, his head swathed in a blood-stained bandage and supported by two of his men, stood shakily at the top of the gully leading down to the ford in the Neretva and stared down, his face masked in shocked horror and an almost total disbelief, at the whitely boiling maelstrom, its seething surface no more than twenty feet below where he stood, of what had once been the Neretva gorge. He shook his head very, very slowly in unspeakable weariness and final acceptance of defeat, then turned to the soldier on his left, a youngster who looked as stupefied as he, Neufeld, felt.

'Take the two best ponies,' Neufeld said. 'Ride to the nearest Wehrmacht command post north of the Zenica Gap. Tell them that General Zimmermann's armoured divisions have been wiped out—we don't *know*, but they must have

been. Tell them the valley of Neretva is a valley of death and
that there is no one left to defend it. Tell them the Allies can
send in their airborne divisions tomorrow and that there
won't be a single shot fired. Tell them to notify Berlin
immediately. You understand, Lindemann?'

'I understand, sir.' From the expression on Lindemann's
face, Neufeld thought that Lindemann had understood very
little of what he had said to him: but Neufeld felt infinitely
tired and he did not feel like repeating his instructions.
Lindemann mounted a pony, snatched the reins of another and
spurred his pony up alongside the railway track.

Neufeld said, almost to himself: 'There's not all that
hurry, boy.'

'Herr Hauptmann?' The other soldier was looking at him
strangely.

'It's too late now,' Neufeld said.

Mallory gazed down the still foaming gorge, turned and
gazed at the Neretva dam whose level had already dropped
by at least fifty feet, then turned to look at the men and the
girl behind him. He felt weary beyond all words.

Andrea, battered and bruised and bleeding, his left arm
now roughly bandaged, was demonstrating once again his
quite remarkable powers of recuperation: to look at him
it would have been impossible to guess that, only ten
minutes ago, he had been swaying on the edge of total
collapse. He held Maria cradled in his arms: she was
coming to, but very, very slowly. Miller finished dressing the
head wound of a now sitting Petar who, though wounded in
shoulder and head, seemed more than likely to survive,
crossed to Groves and stooped over him. After a moment or
two he straightened and stared down at the young sergeant.

'Dead?' Mallory asked.

'Dead.'

'Dead.' Andrea smiled, a smile full of sorrow. 'Dead—and
you and I are alive. Because this young lad is dead.'

'He was expendable,' Miller said.

'And young Reynolds.' Andrea was inexpressibly tired. 'He
was expendable too. What was it you said to him this

afternoon, my Keith—for now is all the time there may be? And that was all the time there was. For young Reynolds. He saved my life tonight—twice. He saved Maria's. He saved Petar's. But he wasn't clever enough to save his own. *We* are the clever ones, the old ones, the wise ones, the knowing ones. And the old ones are alive and the young ones are dead. And so it always is. We mocked them, laughed at them, distrusted them, marvelled at their youth and stupidity and ignorance.' In a curiously tender gesture he smoothed Maria's wet blonde hair back from her face and she smiled at him. 'And in the end they were better men than we were . . .'

'Maybe they were at that,' Mallory said. He looked at Petar sadly and shook his head in wonder. 'And to think that all three of them are dead, Reynolds dead, Groves dead, Saunders dead, and not one of them ever knew that you were the head of British espionage in the Balkans.'

'Ignorant to the end.' Miller drew the back of his sleeve angrily across his eyes. 'Some people never learn. Some people just never learn.'

EPILOGUE

Once again Captain Jensen and the British lieutenant-general were back in the Operations Room in Termoli, but now they were no longer pacing up and down. The days of pacing were over. True, they still looked very tired, their faces probably fractionally more deeply lined than they had been a few days previously: but the faces were no longer haggard, the eyes no longer clouded with anxiety, and, had they been walking instead of sitting deep in comfortable armchairs, it was just conceivable that they might have had a new spring to their steps. Both men had glasses in their hands, large glasses.

Jensen sipped his whisky and said, smiling: 'I thought a general's place was at the head of his troops?'

'Not in these days, Captain,' the General said firmly. 'In 1944 the wise general leads from behind his troops—about twenty miles behind. Besides, the armoured divisions are going so quickly I couldn't possibly hope to catch up with them.'

'They're moving as fast as that?'

'Not quite as fast as the German and Austrian divisions that pulled out of the Gustav Line last night and are now racing for the Yugoslav border. But they're coming along pretty well.' The General permitted himself a large gulp of his drink and a smile of considerable satisfaction. 'Deception complete, break-through complete. On the whole, your men have done a pretty fair job.'

Both men turned in their chairs as a respectful rat-a-tat of knuckles preceded the opening of the heavy leather doors. Mallory entered, followed by Vukalovic, Andrea and Miller. All four were unshaven, all of them looked as if they hadn't slept for a week. Andrea carried his arm in a sling.

Jensen rose, drained his glass, set it on a table, looked at Mallory dispassionately and said: 'Cut it a bit bloody fine, didn't you?'

Mallory, Andrea and Miller exchanged expressionless looks. There was a fairly long silence, then Mallory said: 'Some things take longer than others.'

Petar and Maria were lying side by side, hands clasped, in two regulation army beds in the Termoli military hospital when Jensen entered, followed by Mallory, Miller and Andrea.

'Excellent reports about both of you, I'm glad to hear,' Jensen said briskly. 'Just brought some—ah—friends to say goodbye.'

'What sort of hospital is this, then?' Miller asked severely. 'How about the high army moral tone, hey? Don't they have separate quarters for men and women?'

'They've been married for almost two years,' Mallory said mildly. 'Did I forget to tell you?'

'Of course you didn't forget,' Miller said disgustedly. 'It just slipped your mind.'

'Speaking of marriage—' Andrea cleared his throat and

tried another tack. 'Captain Jensen may recall that back in Navarone—'

'Yes, yes.' Jensen held up a hand. 'Quite so. Quite. Quite. But I thought perhaps—well, the fact of the matter is—well, it so happens that another little job, just a tiny little job really, has just come up and I thought that seeing you were here anyway . . .'

Andrea stared at Jensen. His face was horror-stricken.

Fontana Books

Fontana is a leading paperback publisher of fiction and non-fiction, with authors ranging from Alistair MacLean, Agatha Christie and Desmond Bagley to Solzhenitsyn and Pasternak, from Gerald Durrell and Joy Adamson to the famous Modern Masters series.

In addition to a wide-ranging collection of internationally popular writers of fiction, Fontana also has an outstanding reputation for history, natural history, military history, psychology, psychiatry, politics, economics, religion and the social sciences.